THE PARLOR HOUSE DAUGHTER

THE PARLOR HOUSE DAUGHTER

JOANNE SUNDELL

FIVE STAR

A part of Gale, Cengage Learning

GALE
CENGAGE Learning

Detroit • New York • San Francisco • New Haven, Conn • Waterville, Maine • London

Set in 11 pt. Plantin.
Printed on permanent paper.

LIBRARY OF CONGRESS CATALOGING-IN-PUBLICATION DATA

Sundell, Joanne.
   The parlor house daughter / Joanne Sundell. — 1st ed.
     p. cm.
   ISBN-13: 978-1-59414-722-7 (hardcover : alk. paper)
   ISBN-10: 1-59414-722-1 (hardcover : alk. paper)
    1. Prostitutes—Fiction. 2. Upper class—Fiction. 3. Denver (Colo.)—Fiction. 4. Colorado—History—1876–1950—Fiction. I. Title.
PS3619.U557P37 2008
813'.6—dc22
                                              2008037617

First Edition. First Printing: December 2008.
Published in 2008 in conjunction with Tekno Books.

Printed in the United States of America
1 2 3 4 5 6 7 12 11 10 09 08

For the men in my life:
For my father, Preston L. Gregg
His love ever shines down from above
For my husband, Sy
Always and forever, my Prince Charming
For my son, Zach
No kinder heart beats in any son
For my stepfather, Casey Dean
A man for all seasons

CHAPTER ONE

Nevada City, Colorado Territory, 1863

"You hold on now, Ruby Rose, you hear me? Yer gonna be fine and yer baby's gonna be fine. You just hold on now," Fanny commanded, trying to keep calm in the face of so much blood. Ruby's cotton shift was near soaked with it.

With no doc close in the mining town, it was up to Fanny and the other gals at the end of the line in Nevada City's red light district, to save Ruby and her baby. No call now to get on Ruby for getting pregnant in the first place, her being in such a bad way and all. Fanny knew all about so-called mistakes. Never mind that a body could swallow a whole measure of preventive powders, use sea sponges, beeswax, or even balls of opium if you could afford 'em—mistakes happened easy enough.

Ruby let out another scream, lashing side to side on her simple iron bed, trying to hold onto life—her own and her unborn baby's. But the pain . . . the pain shot through her, poking at her belly and privates worse than any man had ever hurt her. Sweat poured down her face. Her breaths came quick and shallow. Each pain made it harder for her to keep her wits and stay conscious.

"Fan . . . n . . . y," Ruby whispered. "Pl . . . please . . ."

"There, there," Fanny consoled, wiping away Ruby's tears, all the while choking back her own. "Why, yer gonna be just fine. We'll have this baby born and you fit as a fiddle soon enough. You just hold on, like I said." Scared for Ruby, Fanny didn't know if her friend was gonna make it. Lots of ways for a whore to die, sure enough, but to die in a ramshackle crib, with no family around—just other whores—it wasn't right.

"Here, Fanny. Here's my knife. I done washed it good. Need . . . anything else? My sheet ain't any too clean, but I'll fetch it if ya want," Ugly Lulu blurted, out of breath from her errand.

"Take out yer lacing, Lulu. If this baby lives, we gotta tie it off from Ruby. Hurry, Lulu," Fanny spat, putting the knife aside for now. Unless the baby came out soon, likely it would die, and Ruby, too. Fanny had never seen no birthing like this, taking so long and with so much blood.

Another whore, One-eyed Edna, came in from the back kitchen with a heavy kettle of boiling water. She set it down near Ruby's bed and said nothing.

"Edna, help me here, will ya? We gotta save 'em both. We gotta," Fanny pleaded.

Ruby pleaded, too . . . to God. If there was a God, she prayed with everything left in her, for Him to save her baby. Never a churchgoer, Ruby prayed that God wouldn't punish her unborn baby for her sins. If God let her baby live, it would be her—Ruby's—one, pure, decent thing she could do in this miserable world. Her soul might be tainted, but not her innocent baby's. *Not yet, anyways.*

Here she was bringing an innocent baby into a world of lost innocence. Maybe she should have got rid of it, like most of the girls did. But from the first, when she found out she was carrying—with no idea who the father was—she knew she couldn't kill her baby. She loved her baby . . . a pure love . . . a mother's love. She'd never known a mother's love, but her baby would! *All I have to do is hold on, like Fanny says.* The pains stabbed again, each one worse, each one trying to kill. Weak and unable to think clearly anymore, Ruby's last thoughts faded into blackness: *Hold on . . . hold on . . . hold on . . .*

"Rebecca Rose," her mother scolded, "don't touch that pot! You don't wanna burn yerself now, young lady."

Becca jerked her hand away from the kettle and tucked it behind her. Not tall enough yet to reach the top of the modest iron stove, the four-year-old had been curious. And she was hungry, too. The soup smelled good. Her face in a pucker, she turned away from the stove and dragged her feet along the splintered wood floor to her tiny cot in a kitchen corner, and plopped down. She didn't cry at her mother's scolding. She wanted to, but she didn't.

"There, there." Ruby came over to her daughter and knelt down. "I was that worried you'd burn yer little fingers, Becca. Yer my darling girl and I didn't want you to get hurt." Ruby took both of her daughter's small hands in hers, and then kissed each one of Becca's fingers.

Becca started to giggle.

Glad to see her precious daughter smile, Ruby stood, checked the stove, and then passed through the thick curtains to the front room of their pine shack.

Becca watched her mother's every move, knowing better than to try and touch the kettle again. Her mother would catch her at it. She didn't want to be scolded again. It made her sad when her mother was sad. She didn't want to make her mother sad. Becca stared at the heavy curtains, closed full now, keeping everything in the front room hidden from her. If she wanted, she could run through the curtains, now anyway. Her mother hadn't told her she had to stay in the kitchen and play or go to sleep. "This is yer very own, special play room, Rebecca Rose," her mother had always explained. "It's yer secret place. No one can come in here but you and me. There's a magic spell over you in here, with good fairies watching over you. If you go through the curtains without the magic password, the spell will be broken, and the good fairies might fly away."

Too young to realize her mother had contrived the only plan she could think of to keep her daughter with her, and keep her away from the men—the customers—who came in the front, Becca believed in the good fairies watching over her in the kitchen. Instinctively, she knew she had to remain in the kitchen to stay safe.

Becca kept to her playroom in the kitchen until those times when she could play freely in the front room, too. Almost five now, Becca did what her mother said, most times. There were rules in the house and Becca had to obey those rules. If she didn't, the magic spell would be broken. Becca didn't want to break the magic spell and upset her mother, although it was becoming harder for her to stay put when she'd rather run through the curtains. Every day was like a game, waiting for the special password to go play in the front room. Yesterday it was "peppermint" and today it was "gumdrops." Smart as a whip, Becca never had trouble remembering the special password.

What she did have trouble doing was staying inside when she wanted to run out and play in the sunshine or the snow . . . especially the snow. There was a tiny, paned window at the back of the kitchen, next to the door. The door out from the kitchen was always locked. Only her mother could unlock it. Her mother would let her go play sometimes, but the sometimes were never enough times to suit Becca.

There were such wonders outside in back of their house. There were dogs and horses and birds and mud puddles and snow banks and woodpiles and folks walking by. Most folks stared at her. Becca would wave and smile at everyone. Most all of the passersby were men. Some would smile and wave back. She never talked to anyone. Her mother told her not to talk to strangers. But she could wave and smile at the other kids—her mother never said she couldn't do that—if she were ever to see one, that is. Every time Becca went outside she'd crane her neck in every direction, looking for other kids to come and play with her. None passed by. Becca waited every day, but none came.

"Gumdrops, Becca!" Ruby called out from the front room.

In no time, Becca was through the curtains and in her mother's lap. Fanny was there! Oh, what fun. Becca loved her mother's friend, Fanny.

"Hi, you sweet thing." Fanny gave Becca a chuck under her chin.

Becca grinned.

"Here you go. Sweets fer the sweet," Fanny said, handing a peppermint stick to Becca.

"Thank you, Fanny." Becca snatched the peppermint from Fanny, and began licking the confection. Abruptly, she stopped and held her candy up to her mother. "Look, mama! Peppermint!"

Ruby gave her daughter a hug. "I know. Our special peppermint."

"My, my, Ruby, what a polite child. Yer sure teaching her good."

"Manners is . . . are . . . important, Fanny. I want my daughter to have proper manners and a proper life," Ruby intoned.

"All well and good, Ruby, but here? Here yer gonna give yer daughter the good life?" Fanny scoffed.

"Shhh, Fanny. Not in front of the child."

Fanny sat next to Ruby and Becca on the single iron bed in the living area, disturbing the stiff oilcloth draped over the foot when she did. One modest red-curtained window fronted the shack. Ruby couldn't get work anymore in one of the frame houses, the nicer brothels up the line in town, where she could live better and make more money. She couldn't, not with Becca in tow, and not with her face all cut.

At eighteen, when she was still young and beautiful, Ruby worked in one of the nicer bordellos in Nevada City and thought she had it all. It just took one trick—one time with a sorry, mean bastard who was jealous of another miner—to ruin her looks, cutting one side of her face up real bad, relegating her to one of the pine shacks at the end of the line. No lawman did anything about it. Nobody was around to care what happened to a whore.

Ruby still had her dreams for a better life, but now her dreams were for her daughter. Ruby had a plan. It had to work. It was the only way now for her . . . and for little Becca.

Becca hopped out of her mother's lap and sat on the worn trunk at the food of the bed, busy eating her candy and staring out the front window. It was still light outside. But for the trunk, and a little table next to the bed with a kerosene lamp on it, there was no other furniture in the front room. Ruby had talked of getting a chair one day, and of putting in new boards to keep their shack warmer, but money was tight. It was all she could do to keep food on the table for Becca and a safe roof over her head.

Hah. Safe. Ruby thought not.

"You gonna do it tonight, Ruby? You gonna talk to him?"

"Fanny, shhh. I said not in front of the child," Ruby spat.

"No call to get in a dither, Ruby. The child isn't listening to us now, anyways. We gotta talk about this, and I don't have much time. It's Friday and you know what that means. I'll be on my back till sunup. I gotta know what you plan to do and what you plan to say to him tonight." Fanny crossed her arms and waited. She wouldn't leave until Ruby let on exactly what was going on tonight with her special caller. Fridays were Ruby's time with her genteel, rich customer. Fanny was happy for Ruby.

She lived at the end of the line and few men, much less genteel men, had anything to do with throwaway whores.

Fanny had seen Ruby's caller come and go plenty enough, never thinking too much about him other than she wished he'd give Ruby more money for all those hours on her back with him. Damn lucky, Ruby was, to have a man like him, her looks gone and all. But then, Fanny knew why he kept coming. Unlike some, Ruby had never been *burned*—she'd never gotten venereal disease. A lot of whores used a whole lot of concoctions to douche and keep clean, like vinegar, carbolic acid, pearlash or Lysol. It didn't always work, but it must have for Ruby since she'd stayed clean. And, Ruby had a body like no other whore Fanny had ever come across. Other whores would kill for Ruby's soft curves and natural skills at pleasurin'.

Ruby shared with Fanny some of the things her long-time caller said to her, like how she was the best he'd ever had with special ways to please a man, and how he didn't want her seeing anybody else on Fridays but him. He'd been coming to see Ruby a year now and always paid for the whole night with her. Fanny was real curious to find out what he'd say to Ruby tonight, after their "little talk." Anxious for her friend, Fanny tried not to worry. It was so easy for bad things to happen to whores. There wasn't any protection at the end of the line.

"Yes. Yes, I'm talking to him tonight," Ruby spoke up. "It's the only way fer us, Fanny. I know it's the only way now." Ruby swallowed hard, dreading the coming conversation. It was now or never, and she knew it.

Fanny could see Ruby's upset. She knew only too well how high the stakes were for her friend. "Well, good then," Fanny stood. Life was hard on the line and if Ruby had a shot to get out of the business, to make a better life for herself and little Becca, then so much the better. Even whores have dreams, Fanny acknowledged to herself. She'd miss Ruby, no doubt

13

about that. But surviving . . . it was all about surviving.

"Just don't you ferget that I'm right next door. You let out a yell if you need me fer anything. You keeping 'you know what' tucked on yer thigh?"

"Fanny, shhhh. Of course," Ruby said, growing more upset by the minute. She'd never thought there might be any danger involved. She'd never thought he might get mad, and they'd fight. Of course, that wouldn't happen. Of course not. *He'll agree. I know he will. He has to.*

"Keep yer voice down!" Ruby whispered hard. She didn't want Becca to wake up—he didn't know about Becca . . . until now. Ruby had been able to hide the fact that she had a toddler sleeping in the back room all this time. Desperate to remain calm, fighting for control, Ruby rolled away from her best customer and pulled the muslin sheet up, covering her naked breasts. This wasn't going right. None of it was going right. Second to being at Becca's birth, this was the most important moment in her life. She had to make it all go right; she *had* to.

The lamplight flickered on her bedstead. Ruby reached over and turned up the wick, buying time to think of what to say next. She lay back in bed, forcing her insides to calm. There was too much riding on this moment for her to panic.

Her customer suddenly rolled out of bed and began to dress.

She panicked all over again. "Please, honey. Come back to bed. Let's talk and work this out," she pleaded, trying to keep her voice at a whisper.

"There's your mistake, Ruby. There's nothing here to work out. I never promised you anything but the price of a brass check. You don't even use them. Get the point?"

Ruby got it all right. He meant she didn't work at a high-enough level in a decent brothel to use the token exchange for favors. Well, she'd been decent enough for him to bed her for the past year! "You trying to say I'm not good enough fer you anymore?" she spat out, her anger growing. She hurtled out of bed, wrapping the muslin sheet about her, and faced him.

"Yeah," he said, "something like that."

"You bastard," she hissed.

"Yeah, something like that," he said again.

Instinctively, she reached inside the wrapped sheeting, to take her derringer from her thigh. She wanted to wipe that smug smile from his face. She wanted to kill him. Didn't do her any good tonight, with her derringer tucked in her trunk instead of on her!

"Well, hey, Ruby Rose," he came closer. "You want to hurt me, going for your gun. Well, well." He stood facing her now. One quick jerk of the sheeting around her, and he had her naked. "I don't see any gun, do you?" he said, his tone low and dangerous.

Desperate and frightened, Ruby swallowed hard. "Please, honey. Please, make it right by me and my baby. Marry me and give me and my baby a decent life, a respectable life. I'll be good to you, like always. I'll keep you smiling and happy, like always. We can go to Denver City. Nobody knows me in Denver City and we can live all respectable-like. Please, honey. I can't let my baby grow up in this kind of a place. It's not fair to her. Please help give her a chance, oh please, honey."

"Why, Ruby Rose," he rasped. "Didn't I ever mention that I'm already married with children of my own? I just don't happen to need another wife and child. Besides, if I was in the market for another wife, it sure as hell wouldn't be you. You're good in bed, I'll give you that, but do you expect me to look at you any more than I have to?"

Ruby's insides coiled. Her hurt went deep.

"My wife is a fine, elegant, respectable lady, something you'll never be," he went on, his tone deadly. "No way any wife of mine is going to raise a whore's brat." He looked around the tiny room, no doubt for Ruby's child.

"Yer married! All this time . . . and yer married!" Ruby raised her voice. She couldn't control her anger. He'd called Becca a *whore's brat*. "So you have a wife and children in Denver, do you? Well, what if I go to Denver City and find yer wife and tell her what you've been doing with me fer a year now? How do you think yer precious respectable wife would like that?"

"Aw, Ruby girl, now you wouldn't go and do a nasty thing like that to me, would you?" He took hold of her upper arms, his hands like manacles, keeping her from moving away.

"Oh, I would. You bet I would," she promised, her fiery eyes on his, knowing she was on dangerous, deadly ground. She didn't care. All this time—a whole year she'd been planning this—planning to live with him and give Becca the respectability she deserved in life. It was Ruby's last chance, her only chance, and now there was no chance. Or was there . . .

"Would . . . would you take my baby then, and raise her with yers?" she begged. If his wife was a true "fine, elegant lady" then she could raise Becca, and he had a lot of money and all. It would kill Ruby not to have her daughter with her, but if . . . if he'd take Becca to raise—

"You've got sass all right, Ruby. I'll give you that." He laughed under his breath. "One minute threatening to cause me trouble, and the next asking me to take on yours." He looked around the room again. "Where's the brat?" he demanded, tightening his hold on her arms.

"None of yer business, you bastard," Ruby hissed.

He threw Ruby onto her bed like so much garbage. In another swift move, he straddled her. "You stupid, stupid whore," he rebuked, taking out his knife. "You probably think you're my only whore. Honey, you're only my Friday night whore."

Waking up to loud talk, Becca knew something was wrong. Moonlight streamed through the paned window. She'd awakened before to voices through the curtains, but not like this— not these bad voices. The voices were always happy voices, laughing voices, funny voices. Nothing was ever bad like this. She couldn't tell what the voices were saying, but she could tell her mother was scared. The good fairies weren't protecting her mother now and smiling down. As soon as her mother said "gumdrops," Becca could go through the curtains and the good fairies would come, too, and protect her mother. *Mama, say gumdrops!*

Becca curled up on her little cot, holding her doll close. She started to cry. Something bad was wrong. *Something bad.*

Her mother screamed.

Becca bolted off her cot and scuttled across the kitchen floor. Her doll gripped in one hand, she pushed through the heavy curtains with the other—all thoughts of passwords and good fairies frightened away.

She froze in the doorway. A big man stood next to her mother's bed, his back to Becca now. He didn't turn around. Her mother was in bed, sleeping. Becca wanted to run and climb into bed with her mother and snuggle up close. She wanted the big man to leave so she could curl up with her mother. Becca stood very still and waited for the man to leave. He was a bad man. She knew he was a bad man. She wanted him to go before he woke up her mother again and made her sad!

The lamplight shone. The light was dim elsewhere in the front room, but not the circle of light on the little table by her mother's bed. Becca stared at the lamp, and then at the man's back . . . watching him . . . wishing for him to leave. His hand moved. It was right in the lamplight. She saw his hand clearly. It looked funny because some of the fingers were missing. And a ring, there was a big gold, funny-looking ring on one of the remaining fingers. The ring looked like the head of a lion she'd seen in a picture book.

Becca kept staring. The man put something in his funny hand. It was a rag. It looked funny, too. The rag was all red and wet. Becca recognized the cloth. It looked like her mother's white handkerchief with red paint spilled on it. Becca didn't understand why her mother would give the man her beautiful handkerchief! Her mother loved it and told her it was only for "special." Becca kept up her watch on the man and on her mother's handkerchief.

The man dropped the ruined linen on the table by the lamp, and then went over to the door, hesitating as if he knew someone watched him, then opened the door and left. He never turned around to look at Becca.

She was glad for it. She was glad he didn't see her. She padded across the room to her mother's bed, wanting to be very quiet so she wouldn't wake her. Her doll still clutched in one hand, she climbed onto the bed. Her mother lay so still. Becca let her doll fall to the floor. Frightened, she gingerly nudged her mother to wake up. When she did not stir, Becca began to cry. Her eyes clouded with tears. At first it was hard for her to see—to see all the blood at her mother's throat.

"Mama . . . mama," Becca sobbed, shaking her mother again and again, until she couldn't anymore. Needing her mother's comforting arms, she eased down on the blood-soaked bed, snuggling against Ruby's lifeless body. "Mama," she whispered against Ruby's cold skin. "Why didn't you say gumdrops?" she whispered, and then succumbed to exhaustion, falling asleep.

"For the love of God! Oh, sweet Jesus, Becca!" Fanny cried out, discovering the sleeping child cradled in her dead mother's arms the next morning. "I knew something like this was gonna happen. I knew it," Fanny said through her tears. "That no-good murdering bastard is gonna pay for this," she vowed, all the while knowing he wouldn't. His kind never got in trouble for killing no whore.

Becca woke with a start. Her pillow was all dry and sticky against her face. But it wasn't her pillow. It was her mother . . . dead and killed . . . killed by the bad man. Becca sat up, but didn't get out of bed. She couldn't leave, not yet. Her mother was all she had in the world and she wasn't going to leave her mother, not ever.

"Becca, child," Fanny cajoled, trying to gently wrest Becca from Ruby's bed. "Time to get up now, sweet child."

"No!" Becca snuggled against her mother again, hard as she could. "No, Fanny, no!"

"There, there. Hold on now," Fanny soothed, remembering all too well those were the very words she'd said over Ruby the night Becca was born. It had been a night of such promise for Ruby. She'd had her baby—a baby of her very own to love and to love her. And look where it got her. Dead, that's where! It wasn't ever fair, living on the line. It wasn't a life at all, most times. Fanny should get out of the life too, but where could she go now? Too late, past her prime, it was too late for any fresh start. For Becca, too, Fanny realized. The poor child was destined for the same wretched life her mother had lived.

Fanny let Becca have a few more minutes, lying in her mother's lifeless arms. The child was still in shock and would be for a while yet. Fanny went to the trunk at the foot of Ruby's deathbed. Could be there was something of value in it, enough to pay for burial in potter's field and maybe even a tombstone. Potter's field would have to do, since prostitutes couldn't be buried in churchyards; the townsfolk wouldn't allow it. Fanny had to make arrangements today. The bartender at the Nugget would help her. She needed to do this for little Becca. Ruby would want a fitting grave so her daughter could come and pay her respects.

"It's fittin', that's all," Fanny muttered, then began rummaging through Ruby's few possessions.

Becca sobbed against her mother's dead body, her mournful wails breaking the room's tomblike silence.

Fanny worried for the child. After she got Ruby buried as proper as she could, what was gonna happen to poor little orphaned Rebecca Rose?

CHAPTER TWO

"Watch yourself there, Monty!" Morgan called, worried his little brother would get bucked off the big bay again. A scrapper from day one, eight-year-old Montgomery Larkspur was determined to ride their newest horse, despite his brother's warnings. Sure enough, in the next minute Monty lay facedown on the stable ground.

"Get up, little brother," Morgan said, meanwhile catching up the fiery bay's reins.

Monty didn't move.

Morgan knew Monty was playing now. His back turned to his brother, Morgan spoke low and easy to the lathered bay. "There, there, big fella. Atta boy, ease up now." When the animal quieted, Morgan led him to his nearby stall and settled the animal in. Another horse whinnied in the adjacent stall, in a line of a dozen others. The Larkspur Stables "let" horses in Denver City—just one of the family-owned businesses.

Four years his senior, Morgan liked to be around when Monty tried to ride one of the stable horses—not just teaching his brother how to throw on a good saddle and giddy up, but how to treat horses, too. Once in a while Morgan would catch his little brother poking a stick at one of the horses through the stalls and laughing when the horse got spooked. Monty was still young, but he should know better. It was up to Morgan to teach him that.

The afternoon sun beat down hot. It was Saturday, which

meant no school. Morgan spent a lot of his free time in the stable with the horses. He dreamed of owning a ranch some day with horses aplenty. He liked helping out at the stables, although there were hired men to do that. As it was Saturday, Morgan knew the men would be in one of the saloons or hurdy-gurdies along about now, drinking their fill and having a good time with the painted ladies. He'd seen ladies dressed in bright skirts with ruffles, all short to the knee. Heck, he'd seen more than that when he'd peeked through saloon doors—painted ladies with their dress fronts all low, showing their bosoms. One time he even caught sight of a hurdy-gurdy lady's leg, net stockings, garters and all! Still a kid himself, Morgan knew about such things—hard not to with over fifty saloons and gambling houses in Denver City. After all, it was 1867, with at least thirty-five thousand people living in the Colorado Territory. The frontier outpost of Denver City could boast of at least twelve streets now, churches, two schools, and two hotels. Denver City was growing, had done ever since gold was discovered in California Gulch at the confluence of the South Platte River and Cherry Creek. And now the brick city continued to grow, enduring fires, floods, and a grasshopper invasion.

Denver City was Morgan's home, where he was born. It suited him fine. There was enough excitement every day on the city streets to keep a kid busy enough, that's for sure. His parents weren't any too pleased when he and Monty ventured far, often fetching them back home just when their adventure was getting started. Morgan wished his parents would give him more rein, just like their horses needed. He'd argued with his parents more than once, chomping at the bit as only a young boy will.

Eugene and Augusta Larkspur were raising their two boys in a well-to-do section of Denver City, in a fine home. They talked of building "bigger and better" in time, which Morgan didn't understand. What was the need? He and his brother already had it pretty good and he knew it. The kids at school treated him a little different, which Morgan didn't like. He was just like everyone else, and he wanted the other kids to know that. He'd learned to be a scrapper early on. No way would anyone call him a rich sissy. The schoolyards in Denver City were littered with boys with black eyes who'd tried to call him a rich sissy. They never did it twice.

"Spur." Monty had gotten up by now and brushed himself off. He called his big brother Spur because that's what all the school kids called him. Monty was proud that his brother had so many good friends at school. Monty wanted to be just like his brother with friends and all. It wasn't as easy for him to get friends like Spur did. Monty couldn't figure why. He was a Larkspur, too. He should get the same respect his brother did. "Spur, guess what?"

"What, little bro." Morgan joined his brother in the center of the stable yard.

"I hear a big wagon train is pulling into town today, over on Holladay Street. Wanna go?" Monty reset his cowboy hat, with straggles of light brown hair peeking out from everywhere beneath it. He set his hat again, this time running a dirt-covered hand over his forehead to smooth away the strands of hair fallen there, shutting his brown eyes while he did.

"Sure, bro," Morgan agreed. "Might be fun. The folks are out this afternoon. They'll never know." Morgan reset his own cowboy hat, his thick, dark locks, cropped at the shoulder, nearly matching the black of his Stetson. His eyes were every bit as dark as his hair. While the brothers didn't favor each other in hair or eye color, they did in build. Already tall, Morgan was still growing. He figured his little brother would be his same size in time and was glad Monty would have muscle for a good fight. He'd need it, Morgan knew, especially living in Denver City.

About to leave the stable yard with Monty, Morgan looked up when a customer pulled his wagon up to the Larkspur Stables. He and Monty would have to delay going over to Holladay Street, since Morgan needed to see to the customer and the horses first. With the hired help nowhere in sight, it was up to Morgan. He didn't mind, but he knew his parents wouldn't be happy about it. But then, Morgan never told his parents the men were away early, off to Saturday night saloons.

Morgan opened the heavy stable gate, allowing entry for the buckboard and team. Morgan watched the customer, dressed better than most he'd seen renting such an outfit, pull inside and then get down. He looked mean to Morgan. Morgan knew mean. The man wore heavy leather gloves, pushing them on tighter as he approached. Odd, Morgan thought, to be pushing on gloves when a body usually pulled them off after riding. Morgan walked to the front of the team, turning his back on the customer, ready for trouble.

"You there, kid." The big man rapped Morgan hard on the shoulder. "I'm not paying for any of this. Your team was slow and the buckboard near broke apart the whole way," he grumbled.

Morgan didn't look at the man, yelling to his brother instead. "Monty, you go along now. I'll catch up in a few!"

Morgan could see that Monty stayed put.

"Monty, git!"

"Hey kid." The burly man jabbed Morgan in the back again. "Don't you be talking to that kid when I'm the one who's talking to you. You hear me?"

"Yeah, I hear you." Morgan pivoted slowly, all the while keeping his eyes on Monty. Dadgummit. He wished Monty would git!

The stranger glowered down at Morgan, jabbing him in his chest-front this time.

Morgan flinched but didn't step back. The big man towered over him. But still, Morgan didn't step back.

"Spur!" Monty yelled. "Sp-ur!" he yelled again, his voice cracking.

"It's all right, little bro," Morgan gritted out. The big man smelled of whiskey, his hot breath coming at Morgan worse than the afternoon sun.

"Like I said, kid. I'm not paying. You got it?" The man kept up his threatening tone.

Morgan thought he had a chance to make the customer pay— after all, the man wasn't wearing a gun and Morgan didn't see a knife. Just a scrap is all this will be. Just a scrap. Never mind that the man could kill him with one fisted blow to the head or the throat. No, Morgan was worried for Monty now, and not himself.

"Listen, mister." Morgan stood as tall as he could. "You owe five dollars for the day, for the horses and the buckboard. You pay up and there won't be any trouble." Morgan gulped hard and hoped like heck the man didn't see his fear.

"No little whippersnapper like you is going to get a red cent out of me," the man threatened, his tone more dangerous now. "I'm not giving you a cent for this sorry lot I rented. Not a red cent!"

Morgan brushed drops of the man's sour spittle from his face, all the while taking measure of his chances in a fight. When the nonpaying customer turned to leave, steps away now, it was Morgan who yelled at his back. "I'm going for the sheriff, mister! You'll be in jail quicker than you can say jackrabbit!"

The big man stopped in his tracks, then slowly turned. He walked menacingly toward Morgan, reaching him in a few steps. "Kid, you're not going for any sheriff. You won't be able to when I'm through with you."

The last thing Morgan remembered before he blacked out was thinking the man had the eyes of a coward.

"Fanny, please don't send me away. Please. Tell me what I done that you wanna send me away."

"You listen here, Rebecca Rose. You listen good."

It broke Fanny's heart to have this conversation with Ruby's child, but she didn't see any other way. They stood in the little kitchen of Fanny's meager crib, next door to the pine shack where Becca had been born. That crib was occupied by another whore now; in fact it had been occupied by several since Ruby's murder. The morning Fanny found Becca in her dead mother's arms was the last time the child had been in the crib next door. No matter that she was born there, Becca refused to set foot in the place where her mother was killed. Fanny knew the child had murder in her heart for the bastard who'd killed Ruby. So did Fanny, but it didn't do no good. Men like him were untouchable. The law would never believe what he done to poor Ruby. It was the price women paid too often on the line, no matter where they hung out their red lanterns. Sure, a body didn't always get murdered . . . but sometimes they wished they did.

It wasn't any life for little Becca, now eight, and Fanny knew it. Maybe the child couldn't escape the sporting life altogether, but maybe she wouldn't have to live it at the end of the line, neither. There were fancy parlor houses in Denver City, places that might take the eight-year-old in and teach her to be a fine, rich whore. That was the best Fanny could do for poor Ruby's child. With little money or means of her own, Fanny determined to send Becca to Denver City to work in one of the fine parlor houses as a maid or cook or seamstress, till she was old enough to go into the business—around fifteen, give or take, when she'd be a woman—and turn into a rich city lady, dressed all elegant, riding in a fine carriage every afternoon, with genteel men walking by on the street tipping their hats to her.

Besides, Fanny's time was running out and she knew it. It wasn't just her age. Whores aged before most. Her body was rotting away inside. The opium was getting to her, worse all the time now. Opium was her escape from whoring. Having Becca live with her was the one bright spot in all of her no-good thirty years. Sometimes Fanny didn't need to run find the Chinaman who sold opium to her for ten cents a bottle. Sometimes knowing Becca was always around helped her feel like an ordinary woman, a mother even. When she felt good about herself, Fanny didn't need the Chinaman's opium. But when she felt bad about herself . . . hah . . . and now the Chinaman wanted to charge her two bits for the same bottle!

"Fanny." Becca interrupted Fanny's hard reverie. "Tell me what I done that you wanna send me away," she asked, her tone more demanding than tearful.

Becca didn't cry like most would, but then Becca wasn't like most children her age, growing up where she did. Becca knew more than any young girl should. She knew about how men paid for "being alone" with whores . . . about how men smoked and drank a lot of whiskey . . . whores, too . . . about how men sometimes hurt whores . . . even killed 'em . . . like what happened to her mother . . . about how men had the money and whores had to find a way to get their money . . . about how whores were looked down on by so-called "respectable folk" . . . about how whores got sick sometimes, and died . . . about how whores didn't have enough to eat or keep warm or money for a doc, and died . . . about how whores got real sad sometimes and took the opium or drank too much whiskey, and died . . . about how whores were yer friends . . . yer only friends . . . the only ones who cared if you lived or died in this sorry world.

Fanny looked down at Becca, standing before her so brave and strong, the top of her head shoulder level to Fanny. Becca reminded Fanny of her once-beautiful friend, Ruby. Becca was the spitting image of her mother, with luxurious, thick chestnut hair, falling in waves down her back. Her sloe-brown, intelligent eyes sparkled with spirit and spunk, her dark, silky lashes enhancing their loveliness. She had the cutest little turned-up nose, too. The firm set of her jaw just now, as she waited for Fanny to answer her, did nothing to take away from her comely chin. Nor did the hard set of her full, rosy mouth detract from hinting of the desirable woman she'd one day become. Thin as a rail now, Fanny knew Becca would grow up to have her mother's slender yet curvy figure. She was gonna be a beauty all right, no question about it.

But more than Becca's looks, Fanny was worried about the child's insides. Becca was a troubled child, and had been ever since Ruby was murdered. Becca had fears hidden deep down—she had to—but she never let on she was afraid of anything. She never cried, neither. Fanny worried about this the most of all. It wasn't right, a child like her not ever crying, as if she had no feelings inside. She had hate inside her though, Fanny was certain about *that.*

Any child would if they saw what Becca did, and had to go through what Becca went through, her mother dying and all . . . murdered in her own bed! For four years now Fanny had done her best to take care of Becca, with the help of other whores who befriended them. Some didn't want the bother or the worry. Fanny understood. It was business, all about surviving and the business. Whores got jealous and mean and into cat-fights far too easy. Fanny didn't want to stir up any more trouble or worries than she already had trying to raise Becca. But then whores could be generous, too. Some had helped her and Becca out when Fanny knew the women didn't have two bits to rub together.

Trying to protect Becca, yet work and bring in scant money, Fanny had done her best to shield Becca from customers by sending Becca away whenever a man opened the crib door. Becca always flinched and took a step back the moment a man entered, but then she'd walk slowly toward them, close enough to see their hands. Fanny knew what Becca was up to. She was looking for missing fingers and a gold lion-head ring. Becca had promised Fanny more than once that when she found the man who killed her mother, "I'll kill 'im!"

Fanny worried more each day for the child's safety. There was no way Becca would get justice for her mother's death—she would get killed first. Fanny had to do something to get Becca away from Nevada City. Fanny hadn't seen the bastard who murdered Ruby in the bustling mining town for four years now, but no telling if he'd show up again . . . and kill the daughter, too. It could happen. Fanny knew it could.

The best thing for Becca was to get her to Denver City where she'd have an opportunity to grow up in a fine parlor house and become a rich, elegant whore, where she'd have a chance to live a longer life than most on the line. Most were dead by thirty. Fanny wasn't gonna let that happen to Becca.

As soon as Fanny got Becca off to Denver City, she had it all planned for herself. She was gonna buy the finest wine she could afford from a local saloon; go home and clean up her crib all nice, make sure to polish her name out front real good; put on her best dress; eat fine fixings and drink the whole bottle of wine; then lie down on her bed and empty an entire opium vial in her mouth . . . and escape the line once and for all.

"Go around back for a hand-out, child. Seeing as today's bread-baking day, Cook might just have a warm, thick slice for you."

Becca stared mutely at the woman who answered the front door of the big brick house on Holladay Street. She was tired and hungry, and the warm bread sounded real good. But Becca didn't stretch to reach the brass knocker on the massive front door for food. She'd come for work. She'd come down from Nevada City to work in the "fanciest parlor house in Denver City," just like Fanny told her to. She clutched a piece of paper in hand, the paper Fanny had given her. Becca knew what it said; she couldn't read, but she had it memorized:

This child is needing a job. She's a good girl and will work hard. Her mama was murdered and she's an orphan. There's no place for her in Nevada City and no one to care for her on the line. Please help. Fanny Mae Rogers

Becca knew Fanny didn't write the paper herself. She had a bartender do it at the Nugget saloon. Fanny said she couldn't write, but that Becca should learn when she got to Denver City. "Try to get schooling in Denver City, Becca. Reading and writing is fine things fer a fine lady to know," Fanny had said. Surprised about Fanny's full name, Becca had only known her as "Fanny." Becca wondered if *she* had more to her own name than Rebecca Rose, but then thought not; her mother would have said so.

Still having a hard time with her mother's death, Becca didn't like leaving Fanny and Nevada City, the only home she'd ever known. She knew why she had to leave 'cause Fanny told her *and* had it writ down. The paper said she was an orphan and had no place to live and nobody to care for her. Heck. She didn't need nobody caring for her; she'd care for others, like always, and make money till she was old enough to make money like the other whores. She didn't like men—most men anyways—but if she wanted to make money and stay in the Colorado Territory so she could find the bad man who killed her mother, then she'd do what she had to do. When she got older, maybe she wouldn't get sick to her stomach every time a man walked into the room. Maybe she wouldn't want to kill each of 'em till she saw their hands were clean.

"Child, did you hear me?" the mob-capped woman directed. "Now you just go and run on round to the back if you want some bread. Run along, now," the maid said, and then started to close the heavy door.

"No, ma'am, please." Becca placed her slight frame in the doorway, the note in her hand forgotten.

"Land sakes, child." The maid reopened the door. "What on earth has you trying to charge in here? You likely don't even know what this is . . . what kind of house this is, young lady."

"Yes ma'am, I do. This is the Palace, ain't it," Becca declared more than asked, then pushed inside to the entryway of the big house.

The maid closed the front door. "Yes, this is the Palace. How's a bit of a thing like you knowing about such? My, my." The maid shook her head. "All right, I'll take you to the kitchen, but just this once. In the future, you go around to the back door or to the poorhouse over on Blake Street."

Becca walked obediently behind the round woman, happy at the thought of food, but happier still to be inside the Palace. Her whole trip down from Nevada City, she'd never seen any such place. Fanny had gotten her a ride on a supply wagon down from the mines, and the trip had gone well enough. There was lots to see, and Becca took in everything along the ride through the mining towns of Central City and Blackhawk, then on down out of the mountains toward Denver City.

Somewhere between the flatlands and Denver City, she'd fallen asleep in the back of the supply wagon, and was mad at herself for doing so. The day had been hot and she hadn't slept at all the night before, making it hard for her to stay awake.

When she woke up, it was dark and she was in Denver City, the driver told her.

He had his orders from Fanny, Becca knew, to make sure she got to some place called Holladay Street, and then to a fancy parlor house run by Miss Jenny Clayton. It being dark and all, the driver told her she could sleep under the tarp till sunup, then she could skedaddle on her own to Miss Clayton's Palace. They were stopped now on Holladay Street and the Palace was just two houses down. If Becca hadn't been so tired, she would have gone to the Palace straightaway, but she fell asleep instead.

What a sight when she woke up in the morning. The hot western sun already beat down. Needing to relieve herself, she climbed down from the supply wagon and went behind one of the buildings along the bustling, mud-caked street filled with horses and riders and wagons and people walking to and fro, looking for an outhouse.

When she returned to Holladay Street, she saw houses and saloons and different kinds of shops, but no cribs—no pine shacks like she was used to. She'd imagined that Miss Clayton's would look like her mother's crib, only maybe a little bigger, and for the first time realized a parlor house must *not* be like a crib. Dazzled by the sights on Holladay Street, Becca plodded along the dusty thoroughfare, past saloons, houses, and gambling halls, until she came to a big brick house. She stopped in front of it. It had to be the one the driver told her about last night.

And now the maid here had said as much. Becca *was* at the Palace, the "finest parlor house in Denver City," just like she'd promised Fanny.

"Child, don't dillydally," the maid commanded, her tone stern.

Becca couldn't help herself, stopping along the fine, polished hallway, staring into one beautiful room after the other. "Yes ma'am," she answered absentmindedly, knowing she must be in a dream.

How could any place so grand be real? She'd never seen the like in Nevada City. One room had a wall of mirrors with a fancy piano and a spit 'n polish dance floor. Becca stared long and hard at the piano, expecting the Professor to appear at any moment, like in hurdy-gurdies and honkytonks. Whores made out real good when the Professor paid attention to them. 'Course the Professor wasn't as important as the Bartender. Lots of whores tried to get the Bartender to marry 'em.

The room across had beautiful furniture. Becca had never imagined anything like this in a parlor house. She stepped into the lace-curtained, thick-carpeted, Victorian parlor. Pictures hung from wires on all of the walls, some framed in gold, and others in carved wood. The room was beautiful and grand, just like Fanny had said. How Becca wished Fanny could be here with her now, working in the Palace. When she could, Becca determined she'd go back to Nevada City and get Fanny. Running her fingers over one of the fine settees, Becca had never felt anything so soft, like the tummy of a puppy. And cushions, all embroidered and fancy. There was a grand table in front of the settees, with silver on it! She knew about silver, but she'd never seen a real, actual tea set. She'd heard talk, but never seen the like.

In one corner of the grand space there was another fine table with fancy glass containers set atop it. Alongside the glass were two carved, wooden boxes. Becca wondered what might be inside. Next she studied the walls. They looked like silk, a garden of silk flowers. She walked over to the huge fireplace, touching the top of the mahogany mantel as if it were pure gold. Then she ran her fingers over the wall in front of her. It *was* made of silk!

"Child," the maid called from down the hallway. "I said no

dillydallying. Come straight away to the kitchen! You're getting mud all over Miss Jenny's parlor!"

"Clara. Just *who* is getting mud all over my parlor?"

CHAPTER THREE

Jenny Clayton, owner and madam of the Palace, stepped into the parlor.

Becca jerked her hand away from the wall, her forgotten note still clutched in the other. The woman who'd just come into the room was the most beautiful woman she'd ever seen. Becca had never cared about beautiful, especially with her mother's face being cut. It never made her think her mother wasn't beautiful, not for a minute. But the woman in front of her now looked like a fairy princess.

Everything on her seemed perfect, head-to-toe perfect. Her dress was a deep blue silk, with lace at the neck and the cuffs. Her dark hair was pinned up with curls falling just so at her nape. Her face was made up but not all fancy with too much rouge. Becca stared into the woman's deep blue eyes, uncomfortable under her stony scrutiny. Averting her eyes, Becca stared at the woman's hands. This woman had lovely, long fingers with rings on them. Not a gold lion-head ring, but pearls and diamonds. She'd never seen pearls and diamonds, of course, but the whores had told her all about 'em. As for the gold lion-head ring . . . when she saw it again she'd be ready with her own derringer.

"Miss Jenny," Clara huffed, hurrying into the parlor to collect the errant child. "I'm that sorry the child's causing any disturbance. I'll take care of her straightaway, ma'am."

Becca stood her ground, determined to stay put. She wasn't

about to leave until she found out for sure she had work at the Palace. The beautiful woman in front of her, eyeing her up and down, was Miss Jenny Clayton of the Palace. Miss Jenny was the person she needed to talk to, and nobody else.

"Come along, child," Clara pleaded, taking hold of one of Becca's arms. "Miss Jenny doesn't have time for the likes of you. It's off to the kitchen for a bite, and then you're on your way, young lady."

"No!" Becca resisted. "I wanna talk to Miss Jenny," she insisted, throwing the maid a mutinous look.

Jenny said nothing, but kept up her study of the dirty, unkempt child. Never missing a detail about anyone in her place—an absolute necessity in her business—Jenny could see the child was old beyond her years. It was always in the eyes. The eyes never lied. This child had been through a lot. Such a pretty child to have already had such a sad life. Ah well . . . It was no matter to Jenny. She had a business to run, and no time for begging children, especially children bringing so much mud into her parlor.

"Young lady." Jenny addressed Becca now. "You do as Clara says and go to the kitchen. Get something to eat and then run along." Jenny wanted to say run along home, but she doubted the child had a home. Feeling guiltier by the minute, Jenny's agitation with the situation grew. "And for heaven's sake, take off those horrid muddy boots before you take another step in my place."

"What's wrong with my boots?" Becca jerked her arm from the maid and stomped her feet in turn on the ornate, thick carpet. "These is my boots, and they work good, and they're just fine!"

"These *are* my boots," Jenny corrected, ever used to correcting "her girls" to ensure their grammar was letter-perfect.

"Suppose you don't think my dress is good enough, neither,"

Becca fumed, running her free hand over the scratchy burlap.

"Good enough, *either*," Jenny corrected. "Listen, child, your boots are fine and your dress is fine. Just run along now." Her tone softened as she turned to leave the parlor.

"Miss Jenny, please!" Becca yelled, suddenly afraid.

The madam stopped and pivoted, facing Becca.

"Miss Jenny, here!" Becca rushed over to her, escaping the maid's reach, and shoved her note at the madam.

The maid immediately started after Becca.

"It's all right, Clara," Jenny instructed. "Stay while I read this."

Clara obediently folded her hands in front of her starched apron, miffed at herself for the situation.

So . . . Her murdered mother worked at the end of the line in Nevada City. Jenny's heart broke, not just for the pitiable little girl in front of her, but for the poor woman whose life ended in such tragedy. No one knew better than Jenny how easy it was for a prostitute to die young, sometimes murdered, sometimes taking her own life, unable to climb out of the melancholia that often comes with the trade near the end of the line. Jenny's Palace was at the top of the line—the top of the row in Denver City. Her address, at the corner of Twentieth and Holladay, was the best in the city. So was her clientele. It was the only place to be, to Jenny's thinking: at the top.

"Miss Jenny, I'll work fer you. I'll work real good. I can clean and scrub and take care of whores." Becca talked as fast as she could, afraid Miss Jenny would leave before she could finish. "I can get their opium and take care of 'em when they're sick. I can stand watch so's nobody will hurt 'em. I can yell real loud. I can cook a little, too. Soup and such. Then when I'm of the age, like Fanny told me, I can work fer you as a whore. I'll learn real good. I promise," Becca finished, sorry now she'd stomped her muddy boots on Miss Jenny's pretty rug.

Jenny didn't have a choice, knowing what she did now about the child. She couldn't relegate her to the poorhouse. Nor could she let her run along and meet some dreadful end on the city streets. It would be on her conscience forever if she did so. Contrary to the belief of most, prostitutes did have consciences.

Jenny, smart as well as beautiful, had started out in parlor houses at the age of seventeen, choosing her lifestyle, and she'd soon realized her dream of running her own place. No madam on the row in Denver City could claim to be a more astute businesswoman than Miss Jenny Clayton. She'd signed the papers to her house on Holladay Street the day she turned twenty-five, only offering her services from then on to select customers. Not only was it a more lucrative choice for her, but a healthier, safer choice for a longer life. She wanted her girls to enjoy a longer life, too. Nothing second-class in Miss Jenny's Palace. Some day she'd build one even bigger and better.

"Clara," Jenny said to the maid. "Take this child . . . Child, what's your name?"

"Becca . . . Uh, Rebecca. Rebecca Rose is my name."

"Clara, take Becca to the kitchen and feed her; then take her upstairs and wash her down good. I'll send one of the upstairs maids to Joslin's Dry Goods to find some clothes for her. Put Becca in the top attic room with the trundle bed. She can stay with the other children on the uppermost floor. I'll decide what to do with her later. Right now, it's getting late. Our first customers will be arriving and all must be ready. Oh, and Clara, tell all of my girls we have another child with us. Tell them I'll explain later."

"Yes, ma'am." Clara nodded obediently, then took up Becca's arm again, this time determined to shuttle the child off to the kitchen.

Becca, her fear and hunger forgotten, gleefully let the maid take her arm. Relieved she could stay and work and live at the

Palace, she couldn't wait to see other children upstairs. It had been a long time since she'd thought of the good fairies that watched over her. Not since the night her mother was murdered. She'd given up believing in them, or anything else, that very night. But maybe the good fairies did still exist. Upstairs. Watching over the children. Keeping them safe. Suddenly Becca couldn't wait to find out.

Too old to believe in fairies or fairy tales, almost eighteen, Becca finished up her morning toilette, and reflected back on those first days at Miss Jenny's. She thought of the moment she opened the door to her room, three flights up, and discovered the children there: two babies and one four-year-old. It was like magic, being with the other children, though none was anywhere near her age. That didn't matter to Becca. What did matter was to be included with them, to not be shut away and shunned. It was a wonderful time.

In fact, over the nine years she'd been with Miss Jenny—the house had been added on to since Becca first arrived, and now boasted another floor and even finer amenities—the children in the attic room had come and gone. That was the way of it in the world of prostitution, Becca discovered. Children born to prostitutes in a fine parlor house like Miss Jenny's met a much better fate than most. Their mothers could actually keep them for a while in the house, and then often chose to send them East to school or to live with relatives, away from the business. Because the girls working at the Palace were part of an exclusive trade, they made good money and could afford better care for their children, should they have any.

Of course, it wasn't uncommon for children of prostitutes to disown their mothers, once they found out about their true livelihoods. This led to some prostitutes trying to lead a double life, hoping their children would never find out what they really did for a living.

Becca had heard all the stories about children not as fortunate as the ones born at Miss Jenny's. Some prostitutes set their children up in the sporting life, exposing them to alcohol, cursing, and drugs at a very young age. Some were left on doorsteps of churches or on the doorstep of the supposed father, in hopes they'd be cared for. Some died from lack of care, lack of food, and disease caused by living in such poor conditions. Children born into lower houses down the line had a harder time of it for sure. Brothels were a step below parlor houses, and then came saloons, dance halls, and honkytonks or hurdy-gurdies. Near the end of the line were cribs, and at the very end of the line were streetwalkers.

Becca thought of the pine shack in Nevada City where she was born. She didn't care that she came from a crib and felt no shame for it at all. A tear escaped down her cheek. She wiped it away and straightened her spine. She'd yet to find her mother's killer.

In all the years she'd lived at Miss Jenny's, Becca had done her utmost to have a look at every customer entering in the evening. She looked for missing fingers and the gold lion-head ring, but kept it secret. Instinctively, she knew she must keep what she knew about her mother's killer to herself. If she spread the word all along the row in Denver, the killer would find out and run.

Never once did Becca think about the danger she might be in. Never once did Becca think about bringing in the law to help her. Who would help a whore? No one. Becca knew it. So when Becca showed up every time the front bell-pull rang, the bouncer, Big Eddie—the man Miss Jenny had stationed near the door to keep watch for trouble—would tell her to scoot, that she didn't belong off her floor in the house.

"Kids need to git, Becca. So git," Big Eddie would tell her.

Becca got, but then shot down the stairs again the moment she heard the next bell-pull.

"Becca." Big Eddie would shake his head. "Does Miss Jenny know you sneak down here every night, trying to see who all comes in?"

Becca would shrug her shoulders and smile innocently.

Big Eddie would tell her to git yet again.

In fact, Jenny did know of Becca's comings and goings. Jenny knew about everyone's comings and goings at the Palace. A madam couldn't afford to do less. Jenny knew every silver piece exchanged for every brass token; every customer who entered and every girl he came to see; which customer was in mining; who was a politician, a lawman, a rancher, or businessman from the East; which customer liked a particular cigar or wine and which customer preferred a special champagne supper; which customer liked to hear the piano or the violin; which customer liked to watch dancers or jugglers, all before going upstairs to their selected lady's room.

She also knew which customers had a reported malady, or perhaps a festering sore. In those instances her girls had been instructed to call for Miss Jenny. Diplomacy was key here. Miss Jenny didn't want to raise the ire of any in her elite clientele, but she didn't want any of her girls to get burned with syphilis, either.

Jenny kept track of everything going on at the Palace, with her customers and with her girls. She paid good money to make sure her girls stayed in the best of health, requiring them to be checked every month by a doctor. She made sure they operated in a clean, elegant environment, had protection from Big Eddie if need be, wore the finest clothes and spoke properly. No cursing was allowed. If one of her girls uttered a four-letter word, she'd be gone that very day. Jenny didn't give second chances. It wasn't good for business. Why she gave Becca one remained a mystery even to her.

There wasn't any room in the world of prostitution, if you wanted a successful business, for children. A madam had responsibilities, and none of them should be children. Yes, Jenny did allow children to be born in her house, giving the mothers enough time to decide what to do with their babies.

Her heart went out to the prostitutes in brothels and hurdy-gurdies and cribs where it wasn't unusual to do fifty tricks a night. Eighty wasn't unheard of in the mining towns. When a prostitute got pregnant, it was no matter to some who ran boarding houses or to pimps. If a prostitute couldn't be on her back making money, she was worth nothing. A child born to a prostitute had it rough, no matter if it was in a crib or a parlor house, to Jenny's way of thinking. She'd seen too many children grow up to hate their mothers. Maybe that was why she gave Becca a second chance when the child showed up at her door all those years ago: Becca had loved her mother unconditionally; she didn't care that her mother was cut or lived in a crib.

Of course, the world of prostitution was all Becca had ever known, Jenny realized. But something in Becca's thoughtful, intelligent eyes told Jenny that Becca would never have turned her back on her mother, shunning her, condemning her. That fact alone touched Jenny's heart. Try as she might, Jenny couldn't get Becca to open up and tell her about the night her mother was killed or give a description of the man she saw. Jenny knew the reason that Becca scrambled downstairs to see every customer was to see if any of the men entering the Palace might be the man who'd killed her mother. Jenny cautioned Becca more than once to try to stay out of sight.

Jenny provided room and board for Becca, even teaching her to read and write, in trade for Becca helping with the young ones on the uppermost floor, and helping the maids rather than her girls. Better for Becca to learn to cook and sew and clean than take care of the prostitutes on the second floor.

As time went by, however, Jenny realized it was pointless to keep Becca from the prostitutes, especially with everyone gathering in the big, cheerful kitchen for meals and socializing. Becca became invaluable to Miss Jenny's girls and seemed to have genuine affection for anyone in the business. But that's where it stopped. Becca had affection for the girls, but Jenny knew Becca didn't have affection for any of their customers.

Tolerance would perhaps be the better word.

This presented a problem for Jenny. The Palace was all about pleasing men, and Becca wasn't interested in pleasing men. Jenny knew why: her mother's murder. Becca blamed all men for her mother's death, Jenny believed. She certainly didn't want to force Becca into the world of prostitution. If Becca chose the profession, Jenny knew she would be the most requested of her girls. And now, at seventeen, Jenny didn't know what to do with Becca.

Customers had begun to notice her, to ask for her in particular. When men made an appointment at the Palace, especially important men, and they requested a particular prostitute, Jenny's job and livelihood depended on giving them what they wanted.

And there was something else. Some of Jenny's girls coming and going over the years didn't understand why Jenny showed partiality to Becca, despite the fact that Becca helped the maids and prostitutes, working day in and day out. Jenny realized there was jealousy brewing, especially since Becca had grown into a beautiful young woman, with elegant ways, and a classy style all her own. Maybe Jenny *had* shown Becca favoritism, making sure she had enough schooling to learn to read and write well, taking her shopping for just the right clothes, and taking her riding in her carriage on nice afternoons past some of Denver's finest addresses.

Oh, for pity's sake, Jenny scolded inwardly. She *had* taken Becca in her carriage, and that's nothing but pure advertising for the Palace. Taken together with customers spotting Becca's beauty at the Palace in the evenings as she served tea and coffee, clipped cigars, poured champagne, laid out fine buffet suppers, took hats and canes at the door, greeted customers . . . *Oh, for pity's sake,* Jenny scolded again. *My fault. My fault entirely.*

And now one customer—one very prominent customer—had taken particular notice of Becca and wanted an appointment with her that very evening!

For the first time, in a very long time, Jenny didn't know what to do. She'd grown to love Becca, much like the daughter she never had. She understood Becca's hidden hurt, her dislike of men, and she also understood that prostitution was the only world Becca had ever known. Jenny had tried for two years to send Becca to finishing school back East, but the stubborn girl refused, saying she'd never leave Colorado for any reason. And now, with a prominent customer from one of the best families in Denver wanting a special appointment with Becca . . . *What to do, what to do, what to do?*

The reason Jenny had such a successful parlor house, lasting over many years, where others had not, was not only because Jenny took very good care of her girls, paying them well, but also because she had carefully developed an elite clientele, a rich clientele. She catered to their needs and their whims, giving them pleasures they didn't get at home. The dictates of the Victorian era favored prostitution. A wife was not supposed to enjoy sex. She tolerated her husband's touch mainly for the procreation of children.

Business had been good a long time, especially in booming Colorado, and Jenny wanted to keep it that way. She couldn't afford any bad news about her filtering into Denver's lofty circles. She couldn't afford for wealthy miners, rich politicians, or well-to-do Eastern businessmen to hear anything bad about the Palace. If she didn't give the customer who requested an appointment with Becca what he wanted, she wasn't sure what would happen to her and her business and all of her girls. Everything and everyone in her house depended on her. Jenny had been in the business too long to think she was ever safe from being one step away from the poorhouse.

Becca swallowed hard, appreciating Miss Jenny's honesty, yet frightened by her news. She'd known this day would come, and dreaded it.

Becca and Jenny Clayton—parlor house daughter and madam—sat across from one another in the spacious front parlor. It was ten in the morning, and no one else was about. Christmas had come and gone. The new year was upon them. Depression still chilled the bones of many of the girls, making them sleep later than usual. It was hard for some not to be with family, but working in a parlor house during the holidays.

Winter sun shone through the opened gold-tasseled draperies, doing little to warm the chill in the air. Becca straightened on the settee, refusing to cry about this day and what it meant. She never cried, not since her mother's death, not even when she found out that dear Fanny had taken her life. She wanted to, but she couldn't. Her tears stayed buried.

"I'm offering again to send you to finishing school in the East, Becca," Jenny encouraged, knowing the risk she took in doing so.

Becca stared into Jenny's still-beautiful blue eyes. The years had been kind to Denver's most noted madam. What few wrinkles and gray hairs she had were barely noticeable. Her hourglass figure still tempted customers. Becca loved Miss Jenny almost like a mother. She trusted Miss Jenny. She should listen to her. Going East would be a wonderful opportunity, Becca knew, but how could she leave Colorado before she found her mother's killer? She could not. Something in her told her every day she took a breath, the killer was still nearby. No, the killer hadn't walked through the doors of the Palace in the past nine years, but still . . . he was close. She could feel it, and now she was old enough to do something about it.

"Miss Jenny, I'll meet this customer," Becca declared, all emotion hidden. "I'll have an appointment and . . . and—"

"No." Jenny gritted her teeth, and stood up. "I can't let you do this. I know you don't want to."

Becca stood, too. "Miss Jenny, I'm a grown woman now and I can make up my own mind. I've wanted this all of my life, and now I'll have it. I'll earn at least fifty dollars a night. What prostitute could ask for more? Besides, you know I'm not comfortable in the outside world of respectable folk. Respectable folk have unkind hearts. I don't want to be a part of their world. I've no desire to be." Becca walked over to Jenny and took her hand. "You're very kind to care, Miss Jenny. I know my mother would have liked you. I like you," Becca said quietly, ignoring the emotion welling in her throat. She wanted to say she loved Miss Jenny as a daughter would love a mother, but she could not.

"Child, child." Jenny pulled Becca to sit next to her on the nearest settee, all the while fighting her own feelings, her own desire to tell Becca how much she'd grown to love her, as a mother would a daughter. At that moment, guilt settled hard into Jenny's bones—guilt a mother would have to bear for committing a daughter to the world of prostitution. "All right, I'll set up your appointment with the gentleman in question, but I'll tell him there are parameters, and he must stick to them."

"Parameters?" Becca repeated, puzzled.

"Yes, Becca. I'll tell him that the first appointment is only to talk and to get acquainted. In no way can he touch you."

Becca breathed a sigh of relief.

"He can sit with you in one of the parlors and that's all. I'll make it very clear to him. You, young woman, can tell him whatever you wish about yourself, or not. It's up to you how you want things to go. If you don't like him, or if he gives you any problems, just ring for Big Eddie. I won't be far away, either. Is this all right with you?" Jenny softly questioned.

"Yes," Becca answered. "Yes, it sounds fine, and I'll be fine," she reassured Jenny, her hands clasped together so tight now that she wondered if she'd ever be able to pull them apart.

Jenny stood. "Come, child. We've lots to do to get you ready for tonight."

Becca stood, too, and obediently followed Jenny out of the parlor, dreading the night ahead, when really . . . it mattered little. What *did* matter was staying in Denver, staying in Colorado, and finding her mother's killer. If she had to prostitute herself to do it, then so be it.

"Morgan, how is it you didn't invite Lavinia to dinner before now? Shame on you, son."

Augusta Larkspur gently chided her son, then rang the bell for the maid to clear the first course from the table. Impeccably dressed in russet silk, her just-graying auburn hair expertly coiffed, Augusta's brown eyes still held their sparkle. Confident that her son liked Lavinia, the young woman he'd brought— after all, it was New Year's Eve and he wouldn't invite just anyone for the holiday dinner—Augusta smiled inwardly. Entertaining was a main part of Augusta's life, her husband being one of the wealthy, social elite in Denver. Even if she didn't enjoy it, which she did, entertaining was her obligation, a necessity to keep up with business connections and maintain the family's prominent position in the community.

Tonight her son had invited Lavinia Eagleton to their home,

and Augusta couldn't have been happier. Morgan had turned twenty-five and it was high-time her son made a suitable marriage. An engagement to twenty-one-year-old Lavinia Eagleton would be perfect. The blond beauty seated to Augusta's left at their table tonight would be a wonderful addition to the Larkspur family. Augusta knew Lavinia's mother, Mary Ella Eagleton, quite well. They attended the same charity social events and were at many of the same luncheons and parties. The Eagletons came from the East, and were from old family money.

Augusta knew her son wanted to ranch. How silly, especially when he was so adept in the mining business. He'd taken to it from the first trip to the mines with his father back in '75. Well, now here it was 1880, and Morgan managed the family's holdings in Leadville. Tending to family business interests elsewhere, Eugene Larkspur rarely went to the mines anymore, leaving Morgan in charge.

Augusta didn't understand why Morgan wanted to be so hands-on, often working alongside the miners. It made no sense to Augusta that her son wanted to dirty his hands when he didn't have to. Besides, she and Eugene had plans for Morgan, political plans. For that, of course, he needed a suitable wife, a wife like Lavinia Eagleton. *Humph,* Augusta scoffed to herself. If only Morgan wasn't such a difficult son, trying to go his own way all of the time. At least she had Monty. Thank goodness for Monty.

Her younger son, Monty, relished society life in Denver. He made Augusta proud. The easier child by far, Monty loved the circuit of parties, had no trouble delegating work to others, and brought lovely young women—all proper, usually from the cream of society—to dinner. Monty didn't want to dirty his hands any more than he had to, and always did his parents' bidding. *Yes, thank goodness for Monty,* Augusta repeated to herself, switching her gaze to her favorite son. Monty had invited a young lady as well. At twenty-one, it wasn't too early for him to think about marriage, either. Augusta wasn't sure if she quite approved of the young lady Monty had brought this evening; her family wasn't particularly prominent, and Monty could do better.

"Morgan—"

Morgan took up his glass of champagne, interrupting his mother. "A Happy New Year to you all," he toasted, and then took a sip of the bubbly liquid, satisfied he'd quieted his mother for the time being. Returning Lavinia's affectionate regard, he looked forward to his escape to the library after supper when he could join the other men gathered around the festive table for brandy and a good cigar.

CHAPTER FOUR

"Becca, you look beautiful," Jenny declared, stepping away to better admire her handiwork. She'd helped Becca dress for her special customer, and wanted every detail to be perfect.

Jenny had spared no expense in outfitting Becca in the finest silk and arranging her hair just so, but stopped short of jewels or too much rouge. The brunette beauty didn't need them. She already shone more than any girl at the Palace.

"Oh, there's the first appointment." Jenny heard the bell pull at the front door. "I'd best get downstairs." Turning to do just that, Jenny pivoted back around. "Child, are you ready? Are you ready for tonight?"

"Of course I am. Don't worry, Miss Jenny. This is what I want." Becca stared at her own reflection in the full mirror in front of her, rather than face Jenny with her lie.

"All right, then." Jenny heaved a sigh. "I'll let you know when your customer arrives," she said, then turned and left Becca's room, closing the door behind her.

Funny, at such a moment all Becca could think about was money. The money her room and board at the Palace cost, the money her evening gowns cost, the money day dresses cost, how much each bottle of wine or champagne cost, how much for laundry and how much for incidentals, how much for cab fare for customers, how much for fees to the law should they arise, how much to Miss Jenny, then how much money would be left over at the end of the week to put away. By her quick calculations, earning three hundred and fifty dollars a week—seeing a customer every night—she'd have some money left, but not much. Maybe ten dollars. She'd be thrifty, especially since she could do her own sewing. Then she'd have more left over at the end of each week.

Luckier than most, Becca had nothing but gratitude for Miss Jenny's kindness to her over the years. Yes, she worked alongside the maids, helping when there were children, and helping the girls, but in no way did she expect Miss Jenny to provide her with a silk evening gown every night, or cover her room and board now. Not now that she considered herself in Miss Jenny's employ as one of her girls. The Palace was a well-run business, a well-run house of prostitution, and Becca didn't expect favoritism from Miss Jenny. Tonight she'd begin her employment as one of the girls, officially becoming a prostitute.

More dead inside than upset, Becca turned away from the mirror and gazed around her new room. She appreciated the move down from the uppermost floor to room number eight on the second floor. All together, between the second and the third floors, Miss Jenny boarded sixteen girls. Even though prostitutes usually ranged in age from fifteen to thirty, Miss Jenny liked her girls to be at least sixteen, healthy, loyal to the house, in full knowledge that Miss Jenny was in absolute charge, on the up-and-up regarding money exchanged, and willing to learn refined ways—good manners and pleasuring men being the most important of those. Most of the girls were in their twenties, Becca knew.

She'd got along fine with the prostitutes over the years, but lately some seemed upset with her. Becca couldn't fathom why. She thought of the time when she was young, living in Nevada City, when she felt shunned by passersby and was left out of play with other children. That's how she felt now with some of the girls. But then, having a forgiving nature with women in the business, Becca understood better than most that prostitution was a hard life, even in a superior house, and some of the girls just must be having a bad time of it now.

Shaking off such thoughts, Becca walked over and sat down on her full bed. It was brass and wrought iron, with a forest-green satin spread. She knew she'd arrived, since the sheets would be changed every day, in between each customer.

Her insides caught at the thought, as if she'd only now realized its import.

Lace skirted the bed, matching the lace-covered pillowslips. All of the furniture in the room was of the same wood: a dark, high-polished oak. Besides the floor mirror, there was a three-drawer vanity with another mirror along one wall and a changing screen placed adjacent to the vanity. A matching wardrobe stood against the opposite wall, with a marble-topped commode, and all the necessaries for her toilette alongside it. Down the hall, on each floor of the house, was a full necessary, complete with a bathtub.

A small table with a lamp atop it and a single chair had been tucked in a corner by Becca's bed. Two gas-lit wall sconces on opposite walls provided soft illumination. Lace curtains with red velvet tassels and trim adorned the room's only window, under which a window seat had been built in. The wallpaper picked up on the red velvet, with red roses on a white background. It *was* like a palace.

Although not a princess in a fairy tale, at least Becca had made it to a palace—*The* Palace—the best parlor house in Denver. She didn't believe in good fairies or fairy tales, not since the day her mother was murdered. Besides, a prostitute couldn't afford to believe in fairy tales or happy endings. Neither could a prostitute afford to have feelings for any of her customers. *Feelings only get a whore killed,* she remembered Fanny's warning.

Standing now, Becca walked back over to the floor mirror, although she'd no desire to check her appearance. How she looked mattered little to her, but it was an important part of her job now. A prostitute needed to present herself as best she could, to please her customers—her company—and to make good money. Awash in lavender silk, Becca would have preferred a deeper purple. She loved the color purple. *Next time.* Next dress, when she had the money to fashion one. Studying her reflection, Becca scrutinized her appearance, head to foot.

Her low-cut gown clung to her in all the right places, showing off her curvy, yet slight, shape. At five-foot-two, although Becca couldn't weigh more than a hundred and five pounds, her full bosom, tiny waist, and slender hips made for a near-perfect figure. Never very hungry, Becca knew she should probably eat more. What she wished for, what she wanted to do, she'd never done. She wanted to venture outside Denver, outside of the city, and go riding out on the open prairie. She'd never ridden a horse. How odd, to live on the western frontier, and never to have ridden a horse. Becca sighed, and then continued her self-study in the mirror.

The cap sleeves of her dress, resting just so over her upper arms, made her gown more comfortable than day dresses. In a day dress, with long sleeves and high-set arms, one could hardly reach overhead. Evening dresses proved much more comfortable. Becca took pleasure in lifting her arms high and did it now; once, then again. The waistline of her gown, although pulled in, wasn't restrictive, the silk flowing over her hips, then to the floor, pooling at her soft, brown leather-shoed feet.

Eyeing her bodice again, Becca ran her fingers over the cream ribbon floral design across the top of the gown, wishing she could pull the ribbon a bit tighter to perhaps expose less of her. One thing she did like about day dresses over evening gowns— day dresses covered up your bodice entirely. Becca wondered if she'd ever be comfortable exposing herself, trying to be alluring and seductive to men.

Humph. She straightened her spine. She thought not. Glad for the corset she wore, despite the loose flow of her gown, she tried to imagine removing her corset and the rest of her necessaries for a man, suddenly darting her gaze to the changing screen, placed there for just such a purpose. For a split second, regret filled her, washing over her in painful waves. For a split second . . . she was afraid.

Shaking off her fears, Becca turned back to the mirror and her preparations for her customer. Fear didn't have any place in her life. A prostitute couldn't afford such emotions, or any other emotions, for that matter. Not when it came to their male company. A prostitute couldn't risk falling in love or letting foolish passions get the better of her. That's how a prostitute got killed, or worse . . . *having feelings.*

Miss Jenny had helped her with her hair, and not one of the maids. Miss Jenny, an expert in all things, fashioned Becca's long, thick, chestnut hair in a loose topknot, with some wavy tendrils fringing the sides of her face and her forehead. Accustomed to pinning her hair up tighter, Becca fought the urge to do so now, expecting her hair to come tumbling down at any moment.

But that wouldn't do, and she knew it. Wearing your hair down was blatant advertisement and not proper for a parlor house, according to Miss Jenny. Satisfied her hair would stay put, Becca checked her lip rouge. She was wearing it for the first time. Not wanting to look like a painted doll, she happily acquiesced when Miss Jenny said she only needed a bit of rouge on her "sculpted" lips and nothing more.

"Your downy, peach complexion is already perfect. You have unusually pretty eyes, too, Becca," Miss Jenny had continued, extolling her assets. "Not many can boast of such an alluring, soft brown umber, flecked with shadow and seduction. You've no idea of the effect on men, young lady. Every time you bat your lovely dark lashes at them, they'll count themselves fortunate."

Fine. Becca was done with her self-assessment. *Whatever it takes to get my fifty dollars a night.*

She walked back over to the bed and sat down, clasping her hands in her lap. She wore no jewelry at all tonight, even though Miss Jenny had offered to lend her a pearl ring. Becca didn't care for jewelry and refused ever, ever to wear a ring, thinking of the gold lion-head ring on the hand of her mother's killer. The thought of ever putting on a ring, any ring, made her stomach turn.

Something else now made her stomach turn and set her nerves on edge. What if she couldn't remember all the right things to say to her customer when she met him? *Oh dear, oh dear!* She'd best practice while she still had time.

Music reverberated through the floorboards of Becca's room. She was jumpy, and the music played on her frayed nerves. The frequent bell pulls downstairs at the main door had already grated on her, adding to her tension.

A full orchestra had been hired for the evening, as Miss Jenny had a special night of dinner and dancing planned for everyone downstairs. Some evenings there would be a violinist or a pianist only, but tonight, being Saturday night, Miss Jenny made sure the Palace ruled the row in service to her customers. An elegant buffet supper would be set, with the finest food and wine in Denver ready for the enjoyment of all at the Palace.

Miss Jenny had promised Becca she'd keep one of the small parlors reserved for Becca and her customer. Although happy to be on the first floor close to Big Eddie, Becca wasn't happy others could pass by and observe her appointment with him.

Her stomach flip-flopped again. She hadn't thought about what the other girls in the house might think of her and her new job, until now. Some already disliked her. She didn't want to make things worse. All she had in the world, the only home she'd ever known, had been with the girls. To have them disapprove of her hurt. Never once did it occur to Becca that the other prostitutes might be jealous of her—jealous of her generous nature; jealous of her natural beauty; and jealous of her preferential treatment from Miss Jenny.

A rap on the door interrupted Becca's worried thoughts.

"Your company's here," Miss Jenny called through the door.

Becca stood, swallowed hard, collected herself, then walked over to the door and opened it. "I'm ready," she announced to the madam, stiffening her spine, unaware she sounded more like she was being led to her hanging than her first night of work.

"Becca, this is Morgan Larkspur," Miss Jenny said softly the moment she and Becca entered the private parlor.

Becca didn't recognize the name—she never paid any attention to anyone's name, rarely looking at faces, either—but she *did* recognize the man's hands. Her heart raced; her traitorous body instinctively attracted to him.

Angry at her lack of control, she kept her gaze riveted on his hands. He wore no rings on his tanned fingers, and his hands showed scars, telling of work, hard work. Most men entering the Palace, men she'd waited on, wore rings and had smooth-appearing hands. They obviously paid others to do their work. She didn't have to look at this customer's face to know he was the handsomest man she'd ever seen enter the Palace. Well, what did she care? She didn't even like men, handsome or not.

"I'll take my leave now, Spur," Miss Jenny cooed.

"Thank you, Miss Jenny," Morgan politely intoned, his rich,

husky voice echoing in the small parlor.

Becca swallowed hard, trying to keep her composure and her breath. She'd heard him speak once, when she'd served him champagne along with other men gathered in the main parlor a month ago. He'd said the same thing then: "Thank you." One time before that, she'd spotted him from a distance at the Palace. Upset that she'd had any kind of reaction to a man other than dislike, her reaction to Morgan Larkspur wreaked havoc on her insides. She felt every frayed nerve stab at her composure. Why did *he* have to be her special customer? Of all the luck, the *bad* luck!

Nothing to be done for it. She'd best do her job—and do it well, if she expected to be well paid.

"How do you do, Mr. Larkspur? I am Rebecca Rose. I am pleasured to meet you. Please come and sit and we'll have a nice visit," Becca offered, doing her utmost to remember the exact wording of her practiced speech. She'd yet to look the tall, well-built, aggravatingly handsome man in the eye, putting out her hand to direct him to the parlor's only sofa. "Let me pour your favorite wine and clip your favorite cigar, Mr. Larkspur." She kept up her practiced speech, hoping she sounded sweet and syrupy enough, just as she'd heard the other girls in the house with their customers. A table had been set close to the sofa, loaded with her customer's favorites. Becca knew they'd already be there, ready for her to offer. Her stomach churned hard. This wasn't going well.

Morgan Larkspur hadn't moved! He hadn't sat down and he wasn't holding out his hand for a glass of wine or a fine cigar!

Clearing her throat, fighting for calm, Becca decided to repeat her speech. "How do you do, Mr.—"

His deep chuckle stopped her, fueling her anger instead of her fear. How dare he laugh? She'd built up to this moment for years and years. How dare he? Now she looked him straight in the eye.

"I said it all right, didn't I, Mr. Larkspur? I said it like all of the other girls, and you should be sitting down now on the lovely, velvet-cushioned sofa, and waiting for me to serve you wine and clip and light a cigar!" Becca huffed.

I'll be damned, Morgan thought. He believed what Miss Jenny told him now about the brunette beauty. This beauty *was* untried. When he'd first approached the famous madam about the girl in question, never once did he actually believe the girl hadn't worked as a prostitute before. Now he did. No tried prostitute would be reciting the speech he'd just heard, using about as much seduction as a schoolteacher reciting multiplication tables. Whoa. Now Morgan doubted his wisdom in asking for this appointment. He wasn't interested in spoiling any young woman, prostitute or otherwise. He didn't want to be anyone's "first." No matter that this girl took his breath with her looks and her shy ways. He remembered she'd been shy before, barely looking at him. Now anything but shy. She seemed to have no trouble at all lashing out at him.

Becca's customer towered over her, looming now like a great black predator, trying to decide if it liked its prey or not. She hated this. Nothing was going right! She'd done her best to be alluring and seductive, and Morgan Larkspur only laughed at her! She *couldn't* fail at this. She just couldn't. Too much depended on her being a successful prostitute at the Palace.

Gulping once, then again, she forced herself to calm. "Mr. Larkspur, please, won't you sit? Surely you would enjoy some wine." She strained to recapture the moment, taking a seat herself, nervously smoothing the folds of her gown.

"Morgan," he corrected. "Or Spur, if you like." He took a seat next to the nervous girl. "Most everyone calls me Spur." This wasn't going to be easy: getting out of his appointment.

He didn't want to hurt the girl's feelings.

Relaxing a little, Becca turned her head slightly, yet didn't look at him. "Morgan," she repeated in a soft voice.

"And which is it with you?" he tried to make polite conversation. "Are you Becca or Rebecca?"

"Everyone calls me Becca," she responded, staring at her hands clasped tightly in her lap.

"Then I'll call you Rebecca. It's a beautiful name. Your mother's?" he asked, before catching himself. He'd no call to ask a prostitute about her family. At once uneasy, Morgan shifted in his seat.

No one ever brought up her mother. No one in the house ever asked about family. How dare he? How *dare* he? Fighting the urge to get up and run out of the parlor, Becca struggled to retain her control. She needed this job. She needed to please this customer. She needed her fifty dollars tonight.

"Leave my mother out of this, Mr. Larks—Morgan," Becca gritted out, doing her best to hide her upset. She'd only say it once. If he said anything about her mother again, she *would* leave.

"I will have that glass of wine now, Rebecca," Morgan said, in an easy voice. "Join me?"

"Of . . . course," she said, her anger instantly diffused by his simple overture. Flustered that he so easily affected her, she had to keep up her guard. She didn't want anyone—any man—having any power over her.

Reaching for the already open bottle of cabernet, she carefully poured two glasses, then handed one to Morgan. When she felt his fingers contact hers, she nearly dropped the stemmed glass, grateful when he safely held his wine. No, this wasn't going well at all. She never expected to feel anything *good* at the touch of a man; and to feel so . . . so . . . *shaken* just by the brush of his fingers . . . no, this wasn't going well.

"To you, Rebecca." Morgan inclined his glass toward her, and then took a sip.

Becca took a sip from her own glass, grimacing at the taste of the red wine. It was her first.

Morgan couldn't believe it. She was definitely untried. Hell, she didn't even drink! He'd never heard of a prostitute who didn't imbibe a lot and often. Curious now about how Rebecca had arrived at the Palace in the first place, he wondered if he should ask. But then he remembered her reaction when he asked her mother's name. No. He wouldn't ask Rebecca anything personal. Besides, he'd soon be on his way out the door anyway.

"Like it, do you?" Morgan couldn't avoid teasing.

"Why, yes." Becca took another small swallow, as if to prove she did, all the while hoping the distasteful red liquid would go down all right. Until this moment, it never occurred to her that she didn't drink; that she didn't want to drink; and that she didn't want to smoke, either.

Some prostitute she made. A prude of a prostitute would be more apt. Her hands began to shake at Morgan's scrutiny. Quickly, she set her glass down on the table and folded her hands in her lap. Her palms were wet. She fought the urge to run them along the beautiful lavender silk of her gown. Now *that* certainly would not do.

Enchanted by Rebecca, Morgan knew he needed to get out of there, and fast. The next thing he knew, he'd be taking her upstairs and doing the very thing he shouldn't: despoiling a virgin. Sorry now that he'd ever spotted Rebecca all those weeks ago, he regretted this private meeting with her. There were other parlor houses in Denver. He couldn't believe his luck in coming to the Palace and finding this particular girl. All he'd wanted was a little diversion from the mines in Leadville and from his obligation to court and marry Lavinia Eagleton. The more he saw Lavinia, the more he needed to step out for a little distraction. It had everything to do with Morgan's obligation to his family, their business interests, and their standing in Denver, and little to do with the lovely, blond, toast-of-society, lady in question.

Damn, Morgan groused silently. Thoughts of marriage and commitment and Denver society and running for political office soured him every time. But there was no getting around it, and he knew it. He knew his future. His parents mapped it all out for him years ago. No way could he—or would he—let them down. They'd given him a lot, and he wasn't about to turn his back on their hopes and dreams for him.

Once in a while, though, he wished they'd put a little of the family responsibility on little brother Monty. Monty liked to play; he didn't like to work. Monty's irresponsibility had always aggravated Morgan, and now it aggravated him more than ever. No good could come from a grown man not facing up to his duties. Morgan had been trying his whole life to straighten out his little brother, and he hadn't had too much success. He loved Monty, absolutely. But did he like him? Like was another matter.

"It's been a real pleasure meeting you, Rebecca." Morgan stood, only now remembering he ought to pay the girl for her time. Reaching into his pocket, he took out his fifty-dollar token and held it out to her.

Panicked, Becca didn't know what to do. She couldn't take the token. Not yet. They hadn't even sat down and talked for more than fifteen minutes. Everyone in the house would know her customer had spurned her at first glance!

"Mor-Morgan," she sputtered, struggling to draw on every seductive comment she'd ever heard repeated at the Palace. "Please have some more wine . . . hon-honey." She stood, too, but couldn't bring herself to face him. "Why, I just love your name. It's so . . . so manly . . . and strong . . . just like you. I-I can't imagine being with anyone but you. You make me quiver all over." Now that part wasn't a lie. "Come upstairs with me, hon-honey. I need your strong self all close . . . and . . . and—" Becca couldn't finish the rest. She just couldn't. She *didn't* need Morgan Larkspur or any other man all close, no matter if she were all quivers inside. *Hell's bells,* Becca cursed silently. Out of nerve, and out of ideas, she stood stone still, feeling the hangman's noose tighten.

Morgan replaced the token in his pocket, enjoying the insistent girl's speech more than any actress or musicale at the Stephens Opera House. Instinct told him this wasn't an act. Even more entranced by Rebecca now, he knew he should go, but maybe not just yet. His curiosity about her got the better of him.

He'd play this game out with the girl, and wait for her to answer his questions. Breaking her defenses down shouldn't be too hard. He'd no intention of following through and actually bedding Rebecca. That Miss Jenny had this particular girl in her employ intrigued him. He didn't want to leave until he knew why. Besides, he was really beginning to enjoy himself. Being in this slip of a girl's company just now stirred his interest, all right, better than any distraction he could have found with another woman. He caught up her hand, holding it tight enough so she couldn't bolt.

"Well, Rebecca," he said. "I've never had such a welcome invite."

The instant his hand clamped onto hers, Becca felt the noose chaff at her neck. This was it. She had to go through with her "welcome invite," even if it killed her. No use now to remind Morgan Larkspur about Miss Jenny's so-called parameters, either. No use now. She'd taken things beyond rules for the first appointment.

"Yes, well . . . then, fine," she muttered, unwilling to look him in the eye. Staring at his white shirtfront and the lapels of his black gabardine suit jacket, she realized again how tall he was. Why does he have to be so tall and smell so good and be so manly and so strong?

For the briefest of moments, she had visions of running away, but the way her hand was manacled in his, nothing doing.

Morgan read every sign of Rebecca's discomfort, knowing he'd put her out of her misery soon enough and leave her, still a virgin, in her private quarters. But he'd have his answers about why she worked for Miss Jenny first.

Becca took a step forward, glad her legs still supported her weight. If she were the swooning type, she'd be prostrate on the carpet right now. Since she was not prone to the vapors, she did her best to guide her customer, their hands clasped, out of the parlor, into the main hall, past others gawking at them from the dance floor or gathered round the piano or seated in the main parlor, past Miss Jenny's startled expression and Big Eddie's frown, up the carpeted runner to the second floor, through the hallway's flickering glow, to her room, room number eight.

With her free hand, she turned the cold glass knob to open her door. It wouldn't open! *Hell's bells.* She'd locked it before going downstairs, of course. No one left their doors unlocked, in order to keep their possessions safe. It was a rule all prostitutes lived by, no matter their living circumstances. Where had she put her key? She remembered going downstairs, behind Miss Jenny. But what did she do with her key?

"Something wrong?" Morgan shouldn't be enjoying Rebecca's discomfort, but he couldn't help it. The flush on her lovely face, clearly evident despite the hall's dim glow, became her.

"Yes," Becca quietly said. "Could I have my hand back, please?" She needed both hands now to feel around the doorway or under the carpet for her key.

Suddenly she gasped. She realized now where she'd put her

key. Down her bodice! She felt the cold metal press mercilessly against her racing breast. Each time she took a breath, the key poked into her harder, as if heralding her fate. Bowing her head, she looked down at her bodice, mute and otherwise unmoving.

Morgan let go of her hand. "Want me to fetch it for you?" he asked, feigning innocence, doing his utmost not to laugh.

CHAPTER FIVE

"Turn around," Becca said before she realized it—before she realized how silly her comment sounded, coming from a prostitute. Her heart sank right down to her toes. This evening was not going well, and things were just going to get worse.

Morgan did as Rebecca said, not wanting her to see his grin. He hadn't been this entertained in a long time by any woman. It dawned on him that maybe this was all an act, trumped up by Miss Jenny for one of her girls to play out. Well, if so, it was a damn good one. Either way, he'd find out soon enough.

Reaching down her bodice, Becca retrieved the unforgiving skeleton key and fumbled for the lock. Her hands shook and her head hurt. How ridiculous! Here she was about to entertain the handsomest man she'd ever seen, who cut the most impressive figure she'd ever seen, all husky-voiced and tanned complexioned and clean-shaven, with his penetrating, slate eyes and attractively cropped black hair, his mesmerizing, teasing smile revealing white, even teeth, who smelled all clean and earthy and masculine, with just a hint of new tobacco, who didn't seem mean or ill or give reason for suspicion, and who no doubt could easily cause a huge catfight among the other prostitutes downstairs. Here she was, about to entertain this perfect customer and get her fifty-dollar token for the night, and she doubted she could get through this. She doubted her abilities as a prostitute to do the job. She doubted she could let any man, even this one, touch her beyond a brush of fingers against a stemmed glass. Her hands shook worse.

"Let me," Morgan offered gently, taking the key out of her trembling, clammy fingers.

His rich tone at the nape of her neck sent new shivers down Becca's spine. Almost glad he took the key from her, she swallowed hard and stepped inside her room once the door stood open.

Morgan stepped inside behind her, and then shut the door. The room was all shadows. He found her hand and put the key back in it, then closed her fingers over the metal.

Becca stood frozen, holding onto the key now for dear life. Glad for the moonlight streaming into her room, she could at least see how to get to her sconces and turn up the gaslight.

Unfortunately, she couldn't move at the moment. She knew why, but she refused to admit to herself that she hadn't been this scared about anything since she was four years old. Funny. This moonlight made her think of the moonlight that had shone through the little paned window in the kitchen of her mother's crib. Oh, to be that four-year-old child again, and be able to turn back the clock and change what happened all those years ago. Tears welled in Becca's throat, making her almost forget she had a customer waiting. Almost.

Morgan spotted the light fixtures and turned them up enough to provide a soft glow in the well-appointed room. He doubted he had the will to go through with his charade as he witnessed the girl's abject discomfort. It wasn't any act. Still, he wanted to know why she worked at the Palace. Too late to leave now and not find out. She intrigued him.

Without so much as a look at Morgan, Becca walked mutely over to the changing screen, and then stepped behind it. Immediate relief washed over her; being behind the screen and away from his scrutiny. Never a coward before, she hated that she was now.

"Mor-Morgan," she tried to call nonchalantly over the screen. "You take your ease. I'll just be a minute."

Her ivory dressing gown, the one for entertaining, rested over one edge of the screen. All she had to do was remove her clothes and put on her dressing gown, walk out from behind the screen, see her customer ready under the covers, walk over to the bed, and climb in. Simple, right? Then why did her heart pound, her head ache, her breath leave her, and her legs threaten to give way?

Much as he wanted to, Morgan couldn't let this poor girl go through with any more of her "entertainment" plans. Much as he wanted to know everything about her now, he felt sorry for her. She was so obviously upset at his presence. Something told him to back off.

"Uh, Rebecca," he called out, taking up a position by the closed door. "Come back out now. Dressed," he made clear.

Becca froze for a second time tonight, her fingers fighting with the ties on her corset. Did she hear him right? Did he say what she thought he said? "Wh-at?" she whispered.

"Come on out now, Rebecca. And, stay dressed. I want to talk to you."

She had no trouble retying her corset and pulling her gown back up and over her, managing the hooks to her lavender silk. Somewhat relieved, still, she knew she had a problem. If he didn't want her, then what did he want?

Maybe he was a nancy-boy. Maybe he didn't like women, but men. No, that was crazy, she quickly decided.

But then, she didn't understand. Customers might want to talk, but then they wanted to bed prostitutes. She and Morgan had talked a little, had a drink together, and now they were supposed to have sex. That's all there was to it. Talk, have drinks, maybe listen to music, then go upstairs and have sex. Filled with more than a little trepidation, Becca, fully dressed once more, stepped out from behind the screen.

"Can we sit a moment, Rebecca?"

"Yes," she acquiesced, unsure where any of this would lead, but curious herself. She took the chair by her bed, keeping her gaze on him. His handsome features, so serious, stirred more than her curiosity. He unnerved her, and it didn't make any sense. She didn't like men. She shouldn't like this one. Not in *that* way.

Morgan sat on the edge of her bed, near the foot.

Long moments passed. Eye to eye, neither spoke. The first to look away, Becca grew uncomfortable under his careful scrutiny.

"Rebecca, I'll just say it straight out. I've no call to ask you any personal questions, but I want to know what a girl like you is doing in a place like this. I can see you're not a prostitute, so what are you doing working for Miss Jenny?" Morgan kept his gaze leveled on her.

Becca shot up and then sat back down. *No prostitute? Of all the nerve! Yes I am!* He couldn't have insulted her more. Indignant, she fought for composure. She would *never* answer any personal questions, from him or anyone else. Why, she'd never even told Miss Jenny everything about her past. She wasn't about to tell this . . . this stranger! Holding her tongue, she glared at Morgan Larkspur as if he were the devil incarnate.

Morgan was surprised by her obvious anger. Although he expected her to keep some things secret, he didn't get it. Damn, what a beauty she was. Softer, riper, rosier lips he'd never seen on a woman. The way her brown eyes sparked at him stirred him. The image of her luxurious hair, down full—for him, for his touch—roused him.

He liked the challenge she threw out, as if she were daring him to say anything further. Most women made a fuss over him, regaling him with one shallow detail after another of their dull, purposeless lives. Not this one. She definitely interested him.

"Hold on now, Rebecca." He softened his tone, as if he were dealing with a skittish colt. "You don't have to say anything—"

"Damn right, I don't," she interrupted, knowing if Miss Jenny heard her curse, she'd be tossed out of the Palace on her ear. No matter, she'd likely be tossed out anyway, after this customer went downstairs and told tales about her. Hell's bells, she wanted this man up and out of her room. Better to get the whole thing over with now. Ruled by her emotions at the moment, Becca didn't think about the consequences if she really were tossed out on her ear.

"All right then," Morgan stood. He took the fifty-dollar token from his pocket and set it on the table near Rebecca, then turned and walked to the door. He put his hand on the knob, hesitated a moment, then opened the door.

"Wait." Becca stood. At once regaining her wits, she realized she couldn't let him leave. Not yet and not like this. Upset as she was, it wouldn't do. It just wouldn't do. "Please don't leave yet, Morgan Larkspur." She stalled for time, trying to think up some reason to keep him there. The only one she came up with was the obvious one. "I'll tell you why I'm here," she fibbed, knowing she would never trust him enough to tell him the whole truth.

"All right then," Morgan said and closed the door.

Becca took up her chair again.

Morgan took up his same seat at the foot of her bed.

Long moments passed.

"I'm listening," Morgan said, his voice quiet and husky.

Becca searched her mind for the right words, weighing the danger of saying too much. Nothing could interfere with her plans to stay in Denver and find her mother's killer. She certainly didn't want to raise any more questions about her in

Morgan Larkspur's mind than were already there. Smart and socially prominent, he was nobody's fool. She needed to say just enough to satisfy him, but not enough to raise suspicion. She had one thing going for her at least. It was well known that prostitutes kept secrets; their true identities were often secret, too. Customers didn't expect women in the sporting life to do otherwise.

"I was born into this life, Morgan Larkspur," she began. "My true name is Rebecca Rose," she offered, surprised she'd done so. "I came from a mining town. Which one isn't important. I came to Denver to work for Miss Jenny a long time ago. Now I'm of age and now I'm one of Miss Jenny's girls. It's what I've always wanted and the only life I wish to lead. As you can tell," she said, looking him hard in the eye, "you're my first appointment. I can assure you, Morgan Larkspur, you won't be my last," she finished, satisfied with her half-truths, satisfied she'd said just enough.

Hard to believe what she'd just told him, coming from someone living in a parlor house, yet Morgan did believe her. He didn't think she could have made it up; not the way she sat so proud, so defiant, daring him to believe otherwise. He had more questions, but they'd have to wait. She wouldn't say another word to him now, but maybe she would later.

Morgan wanted there to be a later. He wanted to see Rebecca again. Lord knew why. It sure wouldn't be for sex or sweet talk or a full night of pleasure. But it would be for distraction. He'd give her that.

Her last words suddenly rang in his head: "You're my first appointment. I can assure you, you won't be my last." The thought of another man touching her didn't sit well, rousing his protective, even jealous, nature. Damn, he hadn't believed he had it in him to be jealous about anyone or anything. Until now.

Morgan stood and took a step toward Rebecca. He didn't know exactly what he wanted to do with her, but he knew he didn't want her to do anything with any other man.

She stood, too, wary of his intentions.

Leaning over, brushing past her—the fragrant hint of honey and new clover wreaking havoc on his senses—he picked up the token he'd left on the table and placed it in her hand.

She started at his touch, feeling it down to her toes. Staring at him wide-eyed, she waited for the other shoe to drop.

"Rebecca." Morgan cleared his throat, wanting to use the right tone and tact. "I think that's right, isn't it? Fifty dollars for the first appointment? Here," he added, reaching into his breast pocket for his money clip. Deftly removing three bills, he handed her three hundred dollars. "This should cover the next six nights. I'll be away all week, at the mines in Leadville, but I'll be back, Saturday next."

Morgan intended to keep his promise, despite the hazards of spring snow and blocked trails into the mountains. The train to Leadville always managed to make it, as did the branching spur lines to Leadville and the other Colorado boomtowns.

"I'm paying you for every night I'll be gone, Rebecca. I don't want you seeing anyone else right now. Are we good on this?" He searched her lovely face for agreement to his odd proposal.

Wide-eyed and open-mouthed, Becca mutely nodded her head, yes. Utterly and completely stunned at Morgan Larkspur's wishes, she instinctively tightened her fingers around the token and bills in her palm. She had her fifty dollars and more. Much, much more. It was only after he'd left, closing the door behind him, that she collapsed onto her bed, wondering just what she'd gotten herself into.

"This could cause a problem, Becca. Morgan Larkspur's offer to you is not good for business. My business," Jenny said, giving voice to her displeasure over the position Becca's customer put her and her girls in. The moment the others found out that Becca had been paid for a whole week, and that she didn't have to work for it, the trouble would start. Jenny couldn't afford trouble. She had enough of it already, finding out last night from another madam that two brothers—the Blongers—had arrived in Denver and had plans to extort payment for protection all up and down the line. *Humph, payment,* Jenny scoffed silently.

Fines were one thing, and she didn't mind having to pay them on occasion to the law. In a lesser house, monthly fines were frequent, but at the Palace, Jenny made sure her girls stayed out of trouble. Of course, the city of Denver made a lot of money from fining prostitutes, their madams, saloons, hurdy-gurdies and gambling halls. Jenny counted many of the police officials and legislators in the city as customers.

She wondered if she could count on them for protection from the Blonger brothers. Never sure, she needed to be ready if and when the Blongers paid her a visit. She'd talk to Big Eddie this morning, and maybe hire a second bouncer. Most likely the Blongers intended to interfere with business down the line from her place, including liquor sales and opium dens.

Maybe Jenny and all the other madams in Denver, and the thousand or so prostitutes working along Holladay Street between Nineteenth and Twenty-third, would get lucky and the brothers would get arrested and jailed for some crime sooner rather than later. In any event, first chance she had, she'd approach the police commissioner—one of her longtime, *select* customers—and whisper about the Blonger brothers in his ear, along with her sweet and not-so-sweet nothings, perhaps ensuring the brothers' arrest sooner rather than later.

"I don't understand, Miss Jenny," Becca said, despite Miss Jenny's obviously agitated state. Agitated herself after a sleepless night tossing and turning and thinking about what had happened between her and Morgan Larkspur, Becca had hoped for ideas from Miss Jenny, not recrimination. No one else was about. Parlor house daughter and madam sat across from one another in the main front parlor, each sipping her morning coffee, each dressed to perfection in her day dress—Jenny never allowed any of her girls to be on the first floor in dressing gowns or anything inappropriate—and each upset over the events of the night before.

Jenny softened her glare at Becca. The poor girl shouldn't pay for Jenny's upset over the arrival of the unsavory, unscrupulous Blonger brothers. Doing her best to put her own worry aside, she needed to advise Becca on how to handle Morgan Larkspur. This situation needed care, great care. The Larkspur men were power brokers in Denver, not to mention the whole of Colorado. She didn't want to give them any cause to bring negative attention to the Palace, yet she didn't want her other girls to cause a ruckus over Becca's special offer from Morgan Larkspur. A fine kettle of fish, indeed.

"When is Morgan coming to see you again?"

"Saturday," Becca repeated.

"And he never once *touched* you, yet he still paid you for the whole week?" Jenny asked, still incredulous over Morgan's offer.

"No, he didn't touch me," Becca lied. Their hands had brushed, and more. He'd taken up her hand. She could still feel his masterful, warm fingers on hers. "And, yes, he paid me for the whole week," she said, pulling out the bills from the drawstring bag she'd brought downstairs this morning.

Ever the astute businesswoman, Jenny took the money. "I'll give you back thirty dollars on this as soon as we're through with our talk," she said, tucking the bills safely away under the silver tray on which the coffee pot, creamer, sugar, and cups rested. "This will help us outfit you in beautiful things at Joslin's, dear. We must come up with a plan that will make everyone happy. We can't have the other girls jealous of you for getting paid for not working, and we can't have Morgan Larkspur finding out you have entertained other gentlemen." Jenny smiled. "Morgan obviously thinks very well of you, dear. Good work, Becca. Very good work."

Becca understood now what Miss Jenny had meant by "causing trouble." At least she could take ease from knowing Miss Jenny's meaning, if not from her own continued agitation. Morgan Larkspur's nearness had wreaked havoc on her!

For the briefest of moments Becca allowed herself a small bit of pleasure in what Miss Jenny said: "Morgan obviously thinks very well of you." Her heart skipped a beat, causing her to put her hand to her chest in admonishment. She'd no desire to take pleasure in the touch of any man. That she took pleasure in Morgan Larkspur's touch surprised and unnerved her. Unsure of what her next move should be, she was anxious to hear Miss Jenny's plan.

"Wait a moment," Jenny directed, then got up and went into the front hallway, glancing up and down the access. Ever cautious, she wanted this conversation kept private. Satisfied no one lingered about, she returned to the parlor and took up her same seat.

Becca sat on the edge of hers.

"A ruse is called for here," Jenny decided. "We must make up a story for the other girls. I'm going to let it slip that you have a malady in your privates; a malady requiring the doc's attention, and that prevents you from having any more appointments until the doc gives you the all clear. In no way will the girls think you've been burned, or that you got something from your first customer. I'll say it's to do with your monthly, and that's all." Jenny knew everyone would believe her. Her word was law in the house.

Becca remained on the edge of her seat, paying close attention to Miss Jenny's every word. No room here for error on her part.

"In the meanwhile, I'll put you to work helping out in the children's quarters." Jenny brightened at the idea. "Right now your help is needed, Becca. You know that Violet had her twins two days ago, and you've heard by now, I'm sure, that she wants no part of those babies," Jenny said, her disapproving tone obvious. The irony of a madam disapproving of one of her girls not wanting to keep her babies was lost on her.

Becca had heard about Violet's twin boys, and she knew Violet didn't want them. Deep down, Becca understood, but her heart broke for the little ones who would never know their mother's love. She'd had four years of her mother's love, enough to build treasured memories she could carry with her for the rest of her days. The little ones upstairs would have no such memories. It broke Becca's heart.

"I can't just have the boys delivered to the poorhouse or left on someone's doorstep. It would stay on my conscience and I refuse to do it," Jenny said. "It's a pity there's no decent orphanage in Denver where the babies could be taken in and kept together. But in the poorhouse . . . one baby is one thing, but two . . . two brothers who'd likely be split up *if* they survive." Jenny winced inwardly. She already had a pair of brothers, the Blongers, she worried over. It wouldn't do to have the little ones upstairs, another pair of brothers—these newborn innocents—on her conscience. They would be if she did nothing to help them get a better start in life.

Becca kept listening, all thoughts of Morgan Larkspur forgotten.

"Becca, there is something I want you to do this week." Jenny ordered, more than asked. "It's for Violet's twins. I . . . I . . ." She hesitated, her jaw clenched. Straightening, she kept her tone moderate. "There is a church close by here, at Twentieth and Welton. Saint John's. An Episcopal church. The rector there is Father Hart." Jenny shifted in her seat. Prostitutes never talked about God and church. "Father Hart has made it known in Denver that he doesn't much care for our line of work, preaching against 'purveyors of Sunday night amusements.' Humph." Jenny shifted again.

She'd read about Father Hart's opinions on gambling halls and gun sellers and houses of ill repute more than once in the *Rocky Mountain News*. Doubtless other clergymen felt the same. Despite this cold hard fact, there had to be someone among Saint John's well-to-do congregation who needed babies. Better there than the poorhouse. It was worth a try to see if the father at Saint John's would help. If he wouldn't help a prostitute, then maybe he'd help the children of a prostitute. But Jenny wasn't so sure.

Becca would do anything for the little ones upstairs, but what did that have to do with any church? Never in all her days had she been in a church, and she'd no desire to go in one now. Such talk unnerved her. She sat back, not so willing to hear more from Miss Jenny.

"Becca, I believe Father Hart can be convinced to take in Violet's boys and find a good home for them. I'm too well known in Denver to go myself." Jenny laughed. "They'd bar the door if they saw me coming. But you, you're an unknown and would be better received."

Comprehending the drift of Miss Jenny's intentions, Becca fought her growing upset.

"I believe this way, going to Saint John's and asking for help with the twins—I'll leave it up to you what to say—the boys can have a good home and won't be separated," Jenny declared, giving the whole idea a positive nod. "What say you, Becca?" she intoned, as if challenging Becca to refuse her wishes in the matter.

Becca wanted to shout the obvious. Father Hart would turn her away, too, the moment he found out what she was and where she lived. No point in lying.

Although everything inside Becca told her to say no, that she wouldn't set foot in any church, Becca wasn't in a position to argue with Miss Jenny. A part of her *did* want to help the little ones upstairs. A part of her didn't want the twins deprived of a mother's love, even if they weren't natural born to the mother. Maybe she could help find them a good mother at the church, like Miss Jenny said. If there was a God—Becca didn't think so—maybe God would help the boys, even though He'd never helped her mother.

For her own part, Becca didn't care to meet God or Father Hart or anyone else at Saint John's, not needing any of their inspiration to help her get through life. Or meet her death. She believed a body was born hard into this world—the children upstairs were another example of that—a body lived hard, and left this world hard. That was the beginning, the middle, and the end of it, no questions asked.

"All right." Becca spoke low.

"All right, then," Jenny parroted, unwilling to feel guilty over Becca's difficult mission. It needed to be done, and Becca was the better one to try. Otherwise the little ones would be in the poorhouse by the end of the week, lucky to survive out the month. Jenny didn't know of any of her girls who had families or friends who would take in the twins. Saint John's was the only other option.

There were other churches in Denver but, in her heart of hearts, Jenny knew that to enter one, was to enter them all. The response would be the same, no matter the minister or the faith. Besides, if they were to try more than one church, it would be all over the city by nightfall. Prostitution and religion didn't mix. If Jenny wanted to keep her select clientele coming to the

Palace, she didn't want them worrying over the possibility that one of their "appointments" at the Palace might have resulted in a baby that might show up right under their nose, as a constant reminder of their dalliance. No, no more churches. If Saint John's didn't come through for Violet's babies, then so be it. Jenny refused to expend any more time worrying over the little ones. In her line of work, she didn't have the luxury of such worry.

It wasn't unusual for successful houses of prostitution to help out the needy or those in trouble or less fortunate in Denver. Madams, especially, had generous hearts. Miss Jenny was no exception. Just last year, when the townsfolk rose up against the Chinese in Hop Alley over a misunderstanding, with some in Denver wanting to shut the Celestials down and run them out of the city, Jenny and others along the row took up arms and heeled shoes and frying pans and whatever else they could find. They formed a line between the upset townsfolk and the Chinese. The riot abated, thanks to the help of the madams and prostitutes, but the prejudice against the Chinese remained.

Once again, parlor house daughter and madam sat across from one another in silence, each pondering the turn of their conversation. Becca was determined to try her best to find a mother for the baby boys. Jenny tried her best to deny her motherly feelings for Becca.

Becca let out a small laugh. She couldn't help it. Only now did she realize that she had forgotten all about Morgan Lark-spur and her supposed monthly ailment—and that he would return this coming Saturday, and that she actually looked forward to seeing him again!

As if reading Becca's mind, Jenny spoke. "Now, before you set off to Saint John's, we must schedule fittings for you at Jos-lin's Dry Goods for your new gowns. Saturday will be here before we know it, and you must be ready for Morgan Larkspur. By then, I'll have let the others know you are clear from the doc. And Becca," Jenny quietly said, "no word about what you're doing when you leave here today, or where you are going. No need to let on to the others about you going to a church and all. All right?"

"All right," Becca repeated, her thoughts suddenly taking an altogether different turn.

She would be venturing out today, walking the city's streets. Over the years she'd done little venturing out in Denver. Sure, she could have gone to all of the other parlor houses and brothels before, and gone into the saloons and gambling halls, asking after a man with missing fingers and a gold lion-head ring. But that would never do. Not in the world of prostitution. No one asked questions. To do so would only bring trouble.

Then too, if she'd spread the word all over Denver that she was looking for a man with her particular description, her mother's killer would flee. Something in her told her the killer was nearby and hadn't left Colorado. One day she'd find him. When she did, she'd kill him. She wouldn't bring up charges against him. No court would believe a whore.

"Did you hear me, Becca?"

"Of course," Becca said absentmindedly. "It's Sunday."

"Yes. Exactly," Jenny repeated. "Because it's Sunday and the church will be full, you must wait until tomorrow to go to Saint John's. For now, I'd like you to help upstairs with the babies. Clara is older now, and it's much harder for her to do everything. Help Clara for the rest of today. Tomorrow you'll go take care of the church matter, and then on Tuesday we'll go to Joslin's and outfit you in new gowns."

"Fine," Becca agreed. She tossed a smile to Miss Jenny—a smile she didn't feel—and stood. This next week would be difficult, but she did have Saturday. She'd see Morgan Larkspur on Saturday.

CHAPTER SIX

Morgan stepped down off the steam locomotive, onto the platform in Leadville. He'd hopped onto a spur branch of the South Park Line heading north to the mines. It was ten o'clock Monday morning. The gray sky overhead did little to improve his already downcast mood. There were two reasons for it: brewing trouble at the mines, and his recent meeting with a certain beautiful young prostitute. He wasn't quite sure how to handle either.

As he looked out over the town of Leadville over a sea of buildings and houses and tents, smelters spewed out their dark smoke, evidence of ore being successfully mined in the area. Thousands upon thousands of miners called Leadville home, working long hours for little pay—only one of the reasons for labor unrest now.

Leadville had become home to more than one Bonanza King, those who had struck it rich acquiring great wealth from their silver investments. John Routt and Horace Tabor were two of the most noted. Routt's Morning Star Mine and Tabor's Matchless Mine, only two of their respective holdings, hit pay dirt every day they operated. The Morning Star had already paid out one million dollars' worth of silver bullion. Talk was that Routt, with two partners, might sell his mine for three million to a New York investor. For Tabor's part, he was president of the Mining and Stock Exchange in Leadville, which listed fifty names in its membership. Eugene, Morgan, and Montgomery

Larkspur counted among the select names.

Morgan's family had acquired significant wealth with their silver holdings. They owned six mines, each one productive, each one well-built—the timbering through the drifts and workings particularly substantial, with new hoisting facilities planned—and each one turning into a hornet's nest of unrest. Near the trouble brewing among laborers on Carbonate Hill, Morgan worried over what would happen at his own mines. He'd caught wind of the coming strike among the miners. They'd organized the Miner's Cooperative Union, and Morgan knew they meant to confront the mine owners. Hell, Horace Tabor had put together his own militia, the Tabor Light Cavalry, to deal with the coming trouble.

Something had to change with the mine owners and the miners, or there would be bloodshed. Morgan felt caught in the middle. He'd worked alongside the miners, although less now than formerly, and he'd joined forces with the other mine owners to ensure sound mineral transactions. A member of the Mining and Stock Exchange, Morgan abided by their labor rules set down: twelve-hour days, six days a week, three dollars a day. Workers had greater expenses living in the boom town now, and Morgan knew it. One reason for continued low wages was the railroad. Rail service meant the daily arrival of cheap immigrant labor.

His jaw tightened. He could smell trouble in the crisp mountain air. He took up his satchel and left the train platform, heading to his same hotel. Morgan didn't want to build a home in Leadville. He didn't need it. His family had just taken up residence in their new mansion on Fourteenth Street in Denver, on Governor's Row. Morgan still lived there, but not for long. He only stayed now at his parents' insistence that "We must keep the Larkspur family a united force in Denver."

Morgan owed a lot to his parents, as his mother often

reminded him, and meant to fulfill his dutiful family role, no matter that he didn't want to. With his father's attention on the family's banking and railroad interests, and with Monty interested in little involving work, it was up to Morgan to oversee the Larkspur mining interests in Leadville. He meant to do it, more to protect his family than promote his own ambitions.

His mood still somber, Morgan reached busy Harrison Street, the main commercial street in Leadville. He stopped on the planked walkway, nodding to passersby who said howdy, set down his satchel, and then took out his tobacco makings. He didn't like manufactured cigarettes, preferring to roll his own smokes. Tasted better, he thought.

After a clean draw, he exhaled and looked toward the lower end of town just off Harrison Street, toward the parlor houses, dance halls, and cribs, to State Street, where the prostitutes lived and worked. He thought of Rebecca Rose, remembering she was born in a mining town, a hard beginning for sure. Besides her lovely vision coming to mind, he had a lot of questions. Intrigued by her now, he meant to get answers. Too late to take back what he'd done—paying for the whole week. Too late to ignore his attraction to her and the fact that he didn't want other men to bed her, much less touch her.

What he wanted to do right now, he couldn't. He wanted to get back on the train, head down to Denver, and take each appointment he'd paid for with Rebecca—all six of them he had left. He took another draw, inhaling the sweet scent of honey and clover, then blew the smoke out slow, imagining each time with the young beauty. The fact that she was untried stirred him all the more, not because he would despoil a virgin, but that she would be *his,* only his.

His tobacco spent, Morgan stepped on the butt and headed toward his hotel where he'd sleep alone, without the soft, warm body of Rebecca against him all night. *Damn.* Morgan loosened his shirt collar. He'd never spent the whole night with a prostitute. No, he didn't frequent parlor houses as often as his little brother, but when he did, he always left after sex. He didn't want anything else. Just sex, and the promise of passion to come. No other promises.

Soon enough he'd marry Lavinia Eagleton—for too many reasons he cared to think about right now—but he didn't relish sharing their marriage bed. She'd probably be like most wives of the day. He'd heard from more than one married friend at the exclusive Denver Club that wives don't like sex; they just want children. "Sex is to be had at parlor houses. Just keep it quiet so the wife doesn't know," his friends had warned. "There will be hell to pay at home if the wife finds out."

Funny. Morgan only now realized that none of his friends talked about love. Well, no matter. He wasn't interested in love. He supposed his parents loved each other; they seemed happy enough. Still, Morgan didn't think he'd recognize love, much less need it or want it in his life. Now, a good time with a good prostitute, he sure loved *that* well enough. So, what in Sam Hill was he doing bothering with a young, mysterious slip of a girl who was untried, unseasoned, near unapproachable, damn near underage, and the most unlikely prostitute he'd ever thought to meet!

Morgan loosened his collar yet again. He knew why. He knew exactly why.

Saturday couldn't come soon enough.

Outfitted in a conservative day dress and hat, the navy woolen with lace trim covering her from chin to ankle, Becca stepped onto Holladay Street. It was ten o'clock Monday morning. The March day was cold and the air crisp. Her new button shoes were soon covered with dirt and dust from the thoroughfare.

The water wagons trolled Fourteenth Street and Governor's Row, to keep the dust down for all the fancy carriages traveling back and forth, but not Holladay Street. No matter. Becca didn't worry over clean shoes on her mission to Saint John's. It would be a short walk to Twentieth and Welton. She picked up her step. She wanted to get this over with. The idea of setting foot in a church made her stomach churn. The only reason she kept going was for Violet's boys. The gray morning matched her mood.

In little time she'd arrived at Saint John's. The brick cathedral church loomed large. A huge stained-glass window peered down at her, as if watching her, scrutinizing her, and finding her wanton. *Hah,* she scoffed, straightening her spine.

With head held high, she took the necessary steps to reach the front doors of the church. Startled by the creak of the massive wooden doors, she hesitated a moment, then stepped inside. Unprepared for what she saw, Becca mutely shut the doors behind her, then leaned against the ornate wood for support.

First she looked up at the vaulted ceiling high overhead; then at the series of pillars on each side of the cathedral, lined beneath, each creating its own arched section; then at the countless rows of backed seating; then, way ahead, at the opposite end of the cathedral, another stained glass window, this one framed just behind a carved wooden altar of some sort. A gold cross had been placed on the altar, visible from the back of the cathedral. The gold shone, even on this gray day, as if beckoning her to approach. Filled with trepidation, yet curious, Becca pulled away from the front doors and began walking down the center aisle.

She continued forward, only now noticing a raised area near the altar that had steps leading to it. She had a vague notion this must be where the preacher, Father Hart, preached. Not interested in anything a preacher had to say to her, Becca *was* interested in the gold cross ahead. It stirred her. It didn't make her stomach turn, but stirred her emotions, making her remember, making her think of . . . *mama.*

Suddenly frightened, Becca took the nearest seat and shut her eyes against the cross in front of her. She didn't understand what was happening or why she would think of her mother in a place like this, a place where everyone in the church looked down on people like her and her mother. The queerest feeling hit her, as if when she opened her eyes, she'd see her mother. She refused to open her eyes, knowing she'd be disappointed because her mother was *not* there. Her mother was dead. Murdered. How dare God, if He existed, taunt her with the promise of seeing her mother?

"Young woman."

The gruff voice gave her a start. She opened her eyes. A man stood in the aisle by her. A tall, thin, stern-looking, older man, dressed in a dark robe with a white, turned-around shirt collar. This had to be Father Hart, the man looked so disapproving. Becca stood, ready for whatever recriminations would come, finding a mother for Violet's boys foremost on her mind.

"Young woman," the man repeated, "I'm Father Hart."

She knew that already.

"And you?"

"Oh," Becca muttered, stalling for time. Of course she'd every intention of telling him what he needed to know in order to take the babies, but still . . . she didn't want to give her name to any *preacher man.* Stepping out into the aisle to face Father Hart, she looked him straight in the eye, and feeling compelled, spoke the truth. "My name is Rebecca. Rebecca Rose."

"Rose?" Father Hart's brow furrowed. "I haven't heard that name before, at least not in Denver. When did your family settle here, Rebecca?"

Oh dear. Becca could see this wasn't going to be easy. The

father wanted details, too many details, details she refused to give him. If she lied, he'd find out, be mad and not take the children. If she told the truth, he'd be mad and not take the children. She'd little to lose, but the children had a lot to lose if she didn't do this right and say the right thing to the father. "I don't have a family, not anymore. My mother died a long time ago and I'm on my own."

"On your own, you say," Father Hart repeated, his brow furrowing deeper. "Then child, where is your husband? Why isn't he with you today?"

Oh, dear. Oh, dear. Becca wanted to shout, "Hell's bells!" but thought better of it, being in a church and all. Father Hart assumed she was married, all respectable-like. In her eyes she *was* respectable—just not married-respectable. She swallowed hard, trying to think of the right thing to say. All she could come up with was the truth. "I'm not married, Father," she announced, her jaw tight, her throat suddenly dry.

"Is that so?" he intoned, his voice strict.

"Yes, that's so," Becca said.

"Then where do you live, child? What do you do?"

His hard glare bored through her now, threatening to shatter her composure and her purpose. All the things Miss Jenny told her about Farther Hart's opinion of "Sunday night amusements" rang in her head. She knew Father Hart would shoo her out of the church like so much dirt under his feet the moment she told him where she lived and what she did. She must take care. She must! No use in trying to stall for any more time.

"I am here, Father," Becca began, intending to ignore his last question and pose her question to him instead, before he could interrupt, "I am here to find a home for two innocent baby boys in need . . . in need of a mother and . . . and a father," she managed, this last sticking in her throat.

She hadn't thought about a father before, not really. What

did fathers matter? She'd never known any of the girls in cribs or at the Palace to talk about their fathers, and she certainly didn't grow up with one. Men were good for money; as for the rest, she'd no idea.

"I've come to you and your grand church with so many rich families—with so many families that might take in two innocent boys—because . . . because I can't leave the twins at the poorhouse to die. For die they will, if I can't find them parents who will love them and care for them." Fighting tears, tears she didn't think she had in her, Becca kept her chin up and her gaze leveled at Father Hart.

"So, young woman, you are coming here looking to find a home for your babies that you had, outside of marriage, outside the bounds of a moral life, and outside the confines of respectability," he accused, his tone even more gruff than before.

Unwilling to give in to the sudden urge to step away from this whole situation, Becca held her ground. "They are not my babies, but even so, they are beautiful, wonderful babies who need a home," she all but shouted. She could tell from the hard look on Father Hart's face that he didn't believe her. Well, what did she care? She didn't.

"Where are the babies now?" he rounded on her.

Her anger fueled, she told him exactly. "They are at the Palace on Holladay Street, where they were born. We're taking fine care of them now, but it cannot continue. There are . . . there are problems in keeping children for any length of time at our house. We just can't." She dropped her chin at this last.

Father Hart sighed heavily.

Becca waited for his railing on her to begin—railing about the sins of prostitution and immorality and drinking and taking drugs and living a life away from God. *Hah!* What did she care? She didn't . . . except . . . except for the little ones who needed a home.

The father sighed a second time.

Becca looked up at him, reading the unexpected: sympathy and compassion in his eyes, and *not* reproach. She brightened to the change she saw. Maybe there was a chance . . .

"Sit down, child," he gently ordered.

She took up her same seat.

He sat down next to her, rubbing his hands over his face after he did, as if troubled. Minutes passed, with neither of them saying a word.

Her nerves on edge, Becca had to wait. She had to wait for what he would say.

"Child," he finally spoke. Yet he kept his eyes directed forward. "I want to help the babies. They are innocents. They deserve a chance. There is no orphanage yet in Denver, but there will be soon. For now I will help you, because I can do little else. Unlike the children, you are not an innocent. You've lost your way, child." Father Hart looked at her now. "Maybe today you're beginning to find it again."

Becca didn't expect any of this, not Father Hart's understanding attitude, not his willingness to help the babies, and certainly not his belief that she needed religion or God in her life. God never saved her mother from being murdered. Where was God then? Where was God now?

Uneasy with the turn of her thoughts, she refused to think of God any further, wanting to settle things for the little ones now with the rector. That Father Hart had agreed to take the babies was nothing short of a miracle. *Hah! Miracles.*

She didn't believe in them any more than she believed in God.

Becca stepped out of the church office, reentering the cathedral sanctuary, having spent the past half-hour discussing the details of tomorrow. Tomorrow she would bring the newborns to Saint

John's, to Father Hart. He'd assured her that he would find them a good home, and in fact, already had a prospective couple in mind from his congregation. The authorities would be notified, for legal purposes. He'd also assured Becca that he, along with others in Denver, planned to establish charity organizations for just such a purpose, to help those in need: men, women, and children. However, he advised her *not* to bring any more babies to him from her house because it wasn't the right way. "The right way," he'd begun to lecture, "the right way is not to have babies in the first place, and not to have any relations outside of wedlock."

Becca had flinched at his comments, at his inference that she lived an immoral life and should mend her ways. She'd expected as much from the father, but still, she didn't like hearing it. Walking down the center aisle on her way out of Saint John's, Becca suddenly pivoted, face-to-face now with the luminous gold cross at the altar. It shone like sunshine, although the day outside remained gray. At once uncomfortable, even a little afraid, Becca sat down in the nearest seat, much like she'd done when she first entered the church. Shutting her eyes against goodness knew what, she sat for long moments, shivers taking hold of her. She wasn't cold, but she shivered nonetheless. The strangest feeling suddenly washed over and through her, as if . . . as if . . . a presence . . . someone . . . was there.

Mama.

Becca's eyes flew open at the realization that her mother *was* there, in the church with her, and with . . . *God.* At once, she stopped shivering. Hugging her arms in an attempt to keep her mother's presence close, Becca closed her eyes again . . . to remember her *mama.*

Stunned by what had just happened—*a miracle*—Becca leaned against the back of her seat and shut her eyes again. After a few sobering breaths, she reopened her eyes to the knowledge that her mother was here, in this church . . . with God. God *must* exist. He hadn't saved her mother from being murdered, but He hadn't turned her mother away from Saint John's, even though she'd been a prostitute. Of course, Becca had no real proof of this, but she didn't need any. She was convinced her mother had just contacted her from the grave.

Pulling herself up and out of her seat, Becca stared hard at the gold cross. It no longer shone. Gulping hard, Becca knew her mother's presence had left Saint John's. Instinctively, she knew something else, too. Her mother intended for her to come back to Saint John's, and not just to bring the babies tomorrow. Why Becca had this feeling, she'd no idea. It was just that: a feeling.

Exhausted and still stunned, Becca slowly turned away from the cross and made her way to the front doors of Saint John's, this time not hearing them creak open. Her emotions were raw, and she had a lot to think about on her way back to the Palace.

"Oh, honey, you're so sweet to me," the whore whispered into her customer's ear. He was her best customer in the Cripple Creek mining town, and she'd no intention of sharing him with any of the other whores operating in cribs at the end of the line on Myers Avenue. He was older by at least twenty years, but no matter. He was rich. She could tell by the cut of his clothes, if nothing else.

But there was something else. He wore expensive jewelry. Not just his watch and chain, but a ring—a gold lion-head ring. She'd never seen the like; it had to be pure gold. 'Course she didn't like him touching her with that hand, since he had two fingers missing. It gave her the creeps, but she liked the money. He paid real good.

Near the end of her days in operation, at twenty-eight, she'd gotten herself hooked on the opium and there was nothing to be done for it. No way to stop now. Besides, she didn't want to. There was nothing else in her life at the end of the line but the next trick, the next fifty cents. Never really pretty, what looks she'd had were gone. She couldn't believe her luck when the man in bed with her now opened her crib door two weeks ago. A man like him didn't need to find a crib whore when he could have any younger, more beautiful girl he wanted in the fancy parlor houses up the street.

After all of her years in the business, she knew men pretty well. This one was kind of mean. On her guard more than usual, she decided to overlook his meanness for the money—the good money meant more opium. He hadn't hurt her yet. Not really. Sure, he'd been rough, but a lot of men were rough. Accustomed to miners liking hot and heavy sex, she wasn't accustomed to the eerie feeling in her gut when she had sex with this customer. Still, she'd put up with him for the money.

Glad he never paid for the whole night, usually staying only about an hour, she couldn't imagine falling into easy sleep next to him. The thought that she'd never wake up, at least in this world, had occurred to her more than once. Funny, he'd never told her his name. 'Course, most whores didn't use their names—not their real ones, anyway. But she was used to miners in most of the mining towns where she'd worked using their real names, some even coming regular to her crib. This one was no miner, but at least he'd been coming regular. She still couldn't figure why. But best not to try. Thinking could get her killed with this customer—if she said or did the wrong thing. She knew it as sure as she knew how much opium she could buy with his fifteen-dollar visits. Set up real good now, she was, for as long as she could keep him coming.

Rolling out of her bed, his passion spent, her customer got up and dressed. She watched him, admiring his still-fit body and handsome looks. With some men, age didn't affect them as much as with others. 'Course, the same could be said about whores; some aged well and some didn't. She didn't, and she knew it. No matter. She had something this man liked, and she wouldn't question things further.

Getting out of bed herself now, she went into the back room to wash up. Usually she'd wait to wash, but something about this customer made her feel dirty. If she didn't think it would make him angry, she'd laugh out loud at this. Here he was, all rich and well-dressed, having sex with a "soiled dove," and she felt he'd dirtied *her*.

She let out a gasp. His hot breath at her neck and his vice-like fingers pressing at her throat scared her to death. She dared not move, waiting for what might happen next, reminded of how easy it was for a whore to die.

"Listen, girlie," he snarled. "You don't walk out of the room on me, you hear? If you ever do it again . . ."

His fingers tightened at her throat. She knew what he'd do if she did. "I won't ever," she managed, despite his hold on her.

"Good," he rasped, taking his hands from her neck.

She stayed frozen to the spot, listening as he walked across the room then out the door, relief washing over her when he did.

CHAPTER SEVEN

"Clara, are you doing all right?" Becca asked, wanting to make sure the walk to Saint John's with one of the infants in her arms wasn't too much for the aging housekeeper. They only had one more block, and they'd arrive at the church.

"I'm fine, dear," Clara reassured. "Don't you worry over me."

Becca would anyway. She'd come to care for Clara almost as much as she did for Miss Jenny. The baby in Becca's arms stirred, fretting but not crying. "There, there," she cooed, making sure the blanket securely protected the little one. Finding it impossible to ignore her own motherly feelings, she held the baby closer. For the briefest of moments she thought of being a mother herself, but then thought better of it. She'd only be bringing her own babies to the church to give up to someone else. That she could *never* do.

The bells of Saint John's rang out, signaling the noon hour, stemming the downward turn of Becca's thoughts, and reminding her that Father Hart expected her at noon sharp. She and Clara, both with babes in arms, hurried inside the sanctuary. Once inside, they made haste down the center aisle toward the back, to the rectory door. Becca had briefly glimpsed the gold cross, and noted that it didn't shine. She forced her attention back to her meeting with Father Hart. A group of three women waited by the rectory door, their conversation stopping when Becca and Clara approached.

Becca's heart sank. She didn't want to have to deal with anything or anyone besides safely delivering the babies to Father Hart. Uncomfortable under the immediate scrutiny of the three women, Becca could only imagine what they were thinking. One of the young women in particular, the beautiful blonde, stared hard at her, as if accusing her of something. The others held up their noses, then looked away.

So much for respectable folk and their respectable opinions, Becca thought to herself. What did she care? She didn't.

Stepping past the women, Becca knocked on the rectory door. She hoped Father Hart would answer and save her and Clara from the unfriendly eyes of the three women. No one opened the door. Becca's heart sank yet again.

"Father Hart will be here soon, to see *us,*" the blonde condescended to explain.

Becca pivoted, glad the baby in her arms still slept, and caught Clara's eye. "Are you doing all right?" she asked, her voice barely above a whisper so not to wake the babies.

"Of course, dear," Clara answered softly, a smile crinkling at the corners of her mouth. "The little one and I are both just fine."

"I said," the blonde spoke loud and clear, "the father will see *us* next. You and your . . . your *bastards,*" she spat out, "should come back another time. When you do, come in the back way. You've no call to come through the front doors like decent folk."

The babies didn't waken. Becca kept her attention on the child in her arms, ignoring the blonde's ridicule.

"Lavinia!" one of the women whispered in shock.

"Don't Lavinia me," the blonde scolded. "I know a whore when I see a whore."

"Lavinia, you're in God's house! You mustn't use such language!" the other woman warned.

"All right." Lavinia feigned a polite smile. "I know a prostitute when I see a prostitute. Is that better?" Her tone dripped sarcasm.

Becca cuddled the baby closer, keeping her eyes on the child. If she didn't have the baby in her arms, she imagined she'd be punching the blonde right in the face. She'd never hit anyone before, but she could hit *Lavinia*.

"Don't you girls hush me. You both know I'm right. You've seen their ilk riding up and down Fourteenth Street in their fancy carriages, advertising their business every afternoon. It's shocking." Lavinia shot this last at Becca.

At that moment, Father Hart opened the rectory door.

Becca was glad of it, doubting how long she could keep her temper. She doubted, too, that the father had overheard the blonde's nasty comments.

Lavinia smiled at the father, a smile as innocent as the pure-driven snow.

Becca bit her lower lip to stifle her giggles. The blonde was that ridiculous and silly.

"Miss Eagleton," Father Hart said. "You are early. You and the other ladies will have to wait. We'll talk about your charity fund-raiser in due time." He turned then to Becca. "Please, child. Come in," he smiled down at her.

Becca did, with Clara close behind, neither of them giving witness to Lavinia's shocked expression.

Saturday had arrived. Becca fought her nerves, anxious to see Morgan Larkspur again. Would he come this afternoon? Tonight? Maybe he wouldn't come. But then, he said he would.

Oh dear. She collapsed onto her beautifully made bed. She'd set her room in perfect order and tried to do her best with her appearance. She'd donned her finest day dress this morning, since she liked her purple taffeta above all the rest, evening gowns included. The color suited her, she thought. Besides, purple was her favorite color.

Agitated, she stood and began to pace, anxious over Morgan Larkspur's coming—waiting for him to come, wanting him to come. This was all so new to her, and all so *foolish.* Any prostitute who allowed herself to get involved emotionally with a customer *was* a fool. She'd best take care. She'd no desire to be anyone's fool.

A knock broke into her somber reverie. Her heart lurched. But it couldn't be Morgan. Not this early. Still, she hurried to open her door.

"Becca," Mary Beth, who had a room near hers, greeted her. "You didn't come down for breakfast. Are you all right? I know you've been poorly, but you need to eat."

Warmed by Mary Beth's concern, and not a little disappointed it was her friend and not Morgan, Becca opened the door wider. "I'm fine, thank you. I'm much better today, really. I'm just not hungry. You're right. I will come down in a minute. And, thank you, Mary Beth. Thank you for . . . coming by," she said, catching herself before she said *for caring.* She'd no reason not to say the words, but still she wouldn't let herself.

"Be sure that you do." Mary Beth threw her a smile, then turned and headed downstairs.

Becca pulled her door closed and leaned against it, needing another moment before she joined the others. What an amazing week this had been, and it wasn't over yet. In the span of six days she'd met a man who disturbed her in ways she'd never imagined, she'd found a home for Violet's twins when she'd never expected the church to take them, she'd discovered that all these years she'd been wrong about God—wrong about not believing—about not believing that He would accept her mother. She'd felt her mother's presence at Saint John's, sure as she was outfitted now in her purple taffeta, waiting to go downstairs to eat.

That her mother had contacted her from the grave was the true wonder of it all. Becca believed now, after a whole lifetime of *not* believing in God or heaven or going to church. Her mother's spirit at Saint John's was all the proof she needed.

There must be a reason. Why now? Why at the church? Becca needed to return to Saint John's and find out why. Tomorrow was Sunday, which meant church services. No matter. She'd go anyway. She'd go and sit in the back of the sanctuary, and wait . . . wait for her mother . . . wait for her mother's spirit to wash through her, and feel her close. *Mama.*

Suddenly hungry, her appetite improved, Becca pulled away from the door, opened it, and then headed down to the kitchen for breakfast.

"Company, Becca," Jenny rapped on her door, then opened it.

Becca shot up from the window seat, jolted by Miss Jenny's presence, knowing Morgan Larkspur must be downstairs. The clock had just chimed three bells. He'd come early. She hadn't *really* expected him until nighttime, when the other customers would start arriving. What should she do with him at this hour? Should she visit with him in one of the parlors? Should she bring him up to her room? Should she feign illness and turn him away? Fighting her panic, Becca swallowed hard, straightened the folds of her purple taffeta, and gave Jenny her best smile. She *could* do this. She *would* do this. How silly to be so nervous. She was, after all, a parlor house girl. This was her job, for pity's sake.

"Morgan is waiting for you in the same parlor where you met before," Jenny quietly announced, sensing Becca's nerves. "Don't worry, dear. He won't bite. He didn't before and he won't now," she joked, happy Becca had such a fine customer, yet unhappy about Becca's upset. She took heart, however, in knowing Becca chose this lifestyle instead of going East to finishing school and a different life.

"Thank you," Becca at last spoke. "I'm ready, Miss Jenny." She forced a smile, then followed the madam out the door—which she shut behind her but forgot to lock—then down the main stairs, all the while hoping and praying she'd do everything right. It shouldn't matter, but it did.

Morgan stood when Rebecca entered the parlor, forgetting all about his dirty, dusty clothes, his lack of sleep, and the troubles he left behind in Leadville, the second he laid eyes on her. God, she was beautiful. He didn't need reminding, but seeing her now hit him hard all over again. He'd done the right thing, coming here instead of going home first. Being here with this slip of a girl did him more good than any evening dinner party with his family. Yeah, his parents had invited Lavinia to join them tonight, and yeah, he should go home; but damn, right now, seeing Rebecca, he'd no intention of doing so. Not yet, anyway.

"Hello." Becca spoke first. She saw right away how exhausted he looked—handsome, most definitely, but exhausted all the same. "How are you, Mor-Morgan?" she tried to sound nonchalant. Saying his name didn't exactly roll off of her tongue.

"Better now," he teased.

Becca blushed at his inference. She dropped her chin, not wanting him to see.

Morgan chuckled, liking her even more than he already did. She charmed him. He'd never been charmed by any female.

Before she could stop herself, Becca lifted her chin and gave voice to her thoughts. "You look so tired. Is there anything I can get you?"

Before he could stop himself, Morgan said the first thing that came to mind. "A hot bath would suit me fine."

Of course, a bath! Becca brightened to the idea, glad to focus on Morgan and not herself. The necessary upstairs would be perfect. It housed a grand, gilded-edge tub. The staff would help her get things ready, filling the tub with hot water, arranging fresh toweling, and ensuring that he had privacy for his bath. "Please, Morgan, come with me," she asked more than commanded, smiling inside and out.

"No problem," he smiled, too. The prospect of a hot bath, with Rebecca's help, was the most appealing offer he'd ever had from a woman. He'd never looked forward to anything more, he knew that for certain. Following her up the main stairway, it was all he could do not to grab hold of her and pull her close, the sway of her slender hips wreaking havoc on him.

When they reached the second-floor landing, they were met by two of the house girls on their way downstairs. The girls politely nodded, but didn't smile. Mary Beth came out of her room then, and locked her door. She did smile the moment she noticed Becca and her customer.

Becca smiled back, grateful for her friend's support.

Mary Beth hurried past them and went downstairs.

Morgan paid no attention to any of the house girls, his mind on Rebecca, and Rebecca only.

"If you'll wait here," Becca said, opening the door to her room and directing Morgan inside, "I'll get your bath ready."

"No problem," he entered her room, noting she didn't unlock it first.

This fact was lost on her. "I'll be back the moment all is ready," she whispered, in a hurry to escape his dusky scrutiny. Her heart thudded in her chest. Her breaths came quick. If she stood there one moment longer, he'd know! She couldn't have that; she couldn't have any man, much less Morgan Larkspur, knowing he affected her so. Feeling her defenses drain, she fought growing panic. Usually one to face her fears, she wanted to run from this one.

"I'll be waiting," Morgan whispered back, his tone low and husky.

His voice sent shivers down Becca's spine, threatening to topple what little nerve remained. Without another word, she turned on her heels and left, closing her door behind her.

"Where are you going?" Morgan gently asked, confused about her readying to leave the bath area.

Shocked back to reality by his simple question, Becca stood stone cold still. She'd no idea what to do now. If she left, he'd be disappointed, maybe even mad. If she didn't, she'd be all thumbs and embarrass herself, and embarrass Miss Jenny and the Palace. Knowing what she had to do, despite her fear, Becca straightened and met Morgan's scrutiny, yet again. "I'll just fetch your satchel from my room. The staff brought it up, and I know you'll want your clean clothes."

"That can wait." Morgan didn't believe her. He knew she wanted to run. He didn't like it that she did, but he knew it all the same.

Damn, she was more skittish than any colt he'd ever broken. Still, she needed to be broken . . . and he needed to be gentle with her when he did. "Help me with these first?" he asked, trying to keep his tone matter-of-fact. He could imagine her bolting at just about anything he said or did.

"Yes, of course," she managed, stepping toward him, praying her knees wouldn't give out on her.

He'd taken off his jacket and was unbuttoning his chambray shirt. His boots he'd already removed; his hat, too. When he pulled his shirt off, he handed it to her, and their fingers brushed.

Becca pulled her hand away fast, as if she'd been scalded. Hot steam from the bath misted in the air around them. It was becoming impossibly warm in the necessary, so warm Becca fought the urge to unbutton the collar of her dress. Much as she tried not to, she couldn't avoid the partially naked man in front of her, the muscled wall of his bare chest unlike any sight she'd ever envisioned.

Morgan chuckled at her response to him, this time keeping it to himself. Careful so not to spook her, he undid his belt buckle, then the buttons of his pants. In one easy move, he'd stripped down to his bottom drawers. His clothes lay in a pile now on a nearby chair.

No more! Becca couldn't imagine seeing . . . *him* . . . seeing all of him! "I have to go now," she spun around so fast, she made herself dizzy. This way, her back to him, it was easier for her to think. "I must change. I need to put on something else . . . to wear . . . in here . . . with you . . . to help you. I'll be back in a minute," she mumbled this last, then rushed out the door.

Morgan let her leave this time, but only because he knew she'd come back. Skittish, but still she'd come. The idea of what she might have on when she did stirred him up inside all right. Damn. He jerked off his drawers and eased down into the hot bath. He had to keep control and not scare Rebecca off. He wanted her so bad he could taste it, smell it, and feel every bit of her softness against his hardness, but not now; not yet. He pulled a folded towel from the nearby shelf and put it behind his head, then leaned back against the tub and shut his eyes, doing his best to find the control he needed.

Becca had absolutely nothing to change into but her ivory dressing gown. She couldn't waltz into the bath area in her corset and chemise! Well she could, but she wouldn't. It would have to be her dressing gown. All thumbs, she thought of asking for help from Mary Beth or Clara or Miss Jenny to get out of her purple taffeta. That wouldn't do. She didn't want any of them knowing how unschooled she was in the ways of a prostitute, when they applied to her!

Finally she had her dress off, and her corset, and her chemise, but not her pantaloons. They would stay. Quickly now, she slipped on her dressing gown. Once she'd neatly hung her purple taffeta in her wardrobe and placed her button boots in their proper place, she went over to the floor mirror and checked her hair. She'd keep it up. Besides, it would be better in the bath. The bath was already hot enough without her hair clinging to her back and waist, layering onto her misery.

Becca turned away from the mirror, stepped into her kid slippers, then picked up Morgan's delivered satchel. She had nothing left to do now, but join Morgan in the bath.

Her door shut behind her, Becca padded down the hall, glad no one else passed. She didn't feel like seeing anyone, even Mary Beth. She took the hall turn toward the necessary, eyeing the closed door hard, gathering what nerve she had left. Once she'd reached the door, she knocked before going in.

"Come in, Rebecca." Morgan knew it had to be her.

Becca did so, her eyes averted to the planked floor. She set down the satchel.

"Lock the door this time," he gently encouraged. "We don't want the whole house walking in on us."

"No," Becca agreed, all the while frightened to death at his meaning of "walking in on us." She locked the door, immediately relieved that he had immersed himself in the tub. She faced him now. His cropped ebony hair, curled slightly from the heat, attracted her, rousing her senses. This time his stare didn't agitate her; quite the opposite. His handsome features drew her closer, his magnetic expression beckoning her. His arms and chest glistened with moisture, and steam rose from his well-muscled body, conjuring his masculine scent, enticing her, calling her. Unwittingly, she stepped closer.

"Keep coming. I won't bite."

Miss Jenny's same words. Somehow, though, when they came from Morgan, she thought he might. Still, she stepped ever closer. Unsure of herself, she didn't know what she should do next.

Morgan did. The way her silk and satin nightdress clung to her, the moist heat in the room easily allowing him a good view of her comely shape, told him exactly what she needed to do . . . to him. He'd settle for her helping him wash. For now. He leaned forward in the tub. "Mind getting my back?"

Grateful for a task, she refused to look into the water, at *him*. She rolled up the sleeves of her nightdress as best she could, picked up the bar of soap from its dish, and then bent over to wash his back. The moment she did so, the moment she made contact with his skin, the same sensation hit her as before, as if she'd been scalded. Instead of pulling away this time, she relathered her fingers then splayed them over his skin, wanting to feel more of him. It pleasured her, touching him. She washed his shoulders and then farther down his back, reveling in his masculine aura. Lost in her task, she didn't realize her hair had come loose, the pins easily giving way at her movements.

For his part, it was all Morgan could do not to touch her, not to grab her and bring her into the tub with him. The gentle pulsations of her fingers were driving him crazy. If she didn't stop, he'd start something . . . and she wasn't ready yet. "Enough," he all but shouted.

Startled, Becca pulled away from him and stood up, only now realizing her hair had come loose. The soap fell from her hands onto the floor.

"Rebecca," he said, his tone softened. "I'll finish my bath. I'm just tired. You can go."

His comments, surprisingly, didn't bring her relief. She

stepped from behind the tub and walked toward the door, too dejected to worry about fixing her hair or to think about the fact that her wet dressing gown revealed more of her than she'd like.

"Rebecca," he called to her back.

She turned to look at him when she'd rather not.

The sight of her now—with her hair down full, her lovely skin all heated and flush, her shapely breasts jutting against the silk and satin of her gown, her eyes sparking their upset, and her rosy lips trembling slightly—did things to him he'd never thought any woman could do. Women were good for pleasure and sex, but not what else Rebecca made him feel. She mixed him all up inside. Beautiful or not, he wasn't used to having feelings beyond sexual desire. He never intended to have feelings.

Becca hated this, all of it! She hated that she stood practically naked before any man, especially this one. She hated that her entire world depended upon making her fifty dollars a night. She hated that she hadn't found her mother's killer. She hated that she couldn't announce his description up and down the line. She hated that she couldn't go to the law, tell them everything, and have them find her mother's killer. She hated her life, all of it. Most of all, at this moment, she hated that she *didn't* hate Morgan Larkspur!

Face-to-face with him now, aware of him as a man—a man who attracted her, a man who stirred her body in places she'd never imagined, a man who seemed decent, *really* decent, a man who could so easily capture her heart, a man she wanted—a man who didn't want her. This last frightened her. She'd had no idea of it before: wanting someone. Emotions had no place in her world. Feelings for a man had no place in her world. *Feelings only get a whore killed.* Fanny's warning rang out in her head. Becca shrugged her shoulders. No matter. She didn't need Fanny's warning where Morgan Larkspur was concerned. Morgan had dismissed her, telling her to go.

How could three little words hurt so much? *You can go.* Such power the hated words had over her. Uncomfortable at the cruel realization, Becca tried to keep her back straight and her head high in the face of such rejection. She'd hold her ground where Morgan Larkspur was concerned, if only for the next minute. Then she'd leave the bath area and he'd leave the Palace, and that would be the end of her "first appointment" under the employ of Miss Jenny Clayton.

"Rebecca," Morgan said again. "Wait for me in your room. I won't be long."

"Fine," she said, hating that this whole situation would be prolonged.

Why doesn't he just leave from here and get this all over with? As if she needed more proof of his rejection. He didn't say one word about staying. He'd just said to wait. Well, she'd wait, but she didn't want to. She wanted to lock her door against him. *Oh for pity's sake.* It just occurred to her that she hadn't locked her room even one time, all day. Something else occurred to her: she'd been *waiting* all day. For Morgan. For what? So he could come and see her and reject her again after almost as much as telling her she had no skills as a prostitute, who couldn't even please him in the bath!

Still, Becca didn't move. Despite the turn of her tormented thoughts, she stood stock still, waiting. She should wait in her room. He'd said as much. Rebellious at his dismissal of her, then his order to wait for him in her room, Becca decided she'd wait in the necessary. After all, she had some self-esteem left. No man could just waltz into the Palace, pay for her—pay for her for the whole week—cause her to look forward to seeing him, finally show up, then get her in a tizzy over preparing his bath, have her see to him, then tell her, "You can go," and then order her to wait in her room! *Hah!* She had feelings now all right. She'd hold her ground in the necessary to prove it.

Morgan started to rise out of the tub, all the while keeping his eyes on Rebecca. She charmed him, and more. Much, much more.

Becca spun around so fast she almost lost her balance. Already off balance from the downward turn of her thoughts, and already defenseless against Morgan Larkspur, she couldn't imagine what would happen if she saw *all* of him!

In a full panic, she managed to turn the door handle, open it, then pull the door shut behind her. She had to hurry now. She had to hurry up and wait in her room for Morgan. Determined to be fully clothed when she did, she all but ran back to room number eight on the second floor of the Palace.

CHAPTER EIGHT

A knock at her door caught her buttoning the last button of her purple taffeta. Becca's fingers froze. She froze. *Morgan.* Morgan was at the door. She swallowed hard. Her throat hurt. So did her head . . . and her heart. Nothing to be done now but walk over to the door, open it, then have Morgan bid her goodbye. Simple enough, right? With that, she found her composure and her footing and started for her door.

"Took you long enough," Morgan teased, and then he walked past her, entering her room.

Becca said nothing. What was there to say? She closed her door and waited, just as he'd asked her to do. If not a skilled prostitute, at least she'd be an obedient one.

Disappointed to find her dressed and her hair up when he'd rather she still be half-undressed, Morgan sensed something was wrong. He didn't understand her change in mood. "Where are you going?" he blurted out before he thought better of it. Prostitutes didn't like personal questions. This one especially.

"Where am *I* going?" she parroted, incredulous at his question. Glad to find her anger, she faced him squarely.

Morgan fought the urge to grab her and kiss her hard and . . . and bed her hard. Damn, even mad, she got to him. "Yeah, where are you going all dressed? I thought I told you to wait for me," he tossed back lightly, doing his best to keep his hands off her.

"I'm not going anywhere, Morgan Larkspur." She rounded

on him. "You're the one going. So . . . go . . ."

"Hold on now." He didn't get it. The feel of her hands on him, in the bath, told him she didn't want him to go. "Hold on, Rebecca. Why do you want me to go?" He felt a little like a stupid schoolboy right now.

Dumbfounded, Becca tried to decide if she'd heard him correctly. Was it possible she'd got everything wrong? Was it possible Morgan really meant to finish his bath by himself and really meant for her to be there in her room, waiting for him? So they could be together in her room? And finally have their "appointment"? Her heart raced—with excitement and fear—at the prospect. "Mor-Morgan," she sputtered. "Then you *don't* want to go?"

"No, I don't."

"You're sure?" she needed to hear him say it again.

"Rebecca." He took a step toward her, his voice husky. "I am very sure that I want to stay, if you want me to."

"Oh yes," she managed right away, the full impact of his dusky gaze making her tingle everywhere, especially . . . especially in her privates. She'd never known such a feeling, at the same time upsetting yet so . . . so pleasurable. Needing to sit down, Becca all but collapsed onto the nearby window seat. She averted her gaze from him.

"You know what? I'm starving," Morgan abruptly announced. "How about we order up a fine champagne supper?"

She shot him a look of surprise. The last thing she wanted was to eat, with so many butterflies in her stomach, but she'd order up a meal all the same. For Morgan. For Morgan, she would. "Will steak and potatoes be all right?" She tried to think about what might be prepared in the kitchen for Saturday night. Of course there would be more fancy eats, but right now all she could think of was steak and potatoes.

"And champagne," Morgan added.

"Yes, and champagne," she repeated, standing now. "I'll just go take care of it. All right?"

"Very all right." He winked and smiled.

The butterflies in her stomach set to flying all over again.

They sat, parlor house daughter and customer, and had their meal at the little table in room number eight at the Palace. Candlelight flickered between Becca and Morgan while lit sconces softly illuminated the moderate space. Dark out now, music and laughter echoed through the floorboards. More customers had arrived, enjoying themselves downstairs, having their own champagne suppers and maybe a dance or two, looking forward to the night ahead with their chosen house girl.

Morgan leaned back against his chair. No meal had ever tasted so good. No dinner partner had ever listened so attentively. When he'd first sat down to eat he hadn't known what to expect. Dead silence probably, with Rebecca still nervous and him trying to keep his mind on his food, and not her. One simple question to him about his week in Leadville and why he seemed so tired started him talking. He hadn't meant to share anything about himself or the problems at the mines, as he was unaccustomed to opening up to anyone. He kept everything in. Always had . . . until now.

With the burdens of the week weighing so heavily on him lifted now, Morgan felt a lot better than he had when he'd first arrived at the Palace. His improved spirit wasn't all due to a hot bath, a change of clothes, a good meal, and the promise of a soft, beautiful woman in his bed. Much of it was because of who the woman was.

This slip of a girl touched him without touching him. She reached out to him, easing his worries. She was interested in what he had to say, not once taking her attention from him. Most women would have by now, and he knew it, but not this one. This one listened. This one cared. *This one is mine.*

The idea of any other man ordering a bath, sitting down to a meal, then spending the night with Rebecca hit his gut hard. Morgan got up from his seat and walked over to the window, staring blankly out onto Holladay Street. The idea galled him. Hell, he didn't know what to do about it. What was he supposed to do? Lay down money every week to keep her out of other men's beds while he had to be away at the mines? Rebecca wouldn't go for it anyway. He knew she wouldn't, not with her stubborn pride.

Suddenly dog-tired, his fatigue finally catching up with him, Morgan decided he needed a nap, just a quick one, just long enough to figure what to do about Rebecca. He should go home now. He was sure everyone was waiting supper for him. But he couldn't leave. Not yet. He turned away from the window and walked toward the bed. Rebecca, he could see, still sat in her chair . . . waiting . . . waiting for him. No, he couldn't let her wait for any other man. He couldn't. "I'm just going to lie down a few minutes here. All right?" he asked, knowing she wouldn't protest, and knowing she'd understand. Damn, it felt good to know that she wouldn't take offense, and that he didn't need to explain himself.

She smiled at him.

He smiled back.

She kept her seat and watched as he pulled off his boots and lay on top of her covers.

He was asleep in the time it took to do so.

Morgan slept on, so fast asleep, Becca noticed, that he didn't stir at all when she cleared the supper dishes and then set the tray outside in the hall by her door. She'd take it down to the kitchen herself, if she didn't think there would be questioning eyes all around.

Goodness, here she was still in her day dress, for pity's sake. What would everyone think if they saw? She knew what they'd think and shouldn't care, but she did. The kitchen staff would also see that only one meal had been eaten—hers had barely been touched. Everyone knew she never had much of an appetite, but still, she didn't care to have anyone notice her uneaten supper. How could she eat with Morgan Larkspur at her table? How could she eat, watching his expressions, hanging on to his every word, riveted by his disarming good looks as much as his heartfelt conversation?

Becca lingered by her bed, standing close, watching Morgan sleep, watching the rise and fall of his chest, his white shirt unbuttoned enough to reveal that portion of his fit, well-muscled physique. She studied the way he had one strong arm behind his head on the pillow, with the other fallen at his side. She was able to look him up and down now, and yet again his height— what with his feet jutting against the foot of the bed—and know he wouldn't see her blush when she eyed him so carefully all the while fighting the urge to crawl in bed next to him. Letting out a gasp, Becca rushed over and sat down hard on the window seat.

Glad Morgan slept on and didn't wake up to witness her upset, Becca couldn't believe her reaction to him—her feelings for him. She'd only seen him three times in her life, and she didn't even like men. Why she liked this one so much, and why she'd let herself so easily develop feelings for him, frightened her. Feelings for Morgan, or any man, could be her death. The oddest sensation hit her, forcing her to sit back against the window. Maybe it wouldn't be such a bad way to die: in Morgan Larkspur's arms.

She'd no idea of the time. Right now time stood still. She took off her button boots and curled up in the window seat, purple taffeta dress and all, determined to wait for Morgan again, to wait for him to get his needed rest, to wait for him to awaken, to wait to see if he'd pay for the whole week again—not caring this time what the other girls in the house might think of her if he did.

"Rebecca," Morgan whispered, trying to rouse her from sleep. "Rebecca, wake up. I have to go and we need to talk." He gave her shoulder a light shake.

Becca opened her eyes, disoriented by the bright sunshine on her face, slow to awaken. She'd been dreaming—dreaming of Morgan Larkspur—dreaming that he'd stayed the night—dreaming they'd made love, sweet passionate love, all the night through.

"Rebecca," Morgan said again, his voice low and husky.

Still lost in dreams, her eyes open this time, Becca smiled at Morgan, wanting to dream on and on about him. Her desire for him rose, the longer she held his magnetic slate gaze. She let her eyes close to better hold on to him and her dreams of love.

"Wake up, darlin'." Morgan put his hand to her shoulder a second time and gave it another little shake.

Becca's eyes flew open. This time when she spied Morgan fully dressed, she knew it wasn't any dream. Quickly sitting up, ignoring the pain in her stiff limbs, reality rushed to her head with a vengeance. Morgan *had* spent the night, in her bed, alone, without her. What must he think of her this morning—still in her day dress, curled up in the window seat like a little girl? She felt so foolish. A skilled prostitute would have changed into an enticing nightdress, climbed into bed with Morgan, and . . . and . . . done the very things she'd been dreaming about.

"You're not so easy to wake up in the morning," he teased. "I'll have to remember that."

"Remember what?" she answered, too discomfited with her own thoughts to comprehend any meaning from his words.

"Rebecca, stand up, darlin'."

She did, sobering to the moment and the man in front of her. Her hair came undone at that moment, settling around her shoulders and down her back like a mourning veil. Morgan intended to leave. He was going to leave her alone in her room, without her having properly helped him in the bath, without her having whispered sweet nothings in his ear, without her doing her best to look her best, and without their having made passionate love. She'd failed with Morgan. She'd failed as a prostitute befitting Miss Jenny Clayton's Palace.

Morgan caught up her hands.

Startled by his actions, she stared at her hands in his as if she were looking at someone else's hands, and not her own.

"Rebecca, look at me," he gently encouraged, giving her fingers a squeeze.

Slowly she raised her head to meet his compelling gaze, struck again by his handsomeness, by the sensual set of his mouth, the sculpted line of his jaw, by his masterful build, by his masculine scent, all clean, laced with a hint of fresh tobacco—by *him*.

"I have to leave now," he said.

She knew that. He didn't have to say it. It hurt too much.

"I'll be back for you tomorrow. Don't see anyone tonight. Here." He let go of her hands and took a fifty-dollar token out of his pocket. Taking up one of her dropped hands, he pressed the token into it and pulled her fingers closed around the cool metal.

Stirred so by his touch, she had trouble processing what he'd just said. "Did you . . . did you say you'll be back tomorrow?" she asked, incredulous.

Morgan chuckled. "Nothing will keep me away. Count on that. Now do as you're told and don't see any other man tonight. Promise me?"

She stared mutely at him, nodding her head in agreement.

"Good. It's settled then." He grinned.

His disarming smile sent shivers down her spine.

"Tomorrow then, darlin'," he said, placing a quick kiss on her forehead before turning to leave.

She watched him gather his things off her bed, open her door, then close it behind him, the feel of his gentle, warm lips lingering on her skin long after he'd gone.

Jenny watched Morgan Larkspur exit the front doors of her house, not surprised he'd stayed all night with Becca. What surprised her was that Becca had let him. She hadn't figured on that. No indeed.

Jenny knew Becca harbored a dislike of men, which was only one of the reasons she'd tried to send her to school in the East. But, what with her letting Morgan stay last night, evidently she didn't harbor any dislike for him—in fact, quite the opposite. Hoping Morgan would return, for Becca's sake—paying exclusively for her—Jenny would wait for Becca to talk to her. She wouldn't pry the information from the girl. She wanted to, but she wouldn't. Not yet.

Morgan could hear his mother now, nagging at him for missing last night with the family and with Lavinia. Damn. Instead of hopping a streetcar or calling a carriage, he'd walk home. The fresh air went down easy. He thought of Rebecca. Thoughts of her went down real easy, too. He couldn't imagine being anywhere last night but with her.

When he'd awakened and saw her asleep in the window seat, curled up all sweet like a little girl, giving up the comfort of her bed . . . Well, he'd never liked a woman more. He'd never known a woman to put his comfort ahead of her own. He couldn't let that feeling go. He couldn't let Rebecca go.

At least he'd decided what to do about her. It meant delaying his departure for Leadville by a day, but he'd little choice.

Sunday morning. It was Sunday morning and Becca needed to go to Saint John's. No time to try to make sense of Morgan Larkspur. No time to think on the fact that he'd paid for one more night and said he'd be back tomorrow. No time to hope, to wish, to look forward to tomorrow. She had to think on today: on going to church, the church where she'd sensed her mother's presence, the church where she'd begun to believe in a God she never thought existed.

Changing into her navy day dress and hat, she hoped her outfit suited Sunday services at Saint John's. It was the same outfit she'd worn there before, which is the reason she chose it. She'd slip into the church, and sit in the very back, not wanting anyone to notice her. She thought of the beautiful blonde who had noticed her when she'd brought the babies, and for the briefest of moments lost her nerve. How the blonde—*Lavinia,* she remembered—had known she was a prostitute puzzled her. She'd dressed properly. She didn't wear a sign advertising anything. For pity's sake, it didn't matter what the blonde thought of her. Then why did her insults still hurt?

In no time, Becca was out her door, which she forgot to lock yet again, down the stairs, then out the front doors of the Palace, hurrying to make her way to the church at Twentieth and Welton.

Jenny watched her leave, just as she'd watched Morgan leave. This was getting more and more interesting, no question about it.

By the time he set foot inside the family mansion, Morgan had cemented his plans for Rebecca. First thing tomorrow he'd take care of everything then head to Leadville on the next train out, needing to get there as soon as he could. The problems at the mines were only getting worse. If fighting broke out between the miners and mine owners, he needed to be there. Caught in the middle—understanding the issues on both sides while maybe not agreeing with them—he hoped the mounting trouble wouldn't end in bloodshed. If he could do anything to stop it, he would, or die trying.

The dining room was empty except for their housekeeper, Matilda. Ever efficient, she gave Morgan a nod, and then reset the cover over the platter of eggs on the breakfront before going back into the kitchen.

He'd missed breakfast. Matilda must have heard him enter and so reset the morning fare. Next to the eggs she'd put out a tray of fresh-baked scones with marmalade, a platter of fruit, and a pot of coffee. Morgan made a beeline for the silver carafe and poured a cup of the steaming brew. He took a seat at the highly polished mahogany dining table and sipped his coffee, staring at all the empty chairs.

Although he was relieved that his family had left for church as was their custom on Sunday mornings, he didn't relish hearing his mother go on and on about how he wasn't living up to the family name by not showing up last night at this very table. She wouldn't be happy that he'd missed church services, either. Neither would his father. But instead of lashing out at him like his mother, his father would keep silent, giving him a cold, reproachful stare. Morgan hated that worst of all. He put up with his mother's disapproval, tolerating her disappointment in him much better than he did his father's. Morgan finished his coffee and got up for more.

No way he'd ever let on to either of his parents what his plans were for Rebecca Rose.

Becca kept to the sidewalk, making her way past the sea of horse-drawn carriages parked near Saint John's Cathedral. Her insides caught, knowing a crowd gathered in the church and, from the looks of the carriages, a very well-to-do crowd. She relaxed a little, believing few would notice her amid such a large group of churchgoers. She'd stick to her plan, to take a seat in the very back of Saint John's.

She stood a moment outside the front of the church to collect her courage. The large circular stained-glass window loomed overhead, just as it had before. For the first time, she noticed a cross at the very apex of the church roof above the window. Suddenly heartened, she took the necessary steps and went inside Saint John's.

Father Hart stood in the pulpit, preaching to his flock. His commanding voice echoed throughout the sanctuary, as if daring even a church mouse to give challenge to his words. No one turned to look at Becca when she entered. Grateful for anonymity, she tried not to panic when she didn't see a seat free in the back. She could stand, but then she'd be noticed for certain. Creeping forward only enough to see better, she noticed there was an open seat at the end of the last bench row of pews, just to her left. Quick as she could, she took the seat. The woman to her right scooted farther over, away from her, when she did. Too nervous to wonder at this, Becca kept her eyes forward, glad the people in the row in front of her kept their eyes forward as well.

From her position under one of the arched church eaves, Becca stared straight ahead between the pillars, unable to see the stained-glass windows in the front of the church or the altar with the gold cross. Frustrated, she wanted to get up and move to the center aisle for a better look, but didn't, of course. Too many eyes in the back of the church would be on her. She also imagined Father Hart stopping his sermon to preach to her, to tell her to sit down or leave. She must be content to sit and wait for the service to be over, to wait to see the alter, to wait, hoping her mother's spirit would wash over her. *Mama.* Thoughts of her beloved mother calmed her and helped her sit still.

Unable to concentrate on Father Hart's words, impatient for the service to end, Becca glanced around the sanctuary, her gaze settling over the crowd, looking to see if she recognized anyone from the Palace. Surely some of their best customers attended this church. Hadn't Miss Jenny said as much? She knew her thoughts were wicked and that God might not approve of them, but she couldn't help it. Staring at the backs of so many heads, she recognized no one. It suddenly occurred to her how silly she was, trying to recognize someone when she wasn't eye-to-eye with him. No one turned to look at her to make her job any easier—no one but the beautiful blonde, *Lavinia.*

Becca's gut wrenched. She ripped her gaze away. She might have known the mean-spirited blonde would be here, since she'd had the misfortune to run into her before at this very church. Refusing to meet Lavinia's angry glare, Becca stared straight ahead. She knew what Lavinia thought: that she—*a prostitute*—wasn't good enough to be here in the same church with decent, respectable townsfolk. Hah! Becca fought the urge to stand up and shout across the crowd to Lavinia, that she and her mother were both good enough to be here at Saint John's, and that they were welcome here like everybody else.

Mama, where are you? I'm here. Where are you?

Wishing her mother were close, needing the comfort only a mother can give, Becca sat still and as quiet as she could, hoping to feel her mother's presence. But there was nothing; nothing came; no signal from her mother, from her mother's grave. Letting out the breath she'd been holding, Becca tried to resign herself to the fact that what she wished for probably wouldn't happen.

Disappointed and feeling foolish, she suddenly wondered if she'd made it all up, thinking her mother's spirit had come to her here in this church. With a sinking heart, she looked around the sanctuary yet again, suddenly not caring about Lavinia. Her gaze settled on no one, yet she looked over the crowd all the same. The instant she did, the instant she gazed out over the parishioners, a bolt of lightning couldn't have hit her harder, forcing her to sit back hard against her seat. *Mama.*

She knew it was her mother contacting her, not in a spiritual wash of motherly love—but in warning! Becca swallowed hard, her insides trembling, and fought for control. No need now to wait for the service to be over so she could approach the altar and the gold cross in hopes of calling her mother's spirit from her grave. Her mother was here in the church with her now, in the last pew, trying to get her attention, to warn her of something. Stunned by such a revelation, Becca shut her eyes tight, conjuring her mother's image, desperately needing to understand.

Her mother's image came to mind, all right—lying on her bed in her pinewood crib at the end of the line in Nevada City, her throat cut, bleeding to death. Then another image hit Becca—this one of a hand with missing fingers and a gold lion-head ring. Becca gasped aloud. Her eyes flew open.

The woman next to her moved a little farther down the pew, away from her.

Mindless of the woman, Becca shut her eyes again, still not believing what had just happened. She knew now. She knew the why of it all—why she'd been spirited to Saint John's in the first place—so her mother could warn her that her murderer was there in the church, right now, and Becca could be next. Somewhere, amid the hundreds of parishioners, sat her mother's killer!

Becca had always believed the killer was close, and now she knew for sure. She opened her eyes and then stood, abruptly exiting the church. She intended to wait just outside and eye every single man who left, searching for the hand that had killed her mother.

CHAPTER NINE

The warm sunshine outside Saint John's did little to ease Becca's agitation. Her head pounded and her heart thudded in her chest, but no force on earth could move her from her appointed spot near the front doors of the great cathedral. The moment she spied her mother's killer, whom she'd recognize by his murderous hand, she'd kill him.

Fumbling at her bodice for the derringer some prostitutes chose for a hiding place, Becca realized she hadn't brought her gun! She should have hidden it in her bodice or the inside of her thigh, but she hadn't.

Planning anew, she tried to keep calm. She'd follow her mother's killer and see where he lived, and then she'd go and get her gun and kill him. Giving no thought to any consequences for herself once she'd meted out her own justice for her mother's senseless murder, Becca stood outside the church and waited, armed with steely resolve, anxious to finally let her mother rest in peace.

The doors opened. Father Hart stepped out first.

Becca felt dizzy, desperate to hold her ground.

Father Hart smiled at her, and then turned to greet his parishioners.

The men and women exited so fast. One dark suit after another, one elegant outfit after another, gloved hands, ringed hands, hands tucked in the crooks of companions' arm, hands in pockets, hands waving to others, and so many more hands that she couldn't see. For Becca, time stood still although the crowd did not, quickly emptying the cathedral. Parishioners said their goodbyes to Father Hart, got into their carriages, and left.

Dazed by it all, the next thing Becca knew she stood alone out front of Saint John's, plagued by the awful realization that she'd missed her mother's killer. Disappointed, she turned slowly away from the cathedral and headed for the Palace.

Next week. *I'll come back next week, and the next, and the next, until I find him.* When she did, she wouldn't be caught empty-handed. She'd have her derringer within easy reach.

Augusta Larkspur hadn't finished with her older son. Angry with him for not coming to supper the night before and not attending church that morning, she railed at him yet again.

"Morgan, you have obligations to the family, and you know it. You have obligations to Lavinia, too. She will make a good match for you. She comes from fine stock and will be a good addition to our family. You upset her last night. So, Morgan, what do you have to say for yourself?"

Morgan was eye-to-eye with his father now, and not his mother. The look of disapproval in his father's fading blue eyes wore on him, beating him down far more than his mother's rant.

"Mother." He looked at her now, and away from Eugene Larkspur. "I've already told you the business at the mines in Leadville kept me from getting here last night."

"Uh . . . the mines. Of course, Morgan, but that's little excuse," she said, still in a huff.

Morgan didn't expect his mother to understand, or even listen to him about their holdings in Leadville, or any problems at the mines. He didn't expect her to realize that the family name depended on their financial success and not their social comings and goings. A smart woman in some things, he doubted her wisdom in others. Now Rebecca . . . Rebecca was a different story. She'd proved smart in ways his mother and Lavinia, combined, were not, despite her hard life. He'd sensed that about Rebecca from the first, and she'd listened to him, whereas his mother and Lavinia had not.

"Are you keeping things together in Leadville, son?" Eugene Larkspur cut into Morgan's sober reverie.

Morgan looked again at his father. "Yes, sir," he answered.

"Good." Eugene's brusque comment ended any more talk about Leadville.

Morgan knew the drill; he'd been through it before. His father expected him to handle things, not wanting the family's business problems brought home. Failure at anything wasn't an option for Morgan. He'd been given major responsibilities and he needed to take care of them, plain and simple.

Exasperated with this conversation, and more than a little annoyed that Monty lived by different family rules, it struck Morgan again that his parents never held Monty's feet to the fire, as they did his.

"Hey, bro." Monty waltzed into the spacious, elegantly appointed Victorian living room and plopped down on the nearest sofa. "See you finally made it," he teased, throwing Morgan a broad smile.

Morgan shook off his upset at his little brother, forgiving the unfair circumstances as he always did. Besides, he needed to get himself in better spirits. Lavinia would arrive soon for Sunday dinner.

Becca had no idea how long she'd roamed up and down Holladay Street. When she'd first arrived at the Palace from Saint John's, she couldn't go inside, needing more time to walk out her upset. It was early still, and few customers meandered the street, seeking out gambling halls, brothels, and saloons.

She passed more than one "working girl," however. Some were dressed for the day in clothes similar to hers, some in less refined clothing with their pocketed, baggy, one-piece dresses and straw hats. Still others, farther down the line on the row, stood in front of their place of business more scantily clad in low-cut attire. Holladay Street, for the most part, remained quiet, since none of the produce or meat markets opened on Sunday. Becca wished for Monday, not only because she could more easily get lost in the hustle and bustle of the busy marketplace, but maybe on Monday she'd feel better than she did now.

She remembered Morgan. On Monday she'd see him. How she wished for Monday.

Late afternoon when Becca returned to the Palace, she was still upset over the events of the morning at Saint John's. She hadn't spotted her mother's killer at the church, and still feeling the jolt of her mother's warning in her chest, she ignored all the eyes on her when she stepped inside, especially Miss Jenny's. Becca didn't want to explain anything to anyone.

Besides, how could she? Who on earth would believe her? It sounded too crazy to be true. Imagine telling Miss Jenny that her mother's dead spirit came to her at Saint John's to warn her about her killer, and that her killer would murder Becca if he could. Becca had never given Miss Jenny any description or any details about her mother's killer in all the years she'd lived at the Palace, and she wasn't about to now. Miss Jenny would try to stop her from what she had to do.

No one will stop me. No one.

"Becca," Jenny quietly called from behind her.

About to take the main staircase, Becca grudgingly turned around.

"Are you all right?" Jenny spoke low, in order to keep their conversation as private as she could. "You've been gone all day, which is very unlike you. You don't have to tell me where or why. Just tell me if you're all right."

Suddenly Becca wished she could tell Miss Jenny everything that had happened this morning and have Miss Jenny hug her tight and tell her everything would be all right. Thinking better of it, she softened her expression, smiling at the ever-caring madam. "I will be, Miss Jenny, as soon as I get some rest. I'm that tired right now. Oh, here." Becca remembered her Sunday night token, and took it out of her drawstring bag. She handed the fifty-dollar token to Miss Jenny.

Jenny took the token, turning it over in her fingers, knowing it had to be from Morgan Larkspur. Good. At least he wasn't the reason for Becca's upset . . . or was he? All in good time, Jenny would find out. For now, Jenny would cross a line through the name of the man who had asked for an appointment with Becca tonight, and do so readily. She'd take the important customer herself if she had to, since she didn't want any ruffled feathers tonight with her elite clientele.

Business was business. Nothing could stand in the way of it. With the fifty-dollar token in hand, Jenny knew Becca needn't worry about business tonight with anyone other than Morgan Larkspur. Whether or not he would come tonight for Becca remained to be seen.

"Have a good rest, dear. I'll wake you up for supper," Jenny assured her.

"Thank you, Miss Jenny. Thank you," Becca said, close to tears at the madam's kind and understanding nature.

"Go on, dear," Jenny encouraged, her own throat tightening with emotion.

Becca pivoted and started up the stairs, her heart and limbs so heavy, it was all she could do to make it to room number eight on the second floor.

A hard knock on her door woke Becca up. It must be suppertime. Another knock, this one harder, forced her up and out of bed. A quick look out the window told her it wasn't suppertime at all, but breakfast time!

"Becca," Jenny called through the closed door. "Morgan Larkspur is here for you."

Becca opened her door so fast Miss Jenny almost fell through the doorway. Ushering the madam inside, Becca quickly shut the door behind her. "Mor-Morgan did you say? He's here? Now?"

"Yes, dear, he's most definitely here now."

"But . . . but why?" she asked, realizing how silly she sounded, yet asking all the same.

"Sit down, dear, and I'll tell you exactly why," Jenny said, taking a seat alongside Becca on the edge of the tidy bed.

Still garbed in her navy outfit from the day before, having slept the night through on top of her covers, Becca tried to shake the sleep from her addled brain. She couldn't imagine the conversation between Miss Jenny and Morgan Larkspur, and wasn't at all sure she wanted to know.

"Becca," Jenny began, "Morgan has made an offer for you, a grand offer, an offer you cannot ignore."

Becca's insides seized. She'd no idea of it.

"He spoke to me this morning about you, thinking it right to talk to me first, this being my house and you being under my roof. He wants to take you for his mistress, to live in elegant rooms at the new Windsor Hotel, and be solely responsible for your happiness and well-being." At this last, Jenny stopped, then took one of Becca's hands in hers. "This is a great honor, Becca. This is a great opportunity. You will not only live in the finest hotel in Denver at Eighteenth and Larimer, you'll have the finest clothes, ride in the finest carriages, eat the finest cuisine, sip the finest champagne, and live a grand lifestyle. I couldn't be more proud that a man like Morgan Larkspur has chosen you, among all others, to take for a mistress." She squeezed Becca's hand, choking back her tears.

Filled with emotion herself, warring emotions, the last thing Becca felt like doing was crying. She was happy beyond happy at Morgan's offer while at the same time scared to death at the prospect of living *solely* for his pleasure. She loved knowing he wanted her for his mistress, yet also knew she knew nothing of how to be a mistress. Becca shot up off the bed, unable to sit still a moment longer. *Oh dear, oh dear, oh dear!*

"Becca, stop pacing," Jenny ordered. "We don't have time for it. *You* don't have time for it. You need to make yourself presentable, then go downstairs and see Morgan. He's waiting in the same parlor. You know the one." With that, Jenny stood. "I'll leave you now, dear, so you can get ready," she said, and headed for the door. Pausing, her fingers already on the glass knob, Jenny turned and faced Becca. "Child, I am very happy for you, but I am not happy to see you leave me or my house. You're special to me. You always have been. I . . . I—" unable to finish, Jenny quickly opened the door and left.

A tear escaped Becca's cheek, first one, then another, and another. She rushed over to the washstand and poured water from the pitcher into the basin. Dousing her face in the cool water, letting it eclipse her tears, she set to making herself presentable for Morgan.

"Good morning, darlin'." Morgan stood when she entered the parlor.

Becca slowed her step the moment she saw him. Not since her mother, not since Fanny, not since Miss Jenny, had she felt

127

like this—like she was *home*. Right now, with Morgan Larkspur standing before her, showering her with his warmth, signaling his affection in his protective gaze, letting her know she could trust him, even love him . . . Her insides turned. *Love?* She hadn't come downstairs to find love. Companionship, yes. Security in his care, yes. A pleasant enough time with him, yes. But love? No, she didn't want love. *Love can get a whore killed*, she reminded herself. And after all, that's what she was, a whore. Soon to be a mistress, but a whore all the same. She'd best remember that. She'd best remember to keep her emotions in check if she wanted to stay alive. Sobering to the reality of her circumstance, Becca straightened her shoulders, held her chin high, and returned Morgan's greeting. "Good morning, yourself, Morgan Larkspur."

"God, it's great to lay eyes on you again, darlin'."

Morgan's husky words set her spine tingling. It was great to see him, too.

"Come sit a moment, will you?" He took her hand in his and led her to the settee.

His touch wreaked havoc on her insides, setting every nerve on end.

Both seated now, Morgan kept her hand in his.

It was hard enough to concentrate on the situation, much less the upcoming conversation, with his warm fingers encircling hers. She refused to meet his gaze. If she did, she'd no hope of keeping her wits. With her free hand, she played with the folds of her dress, as if she'd not a care in the world.

"Rebecca. Darlin', look at me."

At his quiet command her fingers gripped the navy cotton, which she immediately let go. Smoothing out the folds of her dress again, trying to set the expensive fabric right—buying time to collect herself—she at last turned her head to look at him. The moment she did, the moment their eyes met, her insides folded every bit as much as the disheveled fabric under her fingers.

"Has Miss Jenny talked to you and told you why I'm here?"

"Yes," she answered softly, quickly averting her gaze.

"Are you willing?"

"Yes."

He stood, pulling her to stand along with him.

She took her hand from his, unable to look at him, embarrassed because she didn't know what to do, what to say next.

He put his fingers under her chin, tilting her head up to him. "Rebecca, darlin'—for that you are. You've been my darlin' girl ever since I first laid eyes on you. I want to take care of you and be with you as much as I can, for as long as you'll have me. I know you're still young—"

"I'll be eighteen next week," she interrupted, surprised by her bravado.

Morgan chuckled, and then took his fingers from under her chin, only to take both of her hands in his. "You're quite the old lady then. Had I known I'd have chosen another," he teased.

"I'd like to see you try," she teased back, losing some of her embarrassment.

His expression changing, his smile gone, Morgan brought her hands to his chest, pulling her closer.

Becca had never been kissed by a man. She'd never wanted to be, until now. Her heart raced. Her breaths came short. Her head tilted up to Morgan of its own volition. Her eyes closed. Her tensed body was alerted to him, and waited for his lips to cover hers.

"Not here, darlin' . . . not yet," he whispered.

More than a little confused and upset, Becca opened her eyes. Flooded with disappointment that Morgan didn't kiss her, she couldn't comprehend what he'd said. Nor did she want to. All she wanted to do was run away, upstairs to room number eight, and lock the door behind her.

What she'd been afraid of had happened. She'd let herself have feelings for Morgan Larkspur, when all along she knew feelings were the quickest way for a whore to die. And she refused to die, not until she found her mother's killer.

"Where are you going?" Morgan caught her arm before she ran off.

Becca tried to wrench free, wanting to be anywhere but here, with a man she wanted, but who didn't want her.

"Rebecca, stop," he ordered this time, his hand clamped hard around her slender arm.

Her spirits couldn't dampen further. Slowly, she turned to face him, wounded pride and all, garnering her courage for this last conversation with her first customer. "I . . . I will not stay with someone who doesn't want me," she quietly said.

"Doesn't want . . . *doesn't want you?*" he all but shouted, his tone incredulous. "What are you talking about?"

She gulped hard. The longer she gazed at his handsome visage, the more difficult it was to answer him. "I'm . . . I'm talking about how you . . . you didn't want me . . . just now. You didn't want to kiss me," she finished, glad she'd been able to get the words out.

"Oh my darlin' girl," he said, his husky voice barely above a whisper. "I've never wanted to kiss anyone more than I want to kiss you right here, right now."

"But . . . but I don't understand. You . . . you just—"

"I can see," he interrupted her. "I can see I've lots to teach you," he pulled her close, holding onto both her upper arms. "Sweetheart, I can't kiss you here, not yet. If I did, I wouldn't want to stop."

"Oh," she managed, the full meaning of his words finally sinking in. Flushed from head to foot, embarrassed that he must know it, she wished she could think of something else to say, something to make him think better of her. Was there ever a more ignorant prostitute on all of Holladay Street? She thought not.

Setting her away from him, Morgan checked his pocket watch. "Is an hour enough time for you to pack?"

"Wh—? Yes, of course." She brightened to the change in subject, away from her and onto her things.

"I'll be back then," he said, sealing his promise with a quick nod and a wink.

She flushed all over again.

In the next moment he was gone.

It took her several more seconds to get moving. Her stare was fixed on the empty space where Morgan had been.

Needing little time to get all her belongings collected in her trunk, Becca made sure to spend precious minutes with Clara, then Mary Beth, then Miss Jenny. She'd only be a short ways from the Palace, moving to the Windsor Hotel, but still, she'd no longer be under Miss Jenny's caring, protective roof. She owed Miss Jenny so much, so very, very much. Becca promised the esteemed madam that she'd visit often, and never be far away, should Miss Jenny need her.

Becca had returned to her room, giving it a last inspection to make sure she'd packed everything, especially her derringer and her knife. The next time she stood outside Saint John's, she'd have them with her. She started at the rap on her door, quickly shutting and then locking her trunk. At the second rap, she stood, knowing Miss Jenny's knock signaled the beginning of a whole new life for her. Fighting her upset at leaving, back straight, head high, Becca answered the door to room number eight on the second floor of the Palace for the very last time.

Gaping open-mouthed at the carriage Morgan had waiting for

her, Becca couldn't believe the luxury of it. On her outings in Miss Jenny's carriage, she'd never seen such a fine, ebony-lacquered conveyance, or such a beautiful pair of well-groomed black horses. Their coats glistened in the early afternoon sun. Becca watched as the driver got down from the carriage, set the horses' reins, and then approached. She fought the urge to step aside so the driver could pass by to fetch his party, sure he hadn't come for *her*.

"Masters, let me help you with this trunk," Morgan said the moment the driver reached them.

"Sure thing, boss," his loyal employee said, then took one end of Becca's trunk, while Morgan took the other.

Becca mutely followed them to the waiting carriage, still watching as if in a dream, as if this were all happening to someone else. Only when Morgan took her hand to help her into the carriage did she realize this *was* all real, this was all happening to *her*.

Glancing quickly over her shoulder, knowing Miss Jenny stood outside the door of the Palace, and Clara, too, Becca smiled a last goodbye to her dear companions of oh, so many years. When she heard Masters giddy-up the team and felt the carriage move, she kept her eyes downcast, unable to bear Miss Jenny and Clara's sad expressions.

Morgan took her hand.

Becca looked at him, at once giving him the same trust and affection she'd given to Miss Jenny and Fanny and her mother. Morgan would be her home now. She'd had three others: the crib in Nevada City where she was born, the crib where she lived with Fanny, and Miss Jenny's parlor house on Holladay Street. Excited at the prospect of a life with Morgan, she was scared, too. She'd no way of knowing what her new life would be like living at the elegant Windsor Hotel. She'd no way of knowing if she'd fit in, or if she'd even want to.

She supposed she'd find out soon enough.

"Lavinia, stop pacing."

"It's just so *cruel*," Lavinia huffed, then plopped down in a chair opposite her mother.

"Morgan Larkspur's marriage proposal is cruel?" Mary Ella Eagleton sputtered, incredulous at her daughter's upset.

"No, of course not, Mother," Lavinia rebuked, her tone close to disrespect.

"Then what, pray tell, is so cruel?"

"He's left again to go . . . to go to Leadville. To the stupid mines! Honestly, Mother, what else can I be but upset? He obviously prefers being at the silly mines when he could be with me. How will it look to all of my friends? How can I tell them that my fiancé isn't coming to their parties because he's working? Ugh! How utterly ridiculous." Lavinia spat this last out.

"Daughter." Mary Ella's voice grew stern. "You have just landed one of the finest catches in Denver for husband, and you're complaining because he's minding your future financial interests in Leadville? Think about it," she said, keeping up her lecture. "You'd best realize how fortunate you are, instead of fueling your nonsensical upset. The Larkspurs are one of the most powerful, prominent, not to mention wealthy, families in the whole state. Daughter, think about it, and keep your head."

"Humph," Lavinia scoffed. Yet she knew her mother was right. In a month's time she'd be Mrs. Morgan Larkspur, the envy of all of her friends, and the toast of Denver society. *And when I am*, she fumed to herself, *Morgan will think twice before he goes running off to Leadville or anywhere else!*

"Where do you want to have the ceremony?" Mary Ella broke into her daughter's agitated reverie. "A month is hardly enough time to plan a proper wedding, but we'll make do. I think the ceremony should be at Saint John's and the reception here."

"I want the reception at the Windsor Hotel, Mother. The Windsor has a beautifully appointed ballroom. It would be so elegant." Lavinia suddenly became excited about the conversation.

"Well . . . I thought of our home first," her mother countered, "but you might have a very good idea in the Windsor. Very good indeed. First thing tomorrow we'll settle everything with hotel management."

CHAPTER TEN

Lavinia and her mother exited the Windsor and stepped into their waiting carriage, both satisfied with the venue for the reception, although a bit unhappy with the size of the ballroom. With plans to invite all of Denver's social elite, they worried over the space. Determined that they could never shorten their list, they decided that the grandeur of the Windsor should more than make up for any lack of dance floor or the need to place an extra seat at the set tables. Their errand complete for now, their next stop was Saint John's and Father Hart.

The entire trip from the Palace to the Windsor took no more than ten minutes, with Becca smiling inside and out the whole way. She couldn't help it. Despite her nerves, despite her fears, despite her sadness about leaving her companions of so many years, she felt just like a little girl waking up Christmas morning—or at least what she thought a little girl must feel at such a time, dreaming of being all grown up, and riding in a fine carriage next to her Prince Charming. Here she was now, all grown up, sitting next to the man of her dreams, actually living the fairy tale! She'd no misconception about a happy ending to the fairy tale. Whores never lived happily ever after. But she'd take today and the few tomorrows she'd have with Morgan and try to be a good mistress to him, knowing the end of the line waited for her. For now, she'd be grateful for every day she had up the line.

"Rebecca, why so sad?" Morgan reached for her hand. "Darlin', if this isn't what you want, then tell me now."

She didn't answer, her full attention on her hand in his, on the feel of his strong fingers gently stroking hers, his touch causing a burn deep inside her, a burn that hurt yet didn't hurt, a pain that made her want more. So much more.

The carriage pulled to a stop behind a line of others parked out front of the Windsor. Masters got down, secured his team, then went to the back of the carriage and took down the trunk loaded there.

Morgan didn't get out of the carriage and kept hold of Becca's hand.

Becca didn't move. She didn't want to break the spell Morgan created whenever he touched her. Funny. At that moment she thought of the good fairies, the magic fairies from her girlhood. How foolish to once believe in them. But right here, right now, with Morgan, she thought again that maybe . . . maybe they did exist after all.

"What will you have Masters do with your trunk, Rebecca? Put it back in the carriage or take it inside the hotel?"

"Do you believe in magic?" she asked Morgan, as if it were the most natural thing in the world to do. Lifting her chin, she looked at him instead of their clasped hands, smiling at him, drinking in his handsome features, and luxuriating in the heady power he held over her.

He smiled back, the corners of his firm mouth dimpling ever so slightly.

She nearly died from the pleasure of it.

"Yes, Rebecca."

His simple reply, like magic, sent a current through her, forcing her into believing again. She felt her mother's spirit around her, and Fanny's, and Miss Jenny's. She felt their protective arms enfolding her, loving her, letting her know that Morgan would protect her and care for her, and that she'd nothing to fear with him.

Again, as if it were the most natural thing to do, Becca took Morgan's hand in both of hers. "I believe in magic, too, Morgan. With you, I believe."

"Watch out, Rebecca Rose." Morgan's throat tightened. "Or I just might fall in love with you." He pulled her hands to his lips, kissing the top of one, then the other, never taking his eyes from hers. This slip of a girl did things to him, surprising him, stirring him, every time he was with her. Like now. Like right now. She got to him in places no one else ever had, not any of the other women he'd bedded, and most especially not Lavinia. A cold dunk in Clear Creek couldn't have dampened his aroused mood any more than thoughts of his bride-to-be did. He'd take Lavinia for his wife and fulfill his obligations to the family, but he'd take Rebecca for mistress, and fulfill his obligations to himself. He had needs beyond his family duties, and right now Rebecca was exactly what he needed.

"Come on, darlin'." He spoke low and private, then guided her down from the carriage. Damn, he wished he had more time with Rebecca today, but he needed to be on the afternoon train to Leadville. Already away too long, he worried over the trouble brewing at the mines, his mines in particular. Before all hell broke loose, he wanted to go down into the mines with the laborers, work alongside them, and see if there was any more room for talk. At this point, he wasn't sure. But, he had to try.

Morgan escorted Rebecca inside the Windsor, following behind Masters who managed her trunk handily. Earlier, Morgan had secured rooms on the second floor of the hotel overlooking Larimer Street. He didn't want the top, fourth floor, preferring the second. He'd spent his first night with Rebecca on the second floor of the Palace. He liked the idea of it, intending to spend many more with her on the second floor at the Windsor.

He'd informed management he'd have a "guest" living in his rooms, and that he'd be away on business much of the time. Morgan hadn't expected any eyebrows to be raised on the part of the hotel staff at his listing of a guest, and he'd been right. There had been not one blink, not one faulty turn of the registration page, not one indication that anything was amiss. Enough conversations with his friends at the Denver Club convinced him so. Many married men in Denver went to parlor houses or had mistresses. Such arrangements were no big deal. The big deal came if any of the wives found out. Well, Morgan wasn't married. Not yet, anyway. When he was, he'd no intention of his wife finding out about his mistress. He'd no intention for his private life and public life to intersect at all.

When she first entered the hotel, Becca couldn't help but stare straight up, at the open atrium overhead. She'd never seen such a sight, four stories high, with balconies overlooking each floor. Light poured into the grand space, as if heaven-sent. The guest rooms must face onto the open atrium court. Such a wonder she'd never imagined.

At last remembering where she was, she brought her gaze back down to earth. The moment she did, she felt every eye on her as she walked alongside Morgan across the main reception floor of the Windsor. Oh, most folks just gave her a passing nod, or looked up from their newspapers a moment, but still, she felt they judged her. Silly of her, and she knew it. When had she ever been concerned about what other so-called respectable folk thought of her? Never. Until now. Now she had Morgan's welfare to consider, as well as her own. That thought hit her stomach like a rock, tumbling over and over, unable to find a place to land.

If she wasn't the only mistress Morgan Larkspur had ever moved into the Windsor, she wanted to be the best. She wanted him to be proud of her. His were the only admiring eyes she wanted, and she would make sure others knew it. She determined to pay attention to every detail of proper life at the Windsor, doing nothing to draw undue attention to herself. It would kill her to see disappointment in her on Morgan's face. It would kill her.

Right now she read anything but disappointment on his face regarding her. Her heart skipped still at his earlier comment that he might just fall in love with her. She knew better, of course. Customers didn't fall in love with whores. Happy to be with Morgan—as his prostitute—as his mistress—she'd do well to remember that. Too late not to be attracted to him, not to have feelings for him, at least she'd keep her head and remember who she was and keep to her purpose: to find her mother's murderer—and shoot him dead.

A bellman took her trunk from Masters and then headed up the grand staircase. Becca watched the bellman, forcing her attention onto the details of the mahogany wainscoting along the staircase, the high polish of the carved railing, the etched design of the ornate glass sconces along the staircase, onto anything but the dark deed that lay ahead—onto anything but the man she must kill. Still, she watched her trunk being carried up the steps, remembering precisely where she'd packed her derringer among her things.

At that moment, Masters tipped his hat and bade her goodbye.

Snapped out of her portentous reverie, Becca returned the driver's smile. She liked that he had a sincere, friendly smile for her; she liked that a lot. As for the bellman, he hadn't smiled. She'd yet to take his measure, but all in good time. She hoped she'd have time, a goodly amount of time here at the Windsor with Morgan. With all her heart, she hoped for time.

"Come on, darlin'." Morgan took her elbow and guided her

up the staircase.

His gentle command as much as his touch sent a shudder down her spine. She loved it when he called her "darlin'." It made her feel like *his* prostitute, *his* mistress; it made her feel like she was *his*. Belonging to Morgan Larkspur, for however long it would be, meant more than she could or ever would express to him. She wouldn't tell him. *Feelings get a whore killed.*

Scared to death of her feelings for Morgan, she carefully took each stair, knowing that each step pulled the hangman's emotional noose tighter around her neck, and knowing, too, that no power on earth could make her turn back. Oblivious to anything but Morgan now, and the fact that he held her life in his hands—because she let him—she kept up her forward progress.

"Wh—" Becca gasped, suddenly finding herself scooped up in Morgan's arms. In the next moment, he'd carried her over the threshold of room number eight on the second floor of the Windsor!

"Why . . . good luck. I mean congratulations, Mr. Larkspur." The bellman stumbled over his words. "I didn't know you were just married, sir . . . and ma'am . . . I mean Mrs. Larkspur," he smiled at Becca now.

"That's all right, son." Morgan chuckled, giving Becca a kiss on the cheek before setting her on her feet.

She held onto Morgan for support, stunned that he didn't correct the bellman. Before she could stop herself, she poked her elbow into Morgan's ribs, signaling him to right the situation. Shocked at her action when she realized what she'd just done, Becca looked for the nearest chair then sat down hard. She *was* acting like a wife. She felt the noose tighten around her neck and found it difficult to swallow.

Morgan chuckled again.

She heard him well enough, but dared not meet his slate scrutiny.

"That will be all, son," Morgan said, dismissing the bellman, who quickly left.

Becca had no idea what to say or do, not just to Morgan, but she didn't know how to represent herself to the hotel staff for the remainder of her stay. It hadn't occurred to her until now that she'd need to worry about such things.

Morgan didn't feel like joking anymore. Rebecca's gentle poke at him caught him off guard. It was personal. It felt good. If he wasn't careful, he really could fall in love with her. Most women in Denver would jump at the chance to be called his wife, but not Rebecca. She intrigued the hell out of him. Life with her at the Windsor wasn't going to be dull. As for love, he didn't want love. Companionship and sex, yes, but not love. He didn't think about love. He'd teased her about love outside in the carriage. That's all it was: a tease. He didn't mean it, but something caught at his gut right now, telling him he just might have meant it in spite of himself.

Morgan shrugged off his sober mood. He had no time now to dwell on anything but getting his new mistress settled in, already disappointed he'd have to leave so soon. No time for lovemaking tonight. That caught at his gut, too. He wanted their first time together to be special for Rebecca. He wanted everything to be right. The trouble in Leadville wouldn't wait for him to bed his mistress. Damn. His gut felt like a sore festering, refusing to heal.

"What do you think?" he blurted out a little more harshly than he'd intended.

Becca stood, glad that she could do so without faltering. "Why, it's beautiful." She pivoted, scanning the room with her gaze, seeing nothing really, but Morgan's obvious agitation.

"The bedroom is in there," he blurted out again, wishing he

hadn't said anything about the bed and the bedroom. He didn't want to think about what he wouldn't be doing with her tonight.

Out of habit, he removed his pocket watch and checked the time. Half past three. He had to go. He'd thought they'd have more time before he did. Damn!

"The dining room is on this floor. You can't miss it. There are shops downstairs, and down the street where you can find anything you might need. I've instructed the front desk that you'll be living here, so no questions there, all right?"

"Ye-yes, all right," she muttered, trying to measure what was going on, why he seemed so upset. Then she thought of the mines and the trouble there. She couldn't help but be worried for him. Mining towns and miners could be rough, real rough. No telling what might happen if they got mad. What . . . what if they . . . if they . . . "Morgan!" she cried, scared for him. "Don't go. Don't go to Leadville!"

His chest caught at her tender plea. He knew she was afraid for him. He knew she cared. "Rebecca, darlin', it's all right," he soothed, reaching her in a few steps. When he did, he enfolded her slender, trembling shape in his arms and pulled her close.

Becca laid her cheek against the muscled wall of his chest, feeling each strong beat of his heart, wanting to hold him there, in room number eight of the Windsor Hotel. Forever.

"Darlin' girl," he whispered against her hair. "I'll be fine. Always have been, always will be."

She jerked away and looked up at him. "You promise? You promise that you'll be fine, Morgan Larkspur?" she choked out, fighting tears.

"Yes," he said, his voice hoarse, pulling her to him again.

Becca thought she'd be prepared for such a moment, her first kiss with Morgan, but nothing on earth could have prepared her for the force of his lips on hers. Nothing.

His kiss was hard, hard and driving, deeper and deeper, the

gentle pressure of his warm mouth forcing her to open to him, forcing her to taste him, to feel him, to hunger for him. Deeper and deeper, driving her to madness in places she'd never imagined. She felt swallowed up, deliciously swallowed up. His masterful touch, everywhere she could find it and feel it, forced her to respond to him. Her aroused body was willing to give in to whatever he'd demand of her. She waited for him to teach her, to take her, to love her. Such sweet, sweet madness . . . wanting him . . . waiting for him to demand more . . . and more—

He abruptly let her go.

Dazed, her lips still burning, Becca felt cheated, cheated out of time with Morgan. She wanted more time. It wasn't enough. Not near enough. Struck again by his dark handsomeness, Becca looked up at him, at his warm, gentle, demanding mouth, wanting him to cover hers again. Just once more . . . once more . . . *please.*

Setting her at arm's length, breathing hard, Morgan needed to leave. He didn't want to. God, he'd never been kissed like Becca kissed him. Her innocent body told him all he needed to know—that she'd give everything he wanted of her and hold nothing back. Unschooled in lovemaking, she wanted him to teach her, to take her. That they'd have to wait made him crazy.

Was there a softer, more beautiful, more tender, more caring, more loving woman in all of Denver? He thought not. All clover and honey, she was. She was something else: *his.* "Darlin', I hate leaving you now, but I've got no choice," he managed to choke out, his throat tight again. "I want you to under—"

"Shhh." She put her fingers to his lips. "I do understand, Morgan. I do."

He kissed her fingers, then took her hand in his. "There's money in the desk drawer for you. Buy whatever you want or need. I'll be back this Friday, and we'll celebrate your birthday.

Tell me what you want for your birthday. I'll give you anything," he promised in a husky whisper.

"Anything?" she questioned softly.

"Anything," he agreed.

"Will you come back safe?"

"That's all you want?" Morgan couldn't believe it. Other women, ordinary women he knew—like Lavinia—would want jewels or furs or money to buy out the city; but then he remembered. Rebecca wasn't any ordinary woman.

"All? That's *everything*, for you to come back safe. It's the only present I want," she reiterated, embarrassed now, bowing her head.

Morgan's insides caved. He felt gut-shot, hit hard. He tipped her chin up to him, reminded again of her quiet, classic beauty, inside and out; reminded again that he'd scored big in finding Rebecca Rose at the Palace. What if some other man had found her first? The idea of it grated on him like he'd taken another bullet. What if some other man had paid fifty dollars that first night, claiming her as his? Sure as hell, no other man could claim her now. He'd like to see the son of a bitch try.

Morgan set Rebecca away from him. Each moment he stayed made it that much harder to leave. He studied her, wanting to remember every detail of her beautiful peach complexion, the way shadows played in her soft doe eyes, the dark curl of her silky lashes, the sensual parting of her full rosy lips that waited for his kiss. Delicate wisps of her chestnut hair had come out from their pins, teasing him, begging him to take down the rest of her hair and run his hands through its rich, lush waves . . . and draw her close.

"Darlin', will you be all right?"

"I'll be fine; always have been, always will be." She smiled up at him, using his exact words.

"You promise?" He smiled now, too.

Suddenly unsteady, Becca's knees wanted to give way. Looking up into Morgan's trusting eyes, thrilling under his slate scrutiny, her heart full, with every fiber in her body aching for him, she did her best to keep her footing. Uncertain of so many things in her life till now, Becca was never more certain of anything. She was convinced now that she was born into this cold, cruel world for the sole purpose of hearing Morgan Larkspur utter those two words to her, in room number eight at the Windsor Hotel. For the first time, she felt like a woman, a full-grown woman—a woman in love.

Her insides seized.

This was the best moment of her life, and the worst.

She'd never imagined being with a man like Morgan, or that a man like Morgan would want to be with her. And she'd definitely never imagined falling prey to foolish emotion and falling in love. *Emotions only get a whore killed.*

Despite the danger, Becca stood helpless before Morgan. For as long as he wanted her, she'd stay. She'd no choice now.

"I'll be back Friday, darlin'. Sooner if I can," he whispered, grazing her cheek with his kiss. Without another word, he took the room key from his pocket and held it out for her.

Mutely, she took the key, afraid to say anything for fear she'd cry. She didn't want to cry. She *never* cried, for pity's sake. But when Morgan had gone, she stared for long minutes at the cruel, unforgiving mahogany door, wishing with all her heart he'd come back, unmindful of the tears she wiped away.

"Griff, you'd better be careful whattcha sayin'," the miner warned. "If'n somebody hears you that shouldn't, you'll git fired, or worse."

"Ah hell, Jim, whadda I care? My family's hungry every night. I'm never home, if you can call our two-bit shack a home. The missus has to take care of the kids, 'sides working her fingers raw fer others doin' their cleanin' and laundry where she can. She's been sick, too, goin' on a week now. I cain't be around to help her with nuthin'. I'm workin' in these mines near on twelve hours a day, and fer what? Fer three lousy dollars a day, that's what! It ain't right, Jim, and you know it. When the strike starts next week, I'm gonna be at the front of it with my gun. I'll kill all the son of a bitch mine owners if I have to!"

"Dammit, Griff, shut up," Jim whispered hard, and looked around the dark shaft, making sure no one was near. "We can't let no one know when the strike is startin'. We can't set off no hornet's nest afore next week." The miner set his shovel down against a section of timbering. A torch blazed nearby, allowing just enough light for the men to work. "Listen Griff, I'm just as upset as you are, but we gotta keep our heads and not go off half-cocked. Hell, the owners is bringing in more and more of them Celestials and givin' 'em our jobs as it is. They could just up and fire the lot of us and give the goddamn Chinamen all our jobs."

"Yeah, goddamn Celestials." Griff spat on the ground. "Maybe we'll catch a few of 'em in our sites next week when we're goin' after the owners."

Jim took up his shovel. He heard other miners approaching. "Griff," he rasped under his breath. "Ever occur to you that we just might be the ones to git it next week?"

"Yeah," the miner said, taking his shovel in hand and slamming it hard against the bedrock. The echo vibrated up and down the drift, as if foretelling the danger to come.

Morgan stood just outside the train car door, making sure to keep away from the pinning. Unable to sit still inside, he needed some air and a cigarette. No matter that thick, black smoke from the locomotive's engine drifted over him; he hardly noticed. He took out his cigarette makings, and quickly rolled and lit the tobacco. One draw didn't satisfy. Neither did the next. Still, he smoked the tobacco to its quick. Not yet ready to go back inside his train car, he stared out into the vast night, then at the starry sky overhead.

Damn. It was hard for him to get his mind around what happened with Rebecca Rose today, and what he'd found out about himself. For the first time in his life he worried about his own welfare. Because Rebecca did, and because he wanted to come back to her. He'd never thought about danger before. He'd seen plenty of it, and so what? Never once had he thought about what he had to lose if he took a bullet or met with an untimely accident. Until now. Until Rebecca.

He'd promised her he'd come back safe, and he'd do his best to keep that promise.

The next weeks at the mines were going to be rough, no question; rough for the miners and for the mine owners. He'd already talked with some of the owners, most of whom seemed determined to keep the rules and regulations at the mines the same as always. Easy for the owners, making so much money from all the silver bullion extracted from their holdings, but not so easy for the miners, who'd already felt the sting of Tabor's Light Cavalry. The local militia had rounded up miners they saw as troublemakers, secretly placing their own men in the mines to find out what they could. No mine was safe, and no miner was safe from accusation. The situation couldn't go on much longer.

Morgan had a plan. He'd spend time this week down in his own mines with his miners and find out what he could, not to report anyone, but to gauge the pulse of the miners and find out more about what they wanted. It might not be the best idea to go down into the mines, him being an owner, but it was the only idea he could come up with at the moment. Maybe there was still time for talk. Maybe the mine owners would listen to the miners' union and make an agreement to avoid needless bloodshed. The only way to find out more about what the union wanted was to go down into the mines and talk to the workers himself.

He thought of Rebecca again, all the while trying not to. It did little good. She meant too much to him now. He hadn't intended for things to be this way, but they were. More than anything he'd ever wanted in his life, he wanted to come home to her—not to the family mansion on Governor's Row, not to his parents and his brother, and not to his fiancée Lavinia—but home to Rebecca Rose and their shared apartment at the Windsor.

Morgan went back inside the train car. He might not rest easy, but he had to rest all the same. The sooner he did, and the sooner he dealt with things in Leadville, the quicker he could go home to Rebecca.

CHAPTER ELEVEN

Not a bit hungry, unable to imagine sleeping, too anxious to concentrate on anything but the fact that darkness approached, Becca sat in the desk chair by the window playing with the shade pull. A decision as simple as whether or not to close the shade against the light peeking in off Larimer Street, and she couldn't make it. So much had happened to her today in the span of a few short hours. She'd left the Palace where she had the security of a job with Miss Jenny to move into the Windsor with Morgan Larkspur, where she had anything but security. Her situation was temporary. No security in that. When Morgan didn't want her anymore, he'd move her right out of these elegantly appointed rooms, and she'd be on the street, on her way to the end of the line.

Worse than that, worse than anything today, she'd fallen in love. Love meant death to a whore, and she knew it. Morgan liked her well enough, she could tell, but love? He'd never love her. Not ashamed of being a whore, she certainly wasn't a fool. Men like Morgan didn't fall in love and marry women like her. But it *was* the right thing for her to become his mistress. It was the best offer she'd ever have, and he was the best man she'd ever have. For as long as she could be with him, she would be, all the while saving up treasured memories for the time when he'd be gone. Few whores ever had so much.

A knock on the door startled her.

She didn't move. How should she answer?

Another knock.

She got up from her chair, uncertain of her step in the darkness.

"The night maid," a woman's voice called through the door.

Becca hurried to open it.

"Good evening," the young woman said, then flipped the light switch next to the door, seemingly accustomed to needing to do so. The trim, businesslike maid was dressed in a black frock with a starched white apron and white mob cap covering her pinned-up hair. She proceeded to go to each lamp in the front room, switch it on, then headed for the bedroom and switched on the lamps there.

Becca watched the maid, dumbfounded that the hotel had electric lights, and fascinated by the young woman's efficiency in turning on the lights, turning down the bed, and adjusting the toweling in the bath.

"Is there anything else you require this evening, ma'am?" the maid asked Becca, having finished her duties, ready to leave.

"No," Becca quietly replied. "Thank you."

The maid smiled, out of habit it seemed rather than any heartfelt emotion. "Good night, then." She nodded and left.

Alone now, all at once exhausted, Becca searched the rooms for her trunk, finding it in the bedroom. Too tired to properly unpack or to appreciate the room's lovely décor, she reached in her things and pulled out a simple muslin nightdress. She didn't need silk tonight. Undressed in a matter of minutes, she completed her evening toilette in the bath, then went back into the front room to check the lock on the door, and turn off all the lights. Such a wonder, electric lights . . . a true wonder.

The moment she slipped in between the silk-thread sheets, she was asleep.

"I don't want any business discussed at my breakfast table,"

Augusta Larkspur chastised her younger son. The fact that Monty had even brought up a business matter was lost on her. He'd never done it before.

Monty turned to his father, ignoring his mother.

Eugene Larkspur pulled the *Rocky Mountain News* closer, then took another sip of coffee, ignoring his son.

"Father, there's talk of trouble in Leadville at our mines. Spur's up there in the thick of it. I'm thinking I should go, too."

"Enough!" Augusta stood. "Monty, hurry up and finish eating. My Ladies Aid Society meeting is at ten sharp. You're to drive me. I don't want to be late. I'm the president. How would it look? Hurry, Monty, we've little time." She replaced her linen napkin beside her plate and then exited the dining room.

Even if Monty had had any appetite when he'd sat down, his mother's prodding would have ruined it. Used to her snapping out orders, it grated especially hard on him this morning. He was worried about Spur. He should go. He should help, he and his father both.

"I . . . I think, Father . . ." He faltered. "I think you and I ought—"

"Son," Eugene Larkspur interrupted, setting aside his newspaper. "Like your mother just said, enough. Yes, there's talk of a strike. I know that. I also know that your brother can take good care of himself in Leadville. Tabor's local militia is on top of the trouble, too. No need for us to help. Morgan will be fine."

"I'm worried anyway, Father, and I think we should go. We can be on the afternoon train," Monty encouraged.

"No, son."

"Then I'll go by myself."

"No, son. I'd never hear the end of it from your mother if I let you go. You know how she worries over you," Eugene explained.

"Then why the hell isn't she worried over Spur? He's her

son, too," Monty demanded.

Eugene rubbed his eyes, as if weary of the conversation.

"Why, Father?" Monty wouldn't quit. He knew the answer, but he wouldn't quit the conversation.

"Son . . ." Eugene shook his head. "We've gone over all of this before. You know why." He repeated Monty's thoughts.

"Remind me anyway, Father," Monty said, his tone sharp.

"Spur's the oldest. That's all."

"No, Father, that's not all." Monty raised his voice. He loved his brother, but he'd been jealous of Spur his whole life. He'd been jealous of the way his parents relied on Spur to share in running the family business concerns and not him. He'd been jealous of how strong Spur was, handling anything that came his way, while he wasn't. He'd been jealous of how his mother never harped on Spur to "do this" and "do that." Monty wasn't weak or stupid. Spur never treated him like he was, but his parents always did.

"No call to get upset here, son," Eugene cautioned. "You'd best stay here. Morgan will take care of things. Always has, always will. After you drop your mother off at her meeting, why don't you join me at my downtown office?" Eugene changed the subject.

"Is there a meeting with the railroad today, Father? I'd like to sit in on it." Monty brightened. Maybe now his father would start to give him a little more responsibility, and he could work in the family businesses, just like Spur. Besides, the railroads, more than banking or mining, interested him the most; always had.

"There's my boy." Eugene stood and slapped Monty on the shoulder. "Sure, you come to the office and we'll see."

The clock in the foyer chimed nine-thirty.

"Best get going now, Monty. No need to ruffle your mother's feathers any more than they already are." He grinned.

"No, sir," Monty agreed, getting up from the table. He looked forward to the afternoon ahead with his father, all thoughts of the danger his brother might be in forgotten.

Becca took her derringer out from its hiding place in her trunk, making sure of her bullets, too. From today on she'd wear her gun inside her gartered stocking, at her thigh. No matter that services at Saint John's were five days away. She'd keep her gun with her all the same. Her mother would want her to. Her mother had told her as much in church and more, much more. She knew her mother's killer was one of the congregants.

Becca stood up and tucked the cold steel in her garter. Her jaw clenched. She imagined her mother's spirit forced away from her grave in potter's field in Nevada City and down out of the mountains into Denver, to Saint John's. Becca's jaw clenched tighter. Until she found her mother's killer and brought him to justice, her mother would never be able to rest in peace. Neither would she.

Becca would make sure her mother did rest in peace, or she'd die trying.

She sat down on the side of her freshly made bed. Of course, the maid would likely be there soon to make up the room, but old habits are hard to break. Even at the Palace she'd made her own bed. Such a small problem to consider, whether or not to make her own bed at the fancy Windsor Hotel, but it relieved her to turn her focus onto something trivial. No sooner did she have the thought, than there was a rap at the door.

"Morning maid," a female voice, different from the one last night, called through the door.

Becca got up to answer the door, her thoughts only now beginning to turn to herself and her new life with Morgan Larkspur in room number eight on the second floor of the Windsor.

★ ★ ★ ★ ★

"Don't hurt me, honey, please." The whore was scared to death of her john. Used to a lot in her life at the end of the line on Holladay Street, she'd never let anyone in her door so . . . evil. She wasn't a Bible-learned person, but she knew the devil had come knocking—and she'd let him in. If he killed her, she didn't have anyone to blame but herself. Never more sure of anything in her pathetic life, she knew that his hand with two missing fingers and the gold lion-head ring was the hand of the devil.

"Don't move," he hissed. "You lie there and don't make a move. If you do, missy . . . see this?" He pulled out a knife. "This little blade could cut you up real good. I'd start with your beautiful throat," he threatened, following his words with the tip of his knife over her naked flesh. "Then I'd move lower and cut your budding breasts. Then lower, and cut out your womb . . . and feed it to the dogs." He laughed, jabbing her privates just enough to make his meaning clear.

"Sweet Jesus, save me." The whore shut her eyes and prayed hard.

The devil laughed again. "You want to be saved, missy, you'd best talk to me." He grew hard all over again, knowing how afraid she was. He smelled her fear and fed off it. Tossing his knife aside, he straddled her once more, pinning her arms overhead on her pillow. His brain buzzed with the thrill of the young whore under him, afraid, panicked. She wasn't pretty, but he liked her that way. He knew she'd do anything to stay alive. If she didn't, he'd kill her. He'd killed once and would do it again.

Years ago one whore had died. He still grew hard thinking about that one. A whole year they'd had together, then she up and spoiled it all. He remembered her trembling, sensual, pliant, voluptuous body under him, afraid, yet not begging. Goddammit! Ever since then, he needed whores to beg and beg

154

hard for his mercy. Why hadn't the stupid whore begged? Maybe he wouldn't have slit her throat if she'd begged. She'd spoiled it for so many other whores, because she hadn't begged.

The whore under him now had no one but Ruby Rose from Nevada City to blame for her fear. Poor, stupid Ruby Rose. Her brat was alive somewhere. To this day he regretted not finding the bastard child and killing her. He'd made the mistake of letting the girl live. Goddammit. Stupid prostitutes. Stupid, ugly, filthy whores!

His anger fired, the moment he entered the whore under him, he came. He jutted into her hard, each thrust meant to hurt; each thrust reminding him he risked a lot, doing a whore in Denver. It was too close to home and he knew it, but it was harder to get away as he had before. Besides, his needs didn't wait around for him to travel out of the city. What control he'd had over his sexual appetites in the past, he was losing. He could feel it slipping away, like overturned sands. He had to keep in control. If he didn't, it would be the end . . . for everyone.

Suppertime, and she had to eat. Becca remembered eating a little breakfast yesterday, or did she? The dining room at the Windsor was across the open court from her room. She needn't go far; only a few steps, but it seemed a lifetime away from anything familiar. Here she was, Rebecca Rose of the Palace, about to enter the elegant dining room of the Windsor, filled with the cream of Denver society, all with their prying eyes, sitting in judgment of her and finding her guilty.

She'd spent the entire day in her rooms, her nerves still frayed from the events of the past two days. Drained, even a little confused, she needed to put something in her stomach. Maybe then she could better sort everything out in her mind. She needed to figure out what she had to do and when, what she had to keep secret from Morgan and what she could tell him, what she would do after . . . after her time at the Windsor, if she wasn't in prison or dead after she killed her mother's murderer. Laughter suddenly bubbled up from deep down in her soul. She laughed so hard, her stomach hurt from the irony of it all. Flopping back on the bed, she lay there for long moments, wiping away tears.

Could anything be more hilarious? She didn't have to worry about the end of the line on Holladay Street or anywhere else. She'd never make it to the end of the line. Once she put a bullet in her mother's killer, she'd be arrested or dead. Not once had she ever thought about any clever getaway plan; not once had she given any thought to what she'd do afterwards.

Pulling herself from the bed, Becca checked her appearance in the mirror. She'd no business going in to the dining room a mess. How would that look? If all eyes were turned on her, she wanted to look good, for Morgan's sake if nothing else. Smoothing out the folds of her russet taffeta, she ran cold fingers over the lace at her neck, then made sure her pins were in place to keep her hair styled just so. She practiced smiling. It took her five minutes to get her appearance just so.

Becca opened the drawer of the writing desk in the front room. Morgan had put money in there for her, and she'd need a little to pay for dinner. She'd no idea what anything cost in the luxury hotel and had best be prepared. Putting ten dollars—more than she'd clear in a week's work at the Palace—in her matching reticule, she pulled the drawstrings closed save for her room key. As soon as she exited her room, she put the key in her drawstring bag along with the ten-dollar bill.

People milled around the open court, some heading toward the dining room and some just staring over the balcony, up, down, and all around, apparently appreciating the hotel's majestic architecture. Becca couldn't help but do the same, stopping at the balcony just outside her door, hanging on, looking up, down, and all around with the rest of the guests. Glad to see so many of them, she breathed a little easier, realizing few would notice her in such a crowd. More sure of her step now, she turned away from the balcony and walked toward the dining room. Once there, quickly seated at a table set for two by a window, Becca took the proffered menu from the waiter.

"Thank you." She smiled her practiced smile, desperately wanting to fit in now and not be noticed.

"I'll be back shortly, madam." The waiter nodded, then left

Madam? Becca felt like laughing at the waiter's misconception that she was married. Of course she knew that few women traveled or appeared in public alone unless they were married . . . or a prostitute. That the waiter assumed she wasn't a prostitute made her smile—not her practiced smile, but a genuine smile. When next he returned, she'd give him just that.

It was easy to choose something off the black-tasseled, gilded menu. She'd had a lot of training at the Palace and knew about Denver's finest cuisine. The Dover sole with asparagus would suit her fine. Putting her menu down, she took a sip of water from the crystal goblet in front of her, then straightened against her chair-back and looked around the spacious dining room. Absolutely no one looked at her! At once relieved, she relaxed against her chair and took another sip of water, this one far more refreshing than the last.

The dining room buzzed with conversation, the quiet roar of men and women engaged in discussion audible, yet not too loud. Becca heard music, too, coming from the chamber orchestra situated near the entrance. She loved the violins and cello, appreciating the piece by Mozart. It ever soothed. So did the room's subdued lighting. The multiple chandeliers provided soft illumination, just enough to enjoy a pleasant meal while not glaring overhead. Suddenly hungry, Becca looked around for her waiter. Catching his eye, she motioned the young man over.

Having finished her delicious meal, every bite of it, Becca set her linen napkin next to her empty plate and checked her reticule in her lap, ready to pay. She'd been sure about the meal and how to order, but she wasn't at all sure what to expect at the end of it. Should she leave a tip? How much? Hell's bells, she didn't remember checking the pricing on the menu. Her heart sank when she realized she wasn't as polished as she'd thought. She watched the waiter approach, dreading every moment.

He smiled. "Have you finished, madam?"

"Yes, thank you. I'll . . . I'll just have . . . the bill," she managed, utterly embarrassed at her falter.

"Madam, there is no bill for you," he said nonchalantly.

"I . . . I don't . . . no bill?"

"You are a guest in room number eight on this floor, are you not?" he quizzed, still matter-of-fact.

"Why . . . yes I am," she replied, more confused now than ever.

"Then your bills for this meal and all of the others you might partake of at the Windsor are already paid. No tips are necessary, either, madam," he added, his tone still businesslike, devoid of emotion . . . or censure.

He knows. The waiter knows I'm a prostitute. He calls me madam, yet he knows. Touched by his respectful tact with her, she smiled at the waiter again, not her practiced smile, but her genuine, heartfelt smile.

Grateful for a good night's sleep, Becca wasn't hungry, but a steaming cup of morning coffee motivated her to quickly finish her toilette, dress, and head for the hotel dining room. Last night had been pleasant enough, with the staff and other guests taking little, if any, notice of her. This morning should be equally pleasant. In two days she'd see Morgan, and in four, she'd be outside Saint John's, waiting to find the man who killed her mother.

Only two things mattered in her life now: seeing Morgan and getting justice for her mother. She needed to live each day as if it were her last. Funny. Having such melancholy thoughts didn't upset her so much this morning. Melancholia was a waste of time, time she didn't have.

Hurrying now, she locked her door behind her and started for the dining room. Few guests milled about this morning, but no matter. Becca had other things on her mind, things more important than any discomfort she might feel at the Windsor.

"Good morning, madam," the waiter greeted after she'd been seated at the same table where she'd eaten the night before.

"Good morning." She nodded.

The waiter, different from the one last night, handed her a menu. "I'll be back for your order shortly."

"No need. I'd just like some coffee and perhaps a bit of toast."

"Very good, madam," he said, then took the proffered menu.

Sunlight streaked through the window off Eighteenth Street. Becca warmed to it, her mood somewhat brightened. Carriages rolled by one after the other, each one filled with folks, doubtless out on business or shopping. Horse-drawn streetcars passed by, too, each one brimful with riders. The hustle and bustle of Denver's busy streets cheered Becca, taking her thoughts to Joslin's Dry Goods, the Buckskin Fur and Glove Company, Stephen's Opera House and . . . well . . . to lots of the shops and theater amusements lining the nearby streets.

"Here you are, madam," the waiter returned, coffee and toast in hand.

Becca smiled a genuine smile at the waiter. "Thank you," she said, taking a sip of the delicious brew the moment her cup was set in front of her. Did anything taste better than the first cup of Chase and Sanborn? She thought not.

"By damn, Hollister, things are going to blow any time at the mines. I didn't think things were that bad, but look here, what it says in the *Rocky Mountain News.*"

Becca's cup almost slipped from her hand. As carefully as she could, she set the china cup in its saucer. She put her hand to her toast, needing to think about it rather than what she'd just heard coming from a nearby table. The toast was cold. She jerked her hand away as if it were dead instead of just cold. Panicked, and as much as she didn't want to, she strained to hear more of the conversation between the two men seated nearby.

"The hell you say." The other man spoke now. "Let me see that." He took the morning newspaper from his tablemate's hands and quickly scanned the pages. "It says here that as many as ten thousand miners could strike, and that it could be a real bloodbath coming. I'll be damned, Hollister." The man put down the paper. "I never thought things would come to this. We've all got friends up there in Leadville, not to mention investments tied up in silver and the mines."

"Yeah, I've got money there, and friends," Hollister growled. "I don't know about you, but I think the miners are loco. They've got it damn good, having a decent job. The owners can't give in to their demands. Hell, we'll all be out of money then."

"There's a local militia now, according to the newspaper. Maybe they can help head off any trouble, Hollister."

"Maybe, but I don't think so. I think the miners are the ones who are going to have to pay a high price. With their lives."

"Even so, a lot of our own could get killed, too."

The other man said nothing, nodding his head in agreement.

Becca swiveled back around in her seat.

Killed.

Morgan could get killed.

Panicked, she rose from her chair, unaware that her napkin had fallen to the floor. She had to get out of there. She'd no idea where to go, but she had to get out or she'd suffocate from the close air in the dining room. Hurrying past the bevy of waiters at the door, taking little notice of them or anything else, she rushed down the grand staircase, past reception, and didn't stop until she stood in front of the hotel. Of their own volition, her feet started taking her toward the familiar—toward Holladay Street. She walked on and on and didn't stop until she'd reached the end of the line, in front of all the meager apartments and cribs on the infamous street.

Half-dressed whores stood in front of their doorways or draped out of an occasional window, doubtless waiting for customers. Despite the early hour, the business of prostitution in this run-down part of the row didn't stop at sunrise. Becca didn't see any customers, just whores, and instantly felt better, as if she were home. These women were her kind, and she wanted to be with them now—not whoring, just with them. Every single woman working at the end of the line knew she only had a measure of time left before she'd likely die of violence or disease or loneliness. Becca felt a common ground with these women, some staring at her now, some paying her no mind at all.

Scared to death for Morgan, she wasn't afraid for herself. She knew her end would come soon, but not Morgan's. *Please God, don't let Morgan die.* Falling to her knees on the street, she clasped her hands in prayer. "Please God, please. Protect Morgan. Bring him back to me. Please," she whispered hard into the unforgiving silence all around.

A passing wagon forced her to stand. Other wagons and men on horseback started down the street. Wiping her tears with the sleeve of her dress, her heart so pained she felt faint, she started walking, heading up the line now. She didn't feel like going back to the Windsor, where all she'd have was time—time to sit and go crazy with worry over Morgan. There had to be a place where she could go and keep busy and do some good, if not for Morgan, then for someone.

At that moment she thought of the poorhouse on Blake Street, and was happy to have a direction. She'd go and try to be of some help. The idea of helping the needy was just what *she* needed.

CHAPTER TWELVE

Becca had been right to worry over Morgan.

"Griff, put down the gun. I know you're fired up, but killing me isn't going to help anything." Morgan spoke cautiously.

"Yeah, it will help," the miner spat out. "It'll help me sleep better at night knowin' you and yer kind is dead afore us."

All along Morgan had known it might not sit well with his laborers, going down in the mines alongside them with so much trouble brewing. He'd known, too, they might take him for a spy. Evidently Griff did.

"Listen, Griff—"

"Don't move," the angry miner threatened.

"All right, all right." Morgan stepped back against the closest timber. No one else worked nearby, at least no one he could see. Torchlight blazed down the drift, giving Morgan just enough light to see the fire in the miner's bloodshot eyes. He'd worked for Morgan a lot of years, but he'd snapped now. Morgan didn't have to guess why. Desperate men do desperate things.

Staring down the barrel of the miner's six-shooter, knowing any minute the gun could put a hole in him, Morgan didn't move an inch. Funny, he'd halfway expected some of the men to jump him, beat him up, and give him a good piece of their minds. But he didn't expect this. He hadn't expected to be looking down the barrel of a gun, especially not from a man he'd known for so many years. He'd wait for Griff to make the first move. It could mean a bullet in his gut, but he'd wait all the same.

Other miners joined them now. Maybe they'd heard the ruckus.

Morgan kept his eyes on Griff.

"Griff, what the hell are you doin'?" his friend Jim yelled, stepping out from the group.

"All ya'll stay put," Griff ordered.

Jim stopped a good ten feet from his friend and his boss. "Put the gun down, Griff. Don't get nuthin' started now."

"Hell, I'll help him kill Larkspur." Another miner stepped away from the group, this one dirtier and meaner-looking than Griff.

Griff nervously looked toward the miner, then back at Morgan, his gun hand shaking.

Morgan didn't recognize the other miner. He had to be a new hire. He shouldn't even be in this fight. Things could get out of control real easy with a man like him around begging for trouble, thinking with his fists and little else.

"Go ahead and shoot," the miner egged Griff on.

"No!" Jim countered.

The miner turned on Jim now, shoving him hard against bedrock. The shaft shifted a little overhead, with bits of dirt falling on both men. Despite the well-built shaft, it wouldn't take much for all hell to break loose and kill them all. They fell quiet, each man reminded of where he was and what could happen. The stillness could have been cut with a knife.

"You stupid son of a bitch," Jim snapped. "Yer gonna git us all killed, and fer what? So's you can meet yer maker braggin' that you done killed a mine boss? That'll git you a ticket through the Pearly Gates fer shore." He pulled away from the wall and walked up to the miner.

The miner looked scared and let Jim pass.

"Griff, the same goes fer you. If you pull that trigger, no tellin' if the shaft will hold. This spot ain't exactly stable, and you know it."

Griff's gun hand shook even harder.

Jim came closer.

Morgan waited. He wasn't armed. Even if he had been, he couldn't shoot one of his men, especially since he knew they had a good gripe. The way Griff's hand trembled now, he knew the miner didn't want to kill anyone. Upset as hell, that's all. Upset as hell.

"Stay away, Jim, or I swear I'll shoot you, too!"

"Go ahead then. Shoot me and Spur and all the rest of us. I'm sure that'll help yer wife and younguns just fine. Set 'em up real good fer the rest of their lives."

Morgan watched Griff, relieved the moment he saw the nervous miner's gun hand slip a little, glad to have someone like Jim in his employ. Jim was a union man, and the union was lucky to have him. Hell, he and all the other mine owners should count themselves lucky that there were union leaders as level-headed as Jim. Keeping his eyes on Griff, Morgan pulled away from the timbering, moving toward him, his hand out in friendship.

"Shake hands with me, Griff," he offered. "I promise you I'll do my best for you and the other miners and their families. I promise. I'll be alongside you guys if you strike. If I have to, I'll fight alongside you. Shake on it, friend?" Morgan kept his hand outstretched.

Griff let his six-shooter fall to the ground, its clang echoing up and down the drift.

Morgan saw that the man was close to tears, fighting them, wanting to save face in front of all the other men. He stepped closer and took Griff's hand, pumping it hard. "You're a good man, Griff." He spoke loud enough so all the miners could hear. "I'm proud to have a man like you working for me. Yes sir, proud."

Griff relaxed, his emotions checked, and he stood taller now. "Thank . . . thank you, Mr. Lar—"

"Okay, now you're getting me mad," Morgan joked, "calling me anything but Spur."

Griff stepped away, his hands in his pockets now. "Thank you, Spur," he corrected, nodding in agreement.

"We're all losing good working time." Morgan looked around at the men. "Let's get to it," he ordered, taking up his shovel.

The men disbursed, all but Jim.

"Spur, about Griff and all—"

"It's not a problem, Jim." Morgan looked at Griff now, too. "Let's forget any of this happened." He bent down and picked up the gun at their feet. "Here you go." He handed the six-shooter back to Griff. "Do me a favor and don't point it at me again, at least until I get this empty cart filled and sent up the tracks out of here, all right?"

All three men had a laugh and set to work.

The trouble in the Larkspur's Number-Six mine was over—for today, anyway.

"Hello again, Miss Becca," Pastor Jonah greeted the moment she set foot inside the poorhouse Thursday morning.

"Good morning." She smiled brightly at the kindly clergyman. The poorhouse was his church, she'd discovered out the day before.

Since his arrival in Denver two years ago, he'd put his heart, his soul, and any money he'd collected from donations into caring for those less fortunate than he. He had some help from organizations in Denver like the Ladies Aid Society, but so far none of the ladies had come to work hands on. That Becca had surprised and touched him, even after he found out she was not a member of any respected organization like the Ladies Aid Society.

All in good time. He believed those persons with honest benevolence in their hearts would build orphanages and establish shelters for the needy, the old, and the infirm in Denver, only not yet. Right now, because of her good deeds on this earth—coming to the poorhouse and working as she had the day before—the pastor told Becca, "There will be a special place in heaven for you, my child."

She thanked him, but kept it to herself that she doubted God would let her into heaven once her business in Denver was done.

Yesterday she had worked long hours at the poorhouse, returning to the Windsor just before dark. She'd try to get back earlier today, not wanting to raise eyebrows at the hotel or bring any kind of negative attention to Morgan. *Three o'clock and no later,* she reminded herself.

But there was so much to do. The poorhouse sheltered at least fifty men, women, and children in a space not much bigger than her rooms at the Windsor. Beds were bunked for men in one room and for women and children in another. The kitchen and communal area accounted for the third room. The privy and washing area was located out the back door of the shelter.

She'd spent most of her time yesterday washing and caring for the children. Her heart broke for them, each and every one. Some were with their mothers. Some had no mothers or fathers. Becca wondered if any of the little ones came from the row, from any whores up or down the line. If any did . . . it made her want to hold and love them all the more. Worse still was that a few of the little ones didn't have much time left. Surrounded by illness and poverty and malnutrition, Becca knew that her two hands alone couldn't do much good with the needs at the poorhouse so great. But maybe . . . she had an idea that maybe money could help.

"What's this, child?" Pastor Jonah stared wide-eyed at the three hundred dollars Becca put in his hand.

"It's for the little ones, Pastor. It's to buy food and bring the doc around regular to care for them," she explained. "Of course, you can use the money as you see fit for everyone here, but I especially want the children considered first. All right?"

"Bless you, sweet child." He spoke as if in prayer. "You are an angel sent down to us from above. I . . . I—" His eyes began to water. "I . . . will send for the doc this very minute," he managed; then he charged past her and out the front door.

At that moment two of the children ran up to her, hugging her skirt. Neither one was older than three or four. Becca bent down and hugged them back. She wondered if she'd be able to leave by three o'clock.

Tense about Morgan's safety and about seeing him again, Becca spent most of Friday at the poorhouse on Blake Street, when she hadn't intended to go at all. It was after three now and time to leave. Nighttime would come soon enough . . . and so would Morgan. With a quick goodbye to Pastor Jonah, she waved to the ever-watchful children, and then rushed out the front door before the little ones could catch up with her. A nice hot bath would feel wonderful. She needed to soothe her nerves more than to clean up from her day's work.

In a half-hour she'd arrived back at the hotel, slowing down when she started up the grand staircase, doing her utmost to behave like an elegant lady. Ignoring the stares from onlookers she was sure bore down on her, she kept her back turned and continued up to the second floor. She fumbled for her key, but was unable to find it. She couldn't believe her ineptness. What possible use was her reticule if it didn't hold her key? Out of habit, she felt her dress front, in case she'd slipped the key inside her corset against her bosom.

"Oh, hell's bells," she muttered aloud, "of course not." She wouldn't do that at the Windsor. Someone might see. Trying the knob a second time, she turned it harder. When it wouldn't open, she pivoted slowly; already embarrassed, knowing she'd have to go back downstairs and ask for another one.

The door opened behind her. "Want me to fetch it for you?"

She turned back around so fast she almost fell . . . right into Morgan's arms.

"Hello, darlin'," he greeted, and pulled her inside.

"You're . . . you're . . ." she couldn't finish, her whole body sinking into his warm strength, pressing hard against him, wanting to feel him close. He'd come back safe. *Safe.* She held on tight, never wanting to let him go, never wanting him to be in danger again.

"What's all this?" He spoke low and gentle, hugging her just as tightly as she held him.

The two embraced for long minutes, both lost in the arms of the other; both held by their affection for the other; by their stirred passions. Both of them . . . home.

Morgan was the first to break away. "Rebecca, are you all right?" he asked, his voice hoarse with emotion.

"I am now," she managed, drinking him in with her eyes, her gaze languishing over his broad shoulders and muscled arms, and coming to rest on his face, on his eyes. Those eyes held her, penetrated her, and marked her as his. She felt like she belonged to him, truly belonged to him. It was the most delicious, wanton and wonderful feeling she'd ever experienced. She could die from the pleasure of it. And she would if he didn't take her in his arms . . . and *take* her. No matter that she was a virgin, her body cried out for him. Every part of her ached for him, was willingly drawn in, wanted him and needed him, especially at her female center. Heat began building there, impossible, throbbing, mind-numbing heat; each flame licking, pulsing, penetrating, pulling the aroused woman in her to Morgan. To him. Only him. She'd never hurt like this. But then, she'd never been in love.

"Morgan . . . I . . . I . . ."

"I know, darlin'," he whispered, and pulled her to him, kissing her . . . and kissing her . . . and kissing her.

They weren't enough, his kisses. They weren't nearly enough.

Becca pulled away this time. Her lips burned. She burned . . . for more.

"Morgan . . . I—"

"I know," he took her words, making them his, and scooped her up in his arms. Carrying her to the bedroom, he kissed her once more before gently setting her on her feet.

He said nothing.

She said nothing.

Their bodies did all the talking now. They reached for each other with their eyes, their hearts, their souls.

Becca lifted a trembling hand and touched Morgan's tanned cheek, then his smooth jaw, then his fiery lips. She'd been afraid of this moment for so long. Right now the only thing she feared was not having it, not having him come back from the mines, not having him safe, not having him hold her, not having him make her feel so alive all over. She needed him inside every part of her. She retraced her fingers over his chiseled mouth, gasping when he opened it just enough for her to feel his butterfly kiss against her hand. Gently pressing her hand to his lips, she imagined that same kiss all over her body.

Suddenly hot, Becca put her hand—the same one Morgan had just kissed—to her collar and began ripping open her buttons. She needed to free the woman trapped inside her bothersome, wretched, useless clothes!

Morgan helped her.

Utterly relieved when he did, she tugged at his shirtfront buttons, wanting to help him get rid of the nuisance he wore, too. The taste of his electric kisses—clean, spicy, searing—was still fresh in her mouth, on her tongue, down through her heart, and lower. When she felt her dress slip off her shoulders and fall to the floor, the rush of coolness was exhilarating, because she knew it brought her that much closer to Morgan.

Fighting with her corset laces, the frustrating ties getting caught up in her hands, she was grateful for Morgan's masterful touch. He rid her of the uncomfortable annoyance in no time. When she was down to her chemise and pantalets, the reality of the moment flashed before Becca and she froze just long enough to see that Morgan was down to his long underwear. He was almost naked, like her.

The naked truth was standing in front of her: Morgan was all muscle, all might, all majestic. And all manhood. Embarrassed, she looked up at his face and not at him, growing hard beneath his long underwear bottoms. The look he gave her made her forget her embarrassment, his lazy grin teasing her, telling her, without saying a word, what was to come.

"Oops—" She near fell over her lace-up boots. She stared down at her feet and began to laugh at how silly she looked, standing there practically naked except for her shoes and stockings.

A quick look at Morgan and she stopped laughing.

He wasn't smiling. She watched as he bent down and undid the laces of her shoes, pulling them off in turn. She vaguely remembered her derringer—that she'd not worn it today to the poorhouse. When she felt Morgan's warm, strong fingers hook into the tops of her stockings, pulling them down gently, purposefully, and then brush against the insides of her thighs, her mind drained of all coherent thought. She leaned into him, reveling in the feel of his kisses through the cotton fabric of her chemise—first on her stomach, then her midriff, then between her breasts, then her mouth. She lost herself deliciously in his feel, his taste, his touch. She gave everything inside her to him the instant he swept her up in his arms, then laid her down on their bed of passion.

His mouth was on hers.

Her arms went around him.

His fevered body covered hers, holding his weight off her so as not to hurt.

Her lips tasted him wherever she could.

His skin, wherever it touched, turned hers first to gooseflesh, and then set it on fire. She could disappear into him and lose herself forever. She'd be blissfully lost, burning with him, becoming one with him. Time stood still, then blurred past so fast, it took her breath. Her heart under Morgan's still beat strong against his. Their bodies joined gently at first, then stronger, deeper, harder. Wet. Hot. Harder. Painfully harder. Hurting her womanhood—setting the woman inside her free . . . sending her to heaven and beyond in an explosion of ecstasy. She chased after the stars, never wanting to come back.

Such dreams, such wonderful dreams she'd had. Becca rolled over in bed, hating to wake up and leave her dreams behind— only to roll right up against the hard, muscled wall of a flesh-and-blood man. *Morgan.* It wasn't a dream. It was real, all of it.

He slept on.

She pressed into him, fitting her body to his, snuggling close, her head nestled against his shoulder and her arm lazing across his chest. It was dark out now, and she pressed closer to Morgan, his protective warmth reaching out to her even in sleep. He'd made her a woman tonight, in every sense of the word. A true woman now, she'd given herself, heart and soul, to the man of her dreams. She ached down low. The pulsating sensations felt wonderful. Morgan made her feel this way. Only Morgan. No longer a virgin, she wondered if this was how all whores felt after . . . after . . . She thought not. Most whores didn't let their emotions get the better of them. They ruled with their heads and not their hearts in the business of prostitution. And, most whores didn't let themselves fall in love, as she had.

Too late now. It did no good to deny the truth of it. Besides, what did it matter, really? In a few short weeks she'd either be dead or in jail. For now she'd lie with Morgan, loving him with all her heart, and she'd take her love with her into eternity. Easing even closer against Morgan, her eyelids heavy, one thing was certain in her uncertain world—she was the luckiest whore up or down the line in Denver, to have such a man bed her. She drifted off to sleep then, happy to lose herself again in dreams of Morgan.

Butterfly kisses—delicious, tickling butterfly kisses—at her nape woke Becca up. She turned over, at once finding Morgan's mouth, leaning into him, loving him. Somewhere in the recesses of her sleepy mind, she knew it was light out, and morning had come.

Let it. Let a new day come, another precious day with the man of her dreams. Giving herself over to everything Morgan demanded from her now, Becca melted into him, willingly letting him set her on fire. Their bodies joined, burning together in passionate flames . . . higher . . . ever higher . . . ever brighter . . . ever in love.

When next she awakened, it was dark out. Suddenly afraid Morgan might have left, Becca abruptly turned over in bed to make sure he was still there. He was. Thank God. He was.

"Hungry, darlin'?"

His husky voice sent a thrill down her spine. He lay on his

side next to her, still close, still a part of her. In the dim light she searched his handsome face, remembering every detail, as if when the light went, he might go too. She had to remember. She would.

"Happy birthday, Rebecca," he said, and reached over her to the bedstead, to the birthday cake he'd brought for her. When he returned his hand, his fingers held a dollop of chocolate icing. He put it to her lips.

Still dazed, she licked the icing from him. She couldn't believe he'd actually remembered her birthday! "Thank you," she whispered against his delicious fingers.

"More?" he gently teased, pretending to hold her down while he fed her more of the chocolate confection.

She swallowed the bite of cake, and then reached over to grab some cake herself and put it to Morgan's lips.

He swallowed the offered chocolate, and then tenderly tugged on her fingers. "Mmmm," he muttered in between taking pretend bites of her hand. "I'll never eat anything again unless you feed it to me just this way."

"More?" It was her turn to tease.

"Oh, yeah," he said, pulling her to him, letting her know it was more than cake that he wanted right now.

He tasted like chocolate, dark, savory, satisfying chocolate, at first just at her mouth, then down her throat, then in her belly, then lower. Sweet. Oh, so sweet . . .

The first to awaken as sunshine broke through the half-shaded window, Becca blinked against the light, unwilling to get out of bed and pull the shade down. She shifted in bed, just enough to get comfortable. Sore from two nights of lovemaking, she decided it was a small price to pay for finally becoming a woman. Morgan's woman.

Morgan. It was Sunday morning. He'd leave today! They

hadn't even talked yet, not really talked. She wanted time with him to just sit and talk and share a meal. She wanted to help him bathe and relieve his worries about the mines. She wanted more time . . . much more time.

"Morning, beautiful," he said, opening his eyes, pulling her close.

She broke free of his hold. "Morgan, let's get dressed and go to the dining room for breakfast. Wouldn't that be lovely?" She slipped out of bed and into her robe. "I'll be right back." She hurried now, suddenly shyer than she thought she'd be. Disappearing into the bath area, she closed the door behind her and leaned against it. The thought of him leaving made her sick to her stomach. Fighting tears, she sank to the cold floor, her back smarting against the unforgiving door. It wasn't fair that he had to leave. It just wasn't fair.

When Becca realized what she was doing—wasting time in the bath when she could be with Morgan—she pulled herself up and hastened to finish her morning toilette. Next week she'd make sure Morgan had a relaxing bath on their first night together. She'd do everything right for him next time. She'd massage his back, his neck, his shoulders, wash his hair, and then help dry his powerful body, tenderly patting each corded muscle, making sure of her job. She'd make sure, too, to hang his clothes properly, brush them, and send out to the laundry anything that needed attention. They could take their meals in the dining room or in their rooms, too, of course. She should have thought of that for this morning. Some mistress she made!

They'd had cake. The fact that Morgan brought the cake because he'd remembered her birthday brightened her spirits. She'd have this special memory to warm her all week, whenever she needed to feel Morgan close. It would be enough. It would have to be.

But for right now, for this moment, he was still here with her.

Quick as she could, she finished her toilette, and rushed out of the bath.

"Breakfast is served," Morgan called from the front room of their suite.

Pulling her robe closer about her, Becca walked slowly into the next room. Relieved it was just the two of them, and no waiter was present, she took the seat Morgan pulled out for her at the set-up table.

Morgan poured her coffee.

She put some cream and sugar in it, and took a sip. Delicious, just like the chocolate. Just like Morgan. The next sip didn't go down as easily.

He was leaving today, probably right after breakfast. They'd so little time. Precious little. "Morgan."

She looked up from her eggs and bacon at him. *I love you, Morgan Larkspur. I love you. I love you.* She wanted to be in his arms again, and not sitting at the table. The longer she studied him, his disarming good looks making her heart race, the harder it was for her to stay put. But stay put she would.

"Morgan, tell me about . . . about the mines." Her voice faltered.

"Darlin', what do you want to know?"

"Anything you wish to tell me." She spoke in earnest.

Morgan refilled her coffee cup and his. God, he wanted to tell her everything. But he couldn't. She'd worry. He didn't want her to. It was bad enough he had to leave her alone all week. Telling her the whole truth about the uncertainty in Leadville wouldn't help either of them. Dammit, he resented the time he'd have to spend this evening with Lavinia when she came for dinner at his home. He wanted to stay with Rebecca one more night.

"Rebecca, if there's a strike, I won't be in the thick of it," he lied. "Besides, it might not come down to a strike. It might not," he repeated, knowing it very well could. Men had died for less. Before he'd met Rebecca, he hadn't thought much on the subject of death, especially his own. Now he sure as hell did. He didn't want to leave Rebecca alone. He didn't want to leave her at all.

"Darlin'." He got up and took her in his arms. "Being with you these two days . . . it's the best time I've had in my life. The best." He nuzzled one cheek, then the other, then her forehead, then down to her mouth, kissing her with everything he felt for her. He didn't want to break their kiss, but he had to, their time together over.

Only for now, he hoped. Only for now.

CHAPTER THIRTEEN

Becca stared at the door Morgan had just closed behind him, feeling like she'd been gutted and left hollow inside. A good breeze could send her falling to the floor. What reason did she have to keep standing? Why exist at all without Morgan?

Teetering between all-out panic and overwhelming melancholy, she made herself walk into the bedroom and sit down on the side of the bed, when she'd rather run after Morgan and bring him back to room number eight on the second floor of the Windsor. It was safe at the Windsor. At the Windsor Morgan didn't have to face the dangers waiting for him in Leadville. And Becca didn't have to face the dangers waiting for her at Saint John's.

Saint John's! Sunday morning!

She scrambled off the bed, almost tripping on her robe in her rush to reach the vanity and her watch pin. It read ten-thirty. She had time to get to the church before services were over if she hurried. Just then an eerie calm settled over her, slowing her step, forcing her to think about everything she was doing. She dressed carefully, and remembered her derringer. She had to make sure it was loaded and tucked in place against her thigh.

Services were ending, and people had begun to depart Saint John's. The morning was bright and hot. Becca squinted against the sunshine and moved to position herself close enough to see

178

everyone leave. It was impossible to remain out of sight, although she did her best to blend into the crowd. Shading her eyes with one hand, she kept the other clenched. And ready.

All of the chatter around her buzzed in her ears, droning, building like a hive of bees waiting to sting. She felt faint, but kept steady. It was hard to see everyone's hands, and she tried to move among those brushing past for a better look. Frustrated, desperate now, she began to doubt her own mind. Maybe she'd been wrong about everything—about believing her mother's spirit had come to her in the church, believing she'd warned her that the killer was near. Sick to her stomach, Becca fought the dry heaves and held her ground.

Her whole life had been building to this moment.

She didn't want to fail.

That she might fail made her want to throw up.

The crowd thinned.

Becca's heart sank. Her head hurt. The derringer tucked along her thigh poked against her skin, as if taunting her, as if reminding her she'd failed again. Then something made her turn around. Something told her to fix on the carriage pulling away. There were two men and two women riding in the carriage. The men had their backs to her, and the sun made it difficult for her to clearly see the women's faces.

But it was the men she focused in on. One of them was her mother's killer. She knew it. She knew it.

At first walking slowly, she picked up her pace, then began running after the carriage. Unmindful of anything but the black carriage and its passengers, she strained to remember any detail at all that might give her a clue as to their identity. She ran fast, but the carriage was faster and soon disappeared from sight. Had it turned down Blake Street? Larimer Street? Oh, dear God, which one? She ran until she couldn't run anymore, falling to her knees in the kicked-up dust.

Other carriages passed her by. Breathless, she got up off the street and went over to the sidewalk, hating every black carriage that passed by. Hating them all.

"Morgan Larkspur." Lavinia worked hard not to sound agitated. If she let Morgan know how she really felt about his running off every week to the silly mines and leaving her with egg on her face in front of her friends, he might change his mind about marrying her. She couldn't have that. He represented everything she admired in a husband: money, power, good looks, and a solid reputation among the social elite.

Certainly, her family already had money—*she* already had money—and she was determined to keep it that way. Becoming Mrs. Morgan Larkspur would further her already established position in Denver society. As for love . . . well she supposed she loved him. Who wouldn't? He was handsome, virile, and good at making money.

Of course when they married, she'd have to share the marriage bed with him and have sex. The very thought made her cringe. A proper Victorian lady, she didn't look forward to having some man, even if it was her husband, touching her intimately, forcing himself inside her with his . . . his manhood. How disgusting! Her mother had always told her it was disgusting and degrading, but she'd have to lie with her husband to have children, as many times as it took. Lavinia could only hope it wouldn't take long for her to bear a child.

No, she didn't look forward to her belly swelling and to losing her perfect figure. For that matter, she didn't look forward to motherhood. It all sounded much too painful. What a nuisance children would be. Thank God she could afford to have others take care of any children she and Morgan would have. Thank God for that.

She was grateful for another thing, too. Morgan hadn't tried to kiss her and hold her and touch her everywhere like some of her friends told her their suitors and husbands had. Lavinia always thought her friends were ridiculous to go on so about such nonsense. Well, she didn't have to deal with any of that as far as her husband-to-be was concerned.

Certainly not!

Of course, she'd pretend to fuss over him and get him to kiss her for appearance's sake only. She didn't really want him to, yet a part of her did wonder why he didn't respond to her. But she refused to worry. She knew he loved her. Of course he loved her. All the men did. Morgan was no different. In fact, he was lucky indeed that she'd said yes.

Lucky indeed.

"Morgan Larkspur," Lavinia began again. His family was listening. She didn't want to say anything that might upset any of them, but she wanted them to hear her upset over Morgan being gone so much. "Can't you delay going back to Leadville for a day or so? Can't you, Morgan? For me?" she complained, wanting everyone to know how she hurt because of his absence. "Our wedding is in three weeks and I need you to be here, with me. I miss you so, Morgan." She sniffled, as if on the verge of tears.

Augusta Larkspur got up from the table and came over to Lavinia.

Morgan didn't move.

"There, there, Lavinia," Augusta cooed, gently patting her on her shoulders.

A quick look at Morgan, and Lavinia could see he wasn't convinced. She made herself cry, hoping her tears would convince him. He sat still, clearly unmoved by her show of tears. Hiding her anger, she started to sob.

Morgan exchanged looks with his father and his brother, both apparently as unmoved as he was by Lavinia's upset. But his father, he could tell, expected him to do something about it. Well, dammit, he didn't feel like it. Yes, she was going to become his wife, but that's all she'd be: a wife, and nothing else. It wasn't as if he loved her. With reluctance, he pushed away from the table and walked over to take his mother's place behind Lavinia.

The moment his hand touched Lavinia's shoulder, she grabbed it, continuing to cry. His mother looked daggers at him. His father and Monty rolled their eyes, indicating he should take care of this little problem, and fast. Morgan did feel sorry for Lavinia. He really did. "Lavinia, come into the parlor a moment, won't you?"

She stopped crying as if on cue, and got up from the table. "Yes, Morgan." She kept her voice soft, almost childlike, and obediently followed him out of the dining room. Unhappy they'd be alone now, their audience gone, she didn't think she'd make much headway with Morgan now. Maybe she'd start crying again, or maybe get mad, or maybe say nothing . . . at least for the next three weeks.

Once inside the parlor, Morgan put out his hand, directing Lavinia to take a seat on the deep burgundy sofa. He sat in a chair opposite her. "I know you've the wedding to plan all by yourself. Here." He reached in his breast pocket for money, hesitating a moment, thinking of Rebecca, Rebecca and her fifty-dollar token . . . the woman he'd much rather pay for. "In case you need—"

"Morgan!" Lavinia stood. "I wouldn't hear of you doing any such thing. Why, my father will pay for our wedding, of course." She began fanning herself with her handkerchief. Time enough after they married to spend his money. For now, they must do what etiquette dictated.

Morgan didn't get up. He took his hand from his pocket. "All right, Lavinia, but please understand. I have to go to the mines.

A strike is imminent and there might be trouble. I need to be there to look out for our future interests." He tried to say something, anything, that might resonate with her.

"Oh, imminent schimminent." She sat down. "Why do you need to be there? You have people . . . workers . . . to do all that sort of thing for you. Why can't you be here with me, and go to our engagement luncheons and dinners? They're important to our future, too, Morgan." She looked at him pointedly, forgetting the dangerous ground she trod upon.

Morgan heaved a sigh and got up. He couldn't sit there any longer with a woman who didn't care about him. He thanked his lucky stars he knew one who did.

"Morgan," Lavinia called to his back.

He turned around in the parlor entryway, realizing he at least should say something else.

"Morgan, I'm sorry I got upset. It won't happen again. I know . . . I know you have . . . well . . . business to attend to, and I didn't mean . . . well . . . I didn't mean to—"

"It's fine," he interrupted. "I'm sorry I won't be here for your parties, but it's for our good, Lavinia. It's for the both of us."

"I know," she agreed, still seething inside about his putting work ahead of her.

"Let's go back in with the family," he urged, wanting to change the subject.

"Yes, of course." She swallowed her words, and dutifully followed him into the dining room.

"You know what will happen if you talk, don't you, honey?"

The whore knew. She knew, all right. If she told anyone about her newest customer and his violent tendencies, he'd kill her. When things started to get rough—him tying her up and all— she should have known better than to let him in a second time. Things happened to whores and no one cared . . . especially the law. The law only cared if they didn't get their fines paid on time or if one of their own got hurt in a raid. Other whores cared. She could rely on other whores to help, sometimes anyway. Right now she was alone, and being alone could be deadly. She'd best remember that and do just as her customer said. The money with him was good, but she didn't know how much longer she could take it—take being so afraid.

"There's a good girl." He eased back down in bed with her, holding a knife to her throat, then slicing off each button of her dress. "Don't move," he warned. "Lie still or I'll cut you, and I don't mean your clothes."

She didn't make a move, hating the air she breathed and the rapid rise and fall of her own chest. It might get her killed. He'd told her not to move, liking that she was so scared, aroused by it. She broke out in a nervous sweat and smelled her own fear, the odor hanging in the air like something had just died. Each thud of her heart echoed throughout the tiny room, every anguished beat pushing her closer and closer to the edge of her grave.

If she lived through this hour—this trick—with him, she'd run, leaving Denver far behind her. She'd run to one of the mining camps where she'd be safe from him. She was used to the rough life in mining camps, used to the rough ways of some of the men in mining camps. Never once had she lain with a man this evil, this frightening. Most men loved to love whores, treating them pretty well, all respectable like. Yes, she'd run back to the camps and away from Denver, leaving at first light.

If she made it to morning, she'd never lie with another man, no matter how rich, who had missing fingers or wore fancy gold rings. *Never* for as long as she had left on this earth!

Monday came and went without Becca leaving the Windsor. So did Tuesday. She'd taken her meals in her rooms, not going to the dining room even once. Staying cooped up in her rooms didn't help lessen her worry over Morgan, or her anger at herself for failing to discover the identity of her mother's killer on Sunday, but she couldn't find the energy to go out.

Forcing herself up from her seat at the writing desk, she realized how foolish she'd been to sit there in the first place. Other than Miss Jenny, she'd no one to write to, or call, for that matter. Even if she wanted to use the new telephones installed off the main lobby of the hotel, she'd no one to call. Fascinated by the new device, she'd lingered in the doorway of the telephone parlor and watched others place calls from the Windsor, marveling at such an invention, and wondering who they were calling. How she envied them, connecting with someone on the other end of the wire, probably a loved one, a loved one who had waited all day for them to call.

How she envied them.

Quick to sit back down at the writing desk, Becca pulled the drawer open. She took two hundred dollars from the bills put there by Morgan and shoved them in her skirt pocket. If she hurried, she could get to the poorhouse in time to be of some help today.

"Tabor's miners are going for it!" the miner yelled out, running from the Morning Star mine down the gulch into Leadville.

Morgan stood outside one of his mines near Carbonate Hill, watching men pour out of Tabor's mine, strangely relieved that something had finally broken the volatile silence. He'd known the strike would come. He hadn't been able to budge the other mine owners from their fixed position on working hours and wages, and was disappointed they didn't seem to get it: that the miners would strike, and maybe the smelter workers, too, if the owners didn't give in to some of the laborers' demands. Morgan knew that the Knights of Labor had organized the Miner's

Cooperative Union in secret, pushing for a strike, and pushing hard. Well here it was. Here it was. God help them all.

Word spread fast. Some of his own men brushed past him now, uniting with other miners, pouring out of their respective mines like ants from anthills. He didn't try to stop them, yet he didn't join them either. Not yet, anyway. He had an interest on both sides. But if he had to choose, there wouldn't be a choice and he knew it. The safety of his men came first. That thought started him down the gulch into Leadville along with everyone else. By nightfall ten thousand miners and smelter workers had walked off the job.

Tabor's Light Cavalry spurred into action—the very thing Morgan had warned his miners against. He watched Tabor's local militia move among the sea of strikers, starting fights with some, rounding up others and hauling them off.

"Men, disperse!" Morgan shouted over the crowd. "Go home! Go home!"

Some men listened, passing the word to break up for now. A few miners recognized him as an owner and one spat on him. Another tried to punch him. Another pulled out a gun.

Morgan held his ground, his gun hand ready. One bullet, and the mess around him would get worse, much worse. No, he didn't want the first shot to be on account of him. The kid who pointed a pistol at him was just that: a kid.

"Son." Morgan took a fatherly tone. "Put the gun down. You don't want to kill anyone. You don't want to kill me."

The teen cocked his pistol and aimed it straight at Morgan. He swallowed hard, obviously nervous. "Yep, I . . . shore do." His voice broke.

Others backed away now, circling around Morgan and the youth. Oddly, no one encouraged the kid to fire, but then no one told him not to. Tempers flared in the assemblage around them, random fights breaking out nearby and tensions mounting.

"Son." Morgan kept his tone calm and even. "You have a mama and family, and you need to get home to them tonight. Your dying isn't going to help keep a roof over their heads or food in their bellies. Killing me will just get you killed."

The boy uncocked his pistol and stuck the gun in his belt. *Smart kid,* Morgan thought. *Real smart.* "Say, kid." Morgan cracked a smile. "There will be a job waiting for you in the Larkspur Mines after all this is settled, if you want it."

The boy nodded his head in quick acknowledgement, then turned and disappeared into the concourse of strikers.

The strikers had begun to disperse. Relieved that more violence hadn't broken out, for now at least, Morgan worried about keeping law and order during the strike. There was no telling how long it might last, and no telling how long tempers would hold. He headed straight for the telegraph office, intent on notifying the governor about the trouble—about the sheer size of it—started in Leadville.

"Strike's on! Strike's on! Read all about it!"

Becca ripped open the window shade for a better look at the boy standing below, calling out the morning headline from the *Rocky Mountain News.* Already dressed, she grabbed the necessary coins she needed and rushed out to buy a paper. She had to find out what was happening in Leadville. She had to.

Back upstairs in a matter of minutes, she hurried over to the writing desk and sat down, paper in hand. Carefully placing the paper on the desk, still shaky, she scanned the headline then read on. Too nervous to remember every detail, she got the gist of it: *Ten thousand strikers. The smelter workers, too. Some pockets of violence already. Local militia trying to maintain law and order. Tempers high. Guns pointed.*

187

Morgan! Where was anything about Morgan? She desperately scanned every page, looking for some word telling her he was all right. It wasn't reasonable to expect any word in the paper about him, but she read on anyway, fighting her fears. The paper was all she had connecting Morgan to her now. Her stomach in knots, she got up, taking the paper with her, folding it, unfolding it, and then refolding it.

She went over it all . . . all the reasons she shouldn't care about Morgan. They hadn't known each other long. They came from different worlds. She could never be a part of his world, and never expected him to ask her to be. She was his mistress and nothing more. She wasn't his wife or his sister or any kind of relative to care about, just a prostitute, a prostitute who loved him. At last putting the newspaper to rest on the writing desk, she sat back down.

"I love you, Morgan," she said, giving voice to her thoughts. "I love you," she said again before dissolving into tears.

Someone knocked on the door.

Becca lifted her head and wiped her eyes.

Another knock, this one louder. "Western Union Telegram," a male voice called through the door.

Becca numbly rose from her seat and went over to the door, slowly opening it.

"Telegram for you, ma'am." A young man, clad in an ill-fitting brown suit, greeted her, then handed her the telegram.

"Are you . . . are you sure you have the right room?" she asked, dumbfounded, taking the folded slip from him. She couldn't imagine that he had.

"Yes, ma'am. You're Rebecca Rose, aren't you?"

"Yes," she told him.

"And this is room number eight on the second floor of the Windsor, right?" he clarified, his words practiced. "Your message came through this morning in our Western Union office downstairs."

She ran her fingers over the folded message and managed a slight smile. "Thank you," she said, then watched him leave before closing her door. For long moments she leaned against the hard mahogany, pressing the telegram against her heart, imagining good news . . . or bad. All she could think about, the only person she could think about, was Morgan. The telegram could be about Morgan. He could be . . . he could be—

She never knew she was such a coward until this moment. This was the first telegram she'd ever received in the whole of her life, but it could mean she'd seen Morgan for the last time. She had to know. This was no time for cowardice. Her hands shaking, careful as she could, she opened the message and read it. It *was* from Morgan. He was alive. *Alive.*

Relief washed through her—warm, wonderful, welcome relief. Able now, she walked back across the room to the writing desk and sat down, reading and rereading her message from Morgan:

Can't come home now, darlin'.

Place a telephone call to me Friday night at six from the hotel.

Tell the operator to put you through to the Argo Smelter in Idaho Springs.

Morgan

Unsure how far Idaho Springs was from Denver, Becca traced her fingers over Morgan's telegram again and again. It wasn't just that she had someone to call. She had Morgan to call. He'd be on the other end, waiting for her . . . a loved one waiting for her.

Suddenly energized, she quickly gathered the items she needed then hurried out the door with plenty of time left in the day to be of some help on Blake Street.

★　★　★　★　★

Waking up the next morning, living out the only fairy tale life she'd ever have—her borrowed weeks with Morgan at the Windsor—Becca couldn't wait for six o'clock this evening to place her telephone call to him in Idaho Springs. How exciting to hear his voice, and how exciting to use the telephone for the very first time. She wondered what he'd sound like, and what she'd sound like to him. She couldn't imagine it all.

Six o'clock was hours and hours away. What on earth could she do with herself until then? Rolling over in bed, facing the shaded window, she leaned out as far as she could to reach the shade pull and let in the morning sunshine. Easing back down on her pillow, she'd already decided not to go to the Blake Street poorhouse today. Some of the women from the Ladies Aid Society of Denver were going to tour the shelter. Humph! *Ladies Aid Society.* They'd never come before, and never sent much money either. She wondered what this was all about. She'd find out next Monday when she returned there to work.

For right now, she'd nothing but time on her hands, time to plan exactly what she'd say to Morgan when she heard his voice that night. Hugging herself, closing her eyes, she imagined his handsome face, his hard, muscled body, his clean scent of musk and fresh tobacco, his magical hands, his protecting arms, his demanding mouth. Oh, Morgan. She ached for him all up and down her body. She'd rather have him with her, in their bed, making love all night and into the next morning, but a telephone call would have to do.

Opening her eyes, suddenly needing her morning coffee to calm her nerves, she forced herself up and out of bed to dress for the dining room. She dressed carefully but quickly. It was already half past eight, and they stopped serving breakfast in the upstairs restaurant at nine.

Wearing her best day dress, her navy taffeta with lace trim, Becca felt she should wear her best this morning, for Morgan. He'd be pleased with her appearance, she thought, with her hair arranged in a soft chignon, a bit of rouge on her lips for color, her watch pin placed, just so, on her dress front, and looking every bit the proper lady. She wasn't really worried that she hadn't used the money he'd left for her to build her wardrobe and have more day dresses and gowns made-to-order. She knew she'd done the right thing in using his money for the men, women, and children at the poorhouse. He'd be happy with her; she knew it.

Did anything taste better than her first morning coffee? She thought not. Her nerves calmed immediately. Looking around the spacious dining room, not surprised that few still sat down to breakfast, given the time, Becca unthinkingly returned the nod of a man sitting at a table clear across the room. The good-looking young man reminded her a little of Morgan. He sat with several other men, all finishing their breakfast. His smile was friendly and caught her off guard. She nodded back before she thought better of it. She knew unescorted ladies didn't do such things.

Oh fiddle faddle. He was just being cordial. Nothing wrong with being cordial herself. Miss Jenny would approve, she thought, and so would Morgan. Wouldn't he? Putting the young man and her quandary over what Morgan might or might not think of her nodding to a stranger out of her mind, she took another sip of Chase and Sanborn and stared out the nearby window at the magnificent morning, daydreaming about how Morgan would sound on the telephone tonight.

"Rebecca Rose, you say?" Monty Larkspur leaned against his cushioned seatback, not believing what his friends had just shared with him: that the beautiful young woman who'd just nodded to him was his brother's mistress, *Rebecca Rose,* and that she lived here at the Windsor, in room number eight on the second floor.

CHAPTER FOURTEEN

More than a little astonished that Spur had been keeping a mistress—a stunner, at that—tucked away here at the exclusive Windsor right under Denver society's nose, Monty laughed. Spur pulled off a good one this time, that's for sure. He laughed harder, thinking about what his parents would think when they found out, glad his big brother had finally got them back after all their years of heaping all of the responsibility for the family name on Spur's shoulders. *Good for you, Spur. Good for you.*

"What's so funny?" his friend Archie asked, chucking him on the shoulder.

"Yeah," the rest chimed in, almost in unison.

Monty took a sip of water, needing it to help contain his laugher. He didn't want Spur to get into hot water, but he found this hilarious. For the first time in as long as he could remember, his parents might possibly get their good name a little tarnished, maybe even experience a little scandal.

For his part, Monty didn't worry over the family name. He worried over the fact that his parents didn't think he was good for anything but being Morgan's little brother. Proud of Spur all his life, he was never more proud of him than now. *Good for you, Spur. Good for you.*

Archie gave him another chuck on the shoulder. "Fess up, Monty. What's so funny? Is it about that beautiful girl over there?" Archie seemed surprised that Monty would take any notice of such a common practice as keeping a mistress secreted away. After all, more than one gentleman in his circle did the same thing, if not keeping a mistress, certainly frequenting parlor houses. No big deal, none of it.

Monty straightened in his seat. It was one thing for him to have a good laugh over this, but he didn't want anyone else doing so. It wasn't any of his friends' business what his brother did.

He suddenly wished they didn't know about Morgan's mistress and wondered who else did. His parents didn't, that was for damn sure. Not yet, anyway.

"Arch." Monty forced himself to sound jovial. "I was just remembering my first time with a beautiful young gal, a lot like the one over there." He glanced Becca's way with his made-up story. "The gal threw me and my token out of her room when I asked her to be my mistress. Tossed me right out, she did." He feigned laughter this time. "Said I was too young and too inexperienced, and to come back when I'd learned a thing or two."

Archie grinned at his friend and began sharing a similar experience. Someone else chimed in with his first time with a prostitute, and then another.

Glad to have the attention diverted from him and from Spur and his mistress, Monty joined in with a laugh or two at his friends' stories, only now beginning to worry about the situation. His parents would be furious when they found out. Maybe they wouldn't find out. He sure as hell wouldn't tell them.

Worried all over again now about Spur and the strike in Leadville, Monty wished his brother would return to Denver. Knowing Spur, he doubted that would happen. If it wouldn't cause such a ruckus at home, Monty'd hop on the train today for Leadville. Damn, he'd like to talk this over with Spur, him having a mistress, and see if Spur really knew what he was doing, risking the ire of their parents and of Lavinia Eagleton. Hell hath no fury, and all that sort of thing,

Monty chanced another look at young, beautiful Rebecca Rose, glad she gazed out the window now and not at him. She was a looker all right. He couldn't question his brother's choice in women. He suddenly wondered if Spur had feelings for the girl—which would be ridiculous since she was a prostitute—but then, Monty realized, he might, or else Spur wouldn't take such a risk.

I'll be a son-of-a-gun. The idea that Spur might really care for his mistress made Monty proud of his brother all over again. He wished he could take his coffee over, sit with Rebecca Rose, and find out more about her. About her and his brother. Convention wouldn't allow it. Besides, he'd never hear the end of it from his friends.

Monty called the waiter over to fill his cup, doing his utmost to dismiss his newest concerns over Spur. He wanted to help his brother. He just didn't know how to do it.

Lavinia tried to sidestep the children circling around her at the poorhouse on Blake Street, not wanting the filthy urchins to dirty her new dress. She'd come with two of her friends from the Ladies Aid Society for an in-person tour of the facility, when she'd rather not. Wanting to be the next president of the society, feeling she needed to appear the most benevolent woman in the esteemed organization, she'd decided to visit the shelter to prove to everyone that she obviously cared the most about the poor in the city. Today she'd also give a contribution in front of her friends, to make sure word got back to all in the Ladies Aid Society. No matter that she was only twenty-one and young for the presidency. She would soon be Mrs. Morgan Larkspur, and no one would dare challenge her then. She refused to settle for anything less than being the toast of Denver, its most prominent citizen and the envy of all.

"Good morning, ladies," Pastor Noah greeted, joining the children gathered around the three women. "I'm Pastor—"

"Yes, yes," Lavinia interrupted. "Pastor Noah, I know." She was impatient to get the tour over with and leave. This was all too, too wretched. How she'd endure the next few minutes, she'd no idea. "I've come . . . we've come . . . from the Ladies Aid Society to tour your . . . your facility here." She tried not to scoff, or at least tried not to let on to Pastor Noah how distasteful this whole outing was for her. "So please, if you will, show us where it is."

"Where what is?" Pastor Noah tried not to scoff himself at this unfortunate young woman's visit. He could see insincerity written all over her lovely face, not to mention hear it in her sharp tone.

"Where your shelter is, of course," Lavinia said, incensed at his pitiable intelligence.

"You're standing in the middle of it." He tried to keep God in his heart when he answered her.

"This is all? This is it?" She couldn't believe it.

"I'm afraid so, Miss . . . Miss . . ."

"I'm Lavinia Eagleton," she declared, as if he should know her name like everyone who was anyone in Denver did. Obviously, Pastor Noah wasn't anyone of importance.

"Children." He spoke so everyone in the group could hear. "Go outside and play now. Go along," he encouraged, shooing them away so they wouldn't hear any more of his conversation with the women from the Ladies Aid Society. Once the children disbanded, he turned again to the society women, Lavinia in particular. "Miss Eagleton, just what is it I can do for you?"

"As I said." Agitated, she tried not to sound unkind. "We came for a tour. I want to make a contribution, too," she stated, loudly enough so everyone in earshot could hear her. Opening her reticule, she handed the bills to Pastor Noah. "Here's twenty-five dollars for you, *personally* from me. I know it's a large sum, Pastor, but I feel I must help you and the unfortunates here. It's the Christian thing to do," she finished, feigning emotion.

"Well, thank you," he said, taking the bills. "I'll add it to our other charitable contributions."

"What other charitable contributions?" she asked, flabbergasted. "No one gives money to you but the Ladies Aid Society, I thought," she blurted out before she thought better of it.

"There are others in the community, Miss Eagleton, who think to help us, too." The ordinary man in him, rather than the clergyman, wanted to put this snip of a girl in her place. He didn't want to be uncharitable to her, but he couldn't help it.

"What others?" Lavinia raised her voice. "Who?" Angry that someone else might usurp her plans and her position, she wanted him to tell her who had done so. It had to be another member of the Ladies Aid Society. Could be that haughty Prunella Winters, for all she knew.

"It's not important who, Miss Eagleton," he told her.

"Oh, but it is," Lavinia gritted out. "If it's another member of our Ladies Aid, you have to tell me. I'm sure it will be put down in the notes at our next meeting, so you might just as well go ahead and tell me," she insisted.

Frustrated, wanting her to leave and to take her friends with her—although they didn't appear condescending, as she did—the good pastor didn't see any harm in letting the renowned Ladies Aid Society know that one outside of their ranks was, by far, much, much more charitable. "A kindly young woman, indeed. Miss Rebecca Rose of the Windsor Hotel has contributed of her time and her money. She comes over here many a day and works hard, rolling up her sleeves to help. Why, she's donated hundreds of dollars to us for food and medicine. She's a saint, that Rebecca Rose," he opined, making sure he had Lavinia Eagleton's eye when he did.

"Well, then, you won't need this," she snipped, grabbing her twenty-five dollars right out of Pastor Noah's hand.

He let her take it. He didn't want anything from this disagreeable young woman.

"Ladies." She turned to her two companions. "Our business here is quite finished. Pastor." She nodded curtly, and then left with her friends close on her heels.

Unaccustomed to approaching the reception desk at the Windsor, Becca had to ask about placing her telephone call to Morgan. She needed to know how to do it and how to pay. She waited in line behind a well-dressed couple apparently registering at the hotel, checking her watch pin. *Fifteen minutes to six.* Nervous, more about talking to Morgan than standing right in the middle of busy reception, she fidgeted with the folds of her dress, much as she did when she'd first met Morgan. It seemed like months and months ago, when it was only weeks. Some needed a lifetime to find the man of their dreams. Becca didn't have that luxury, and not just because of her chosen profession, but because she had a deadly mission to carry out.

Suddenly she let go of her skirt fabric and shot her glance around the spacious area. The killer could be among the crowd right now. Scrutinizing the hands of all the men who walked by, she was angry at herself all over again for failing to track the killer from the cathedral. She should have kept up with the carriage and its passengers, at least seeing which street the expensive carriage turned down.

A bellman brushed past, ending her somber reverie.

The young man abruptly stopped, turned around, and smiled broadly. "Good evening, Mrs. Larkspur," he greeted, and touched his cap to her.

She recognized the bellman. He was the young man who'd helped her with her trunk when she first arrived at the Windsor. Morgan never bothered to correct him about her *not* being Mrs. Morgan Larkspur. It didn't upset her anymore, that the young man believed her to be Morgan's wife. It made her feel wonderful inside, nothing short of wonderful.

"Good evening." She returned his smile.

"Is there anything I can do for you this evening, Mrs. Larkspur?" he asked, somewhat sheepishly.

"No, thank you. I'm just waiting to make a telephone call." Nervously checking her watch pin again, she changed her mind. It was five minutes to six! "Could you help me make my call? I've never made one before," she explained, worrying that she'd be late and Morgan wouldn't be waiting on the other end. Upset she hadn't come downstairs sooner, she tried to keep her nerves in check.

"Oh, I can help you with that." The bellman brightened to her plea, as if happy he actually knew how to help. "Come with me to the telephone parlor. I'll show you how to ring the operator."

"What of the charges? How do I pay?" She hurried with her questions.

"The call will be charged to your room here. That's how it's done," he told her confidently. The young man looked over at the front desk. The hotel clerk still dealt with the couple checking in, and the other evening clerk was nowhere in sight. Really, it wasn't up to him, a bellman, to direct any guest to anything other than their room with their bags. Not the first time he'd been a little overzealous in his job, but he didn't see anything wrong with helping Mrs. Larkspur make her call. After all, the staff seemed busy or unavailable. "Follow me," he instructed Becca.

She did, all but running behind the speedy bellman.

The telephone parlor was just off the main lobby. There were three telephones installed, each affixed to the wall, and each placed far enough apart to afford some privacy. A desk and chair had been provided near each phone. One phone was in use. Becca heard the man, but didn't hear him, too concerned about her own call.

"Here, use this one," the bellman said, guiding her over to the telephone in the far corner.

It was impossible for her to reach the phone properly, since she was a little too short for comfort, she looked around for a stool.

"Here, ma'am," the bellman offered, placing a small wood crate at her feet.

Becca stepped onto the crate, grateful for the added height. "All right, young man, how do I do this?"

"Here's where you talk." He pointed to the speaker. "And here's where you listen."

Becca took the receiver in hand and put it to her ear, then returned it to its hook on the phone.

"Just turn the ringer here." The young man showed her the handle on the right. "The operator will come on and tell you exactly what she needs."

The clock just outside the telephone parlor chimed six.

"Thank you," Becca said in earnest.

"You're welcome, Mrs. Larkspur." He tipped his hat, and then quickly left. He'd be needed in reception now, for sure.

Becca put the receiver to her ear and turned the ringer on the phone . . . once . . . then again . . . then again.

"Colorado Telephone Company." A distinct woman's voice came through the receiver.

"Yes. Good evening," Becca said into the speaker, her mouth so close she could feel the cold metal against her lips.

"How may I direct your call?" the operator said.

Becca's ear tickled. The woman's voice vibrated close in her ear.

"How may I direct your call?" the operator repeated.

"Yes . . . I . . . my name is Rebecca Rose and I'm calling from the Windsor Hotel in Denver." Becca didn't know what else to say.

"Yes, thank you. Rebecca Rose from the Windsor," the operator repeated, very businesslike. "We have your exchange noted, ma'am. How may I direct your call?"

"Oh . . . yes. I am calling Morgan Larkspur in Idaho Springs."

The operator came back on. "Is Morgan Larkspur a personal number or are you calling a business?"

"He's a business. I mean I'm calling a business. The Argo Smelter," Becca said, grateful she could remember anything now.

"One moment, please," the operator said.

Becca held the receiver tight against her ear and kept her mouth close to the speaker, hard to do with her hand trembling so. A distant ring buzzed once, then again. She almost dropped the receiver when another voice came on the line, not Morgan's.

"Argo Smelter," a gruff male voice said.

"I have Rebecca Rose on the line for a Morgan Larkspur," the operator told him.

"Yeah, just a minute," the man replied.

Becca's heart thudded in her chest. Her knees wanted to give way. She couldn't imagine talking to Morgan. But then, she couldn't imagine *not* talking to Morgan. Something might have gone wrong; he might not be on the other end. She pressed the receiver even harder against her ear. Waiting . . . waiting . . .

"Rebecca?"

"Morgan?" she answered back, putting her mouth closer to Morgan, closer to his cherished, magical, magnificent voice.

"Hi, darlin'," he said, his tone husky and low, heavy with

emotion. "Are you all right?"

"I am now." She wanted to melt into the telephone.

"Good." He chuckled. "I miss you, darlin'."

"Me too, Morgan. Me too." She tried to speak clearly in spite of the emotion welling in her throat. "Morgan, you sound wonderful."

"No more than you do," he quipped on the other end.

"I love you!" she blurted out, instead of all the other things she'd practiced to say to him. She never meant to say I love you. Never.

Silence on the other end.

Her heart sank to her feet, dread rising up inside her like a cloying, wet blanket, heavy and oppressive. She was afraid now. Any second she expected him to hang up on her. Any second.

"Me too, Rebecca. I love you, too," he came back, the passion in his rich, hoarse tone obvious.

Silence on her end now. She had no words, only tears.

"Don't cry, darlin'," he said, his voice barely above a whisper now. "I don't ever want to make you cry."

"Morgan. Oh, Morgan," she sobbed, the impact of his words breathing life into every part of her, filling her, healing her, giving her strength. "I'm just happy . . . so happy . . . that you're all right. Are you? Are you . . . all right?" She tried to collect herself, not wanting to spoil their call.

"I'm fine. Didn't I tell you I'm always fine?"

"Yes." She sniffed.

"The strike has started, but I think things will get settled before there's more trouble," he told her.

"Has there been much trouble so far?" she asked, needing to know.

"Some."

Afraid for him, she had more questions, questions she knew he couldn't answer. "Morgan, promise you'll come back to me.

Promise." She had to hear him say it, even knowing it was a promise he might not keep.

"I promise, darlin'," he answered, knowing she needed to hear him say it, hoping with all his heart he could keep his promise.

Becca held back more tears; they wouldn't do her or Morgan any good right now.

"Rebecca, how about you?" he asked.

"Me?"

He chuckled.

She felt the vibration in her ear, then it tingled down her spine, making her want to touch him, to feel him close, to feel him inside her. Loving her. Stirred and frustrated, she could rip the telephone, the obstacle keeping her from Morgan, right off the wall.

"Rebecca?"

"Yes?" she managed to answer.

"Darlin'—"

"I'm all right, Morgan." She hurried with her reply, realizing that he worried for her, too.

"I have to go, but I want you to call me the same time next week. If things settle before then, I'll telegraph you and take the next train out."

Clutching the phone harder now, with all thoughts of ripping it off the wall gone, Becca didn't want to let go. "Yes, Morgan. Next week. Next Friday. I'll call you," she reassured him, fighting her fears for his safety all over again.

"That's my darlin' girl," he said.

"I love you," she whispered, meaning to say it this time.

"I love you, too, darlin'," he whispered into the receiver.

She heard the phone click. And then he was gone. Mutely, she put the receiver back on its hook and stepped off the wood crate. There were others in the parlor now, making calls. She saw them but didn't see them, heard them but didn't hear them. Doing her best to hold back her tears, she left the telephone parlor and headed straight for room number eight on the second floor of the Windsor. Her tears were private, meant for no one but her and Morgan.

Saturday came and went.

After another fitful night, Becca awakened Sunday morning before dawn but lay in bed, unable to get up and face the day. Today could mark the end of everything for her if she shot her mother's killer at Saint John's and got shot herself, or arrested, and she didn't think she could face not having at least one more day—one more night—with Morgan. The idea that what they had together would end so fast played hard against her breast. The notion, too, that she needed to stay all right swirled around in her troubled thoughts. What if Morgan came home early and she wasn't there? It wouldn't be right. It wouldn't be fair to him, to pull such a surprise. Another notion struck her. She needed to make sure of Morgan's safety before she took action against her mother's killer. She couldn't go to her grave without making sure. She couldn't.

Eyes wide open, her decision to stay at the hotel through church services made, Becca then scrambled out of bed. She determined to do one thing today, at least, and needed to set about doing it. Monday morning, she'd go see Miss Jenny and have it over and done with.

"What's this?" Jenny asked, remembering the time all those years ago when Becca stood in her front parlor, a pitiable orphan of eight in her shabby dress and dirty boots, and handed her a note, much like she'd just done now. Jenny remembered the note word for word, as upset now as she'd been then that Becca's mother had been murdered in Nevada City.

No longer a forlorn child, Becca had grown into a beautiful, refined, compassionate, young woman, one who should be happy now that she was a woman kept by one of Denver's finest gentlemen. Looking at Becca, Jenny could tell she wasn't happy. It broke Jenny's heart that she wasn't, and she guessed the reason.

"Read it, please." Becca sat stone-cold still on the settee in the Palace's fine front parlor.

Jenny unfolded the paper, reluctantly reading Becca's near-perfect penmanship:

> *I, Rebecca Rose, currently of the Windsor Hotel on Eighteenth and Larimer Streets, being of sound mind and body, request that in the event of my death, my body be buried in potter's field in Nevada City, alongside my beloved mother. I have put money aside for this purpose, which I am giving to Miss Jenny Clayton of the Palace, the finest parlor house in Denver.*
>
> *I would like to leave any worldly goods and any monies I have to Pastor Noah at the poorhouse on Blake Street.*
>
> *I sign this willingly in the presence of Miss Jenny Clayton, my most trusted confidante, herein on this date, July 15, 1880.*
>
> *Jenny Clayton* _____
> *Rebecca Rose* _____

CHAPTER FIFTEEN

"Miss Jenny, don't!" Becca snatched her will from the madam's hands, seeing she was about to rip the paper in half. She smoothed out the document, making sure it was intact. Becca had hoped things wouldn't go like this although she'd known better.

"Becca." Jenny swallowed hard, fighting for composure. The lump in her throat hurt clear down to her heart. She couldn't imagine Becca in some pine box in potter's field. She couldn't imagine Becca dead. Bright, beautiful, blessed Becca. Her daughter—her parlor house daughter—should have a long life, much longer than most on the line. "What's the reason for this?" Jenny said, her anger obvious.

Becca needed to take care with her words. She needed Miss Jenny to accept her last will and testament, and she needed Miss Jenny to understand. But she didn't need Miss Jenny going to the law and trying to stop her. She guessed that was precisely what she would do, being so well-connected to so many higher-ups in the police department in Denver, not to mention legislators. For her part, Becca had no faith that any lawman would help a prostitute, not really help. No, she didn't want Miss Jenny to stop her. Dear, dear Miss Jenny. She owed the kind, generous madam a lot, but not the whole truth. Becca couldn't risk it. She'd chosen the path she must take long ago, and there was no turning back now.

"The paper is just what it says: my last will and testament,"

The Parlor House Daughter

Becca put forward her explanation. "In our business, I thought it right to get my things in order so I could be buried proper next to my mother in Nevada City. That's all, Miss Jenny, really."

"No, that's not all." Jenny didn't buy it. This had everything to do with her mother's murder and nothing to do with any early demise because of the sporting life. This child was going to go out and get herself killed, trying to kill her mother's murderer. The bastard must be close, Jenny figured. *Becca must have found him.* "Child." Jenny prayed Becca would listen. "I have friends in the police department, as you know."

Becca knew where this was going and tried not to listen. She wanted to put her hands over her ears to shut out Miss Jenny's voice, but made herself sit still.

"You've found your mother's killer, Becca. I know you have."

Becca heard Miss Jenny now, loud and clear.

"My friends can—"

"Stop, please, Miss Jenny!" More upset than she thought she'd be, Becca refused to listen to how the police would help a whore. "I don't believe the police would help me. I don't believe the police would *believe* me. I'm a whore, plain and simple. What lawman would believe a whore over . . . over—" She couldn't finish.

"Child, don't call yourself a whore," Jenny said soothingly.

"That's what we are, Miss Jenny. That's what my mother was and that's what I am." Becca started to cry, hating herself for it.

"I am a madam and you are a parlor house daughter. We are in the sporting life, yes, but we are not whores, and neither was your mother. Your beloved mother was a soiled dove, a legend in lace, a lady of the tenderloin, but not a whore, my sweet child," Jenny consoled, wiping away her own tears.

Becca listened to Miss Jenny now, and her words were like a balm on an open wound. "Thank . . . you," she sniffled. "Thank you, Miss Jenny." As much as she appreciated what the madam said, she still didn't believe the law would help a soiled dove, a legend in lace, or a lady of the tenderloin. Not really.

Jenny thought of Morgan Larkspur. Becca's affection for him might stop her from this dangerous path. "And what of Morgan Larkspur?" she asked straight out.

"What about him?" Becca's insides caved.

"Child, I know you care for him and I'm guessing he cares for you. The moment I met him, I could tell he was a fine gentleman with a good heart. I'm guessing he's already given you his. Have you done the same?"

"Yes," she said, owing Miss Jenny at least that much of the truth.

"Are you willing to give him up, and everything you might have with him, in order to be killed yourself hunting down your mother's killer?"

Miss Jenny's words stung like a swarm of bees, all at her, all at once.

Jenny could tell her words hurt, but she refused to hold back. Becca's life was too important. "*Are* you, Becca? Are you willing to put justice for your mother over your love for Morgan Larkspur?"

Sick inside, the coffee and biscuit she'd had this morning threatening to come up, Becca took a deep, cleansing breath, and then let it out. She needed to have a clear mind and body for the task ahead. Facing Miss Jenny's question as if it were a firing squad, she answered simply, "Yes."

"I won't hear this anymore." Jenny got up. "I can't sit here and let you do this. I can't stop you, but I don't have to bear witness!" she shot at Becca, too upset to hide her fear.

Becca got up, too. "Miss Jenny, please." She put her hand on the trembling madam's arm.

Jenny jerked her arm away, and then forced herself to calm down. "Child, is there anything . . . anything at all I can do or say to stop you? Anything?"

"Dear Miss Jenny, for dear you are to me . . . no." Becca looked her straight in the eye. She put her last will and testament back in Jenny's hands.

"Well then," Jenny muttered, accepting the will, every bit the mother now and not the madam. "I'll just go along. You just go along. I have to—" Jenny started to cry, hating herself for it. She turned away from Becca and hurried up the stairs, leaving her parlor house daughter alone to meet her maker.

Morgan stood outside Larkspur Mine Number Five, an uneasy feeling gnawing at his gut. Things were quiet—too quiet. He stared off in the distance at other mines lying fallow, wondering if any men still labored inside. If so, the conditions would be dangerous, even more dangerous than before the strike. The men would be working down in the deep shafts along dark cavernous drifts, trying to find a good footing, smashing their picks in the bedrock, wiping the sweat away so they could see through the salty sting in their eyes, praying the timber overhead would hold, thirsty as hell, tired and dirty and . . . alone.

If something happened—a slip of the foot, a cave-in, or an explosion—they'd be dead. Dead was forever. Dead meant they'd leave grieving widows with hungry children to feed. He thought of Rebecca and swallowed hard. Dead meant the end for a family that had come all the way up to Leadville, willing to endure one hardship after another to find steady work in the silver mines.

Pulling out his tobacco makings, Morgan rolled a cigarette. Once it was lit, he inhaled deeply, imagining the hardships of the miners. Yeah sure, he along with other mine owners had lost thousands of dollars every day the mines were not in operation, but they'd only money to lose, not their lives.

To Morgan, an ounce of silver wasn't worth a pound of flesh.

The miners had a decent gripe. He'd gone over all of this in his mind before and did so again. To him, working twelve-hour days, six days a week in precarious, unsafe, unhealthy conditions for three dollars a day constituted a decent gripe, all right. The strike was bound to come, especially with so many Celestials from the railroad being hired on now, willing to work for three dollars under the same conditions.

Damn. Morgan took another deep draw. All they needed now, on top of everything else, was for something—someone all caught up in hate and prejudice—to start a race riot over the Chinese presence in Leadville. In Denver, too. The Chinese population was on the rise, and not just in Hop Alley where the opium dens existed. Most immigrants came willing to work and work hard, much like the railroad laborers who wanted to work in the mines now. Men were the same, no matter where they came from, to Morgan's thinking. Most just wanted to lead a halfway decent life, work hard, make a decent wage, and provide for their families.

To be fair, giving credit where credit was due, Morgan didn't begrudge the mine owners—including himself—success in ore production and sales. It took hard work on everyone's part to keep operations running smoothly and keep the mines financially solvent. If not for the mine owners, there wouldn't be any jobs for the thousands living in Leadville now. Morgan did feel a responsibility, however, as a mine owner. He had a responsibility to the miners to help provide safe working conditions and pay a fair wage. He threw down his cigarette butt and stomped it out, the tobacco taste suddenly bitter in his mouth.

Things were quiet—too quiet.

Help would come soon, from the governor. Tabor's Militia would likely back off if the state militia arrived to help calm things down and bring everyone to the negotiating table. The union and the mine owners needed to hold a conference, but how to get everyone to the table without guns drawn was the problem. Morgan hoped the state militia would arrive soon, as promised, before it was too late. No one needed to die over this strike, spilling his life's blood over even one ounce of silver.

Starting back down Carbonate Hill into Leadville, he thought again of Rebecca. Beautiful, soft, loving, lovely Rebecca. Friday was only a day away. He'd hear her voice soon and life would be good—perfect—for those few moments with her.

Laying her head against the silky cotton of her pillow, Becca hoped she'd rest easier tonight, knowing she'd set things in order with Miss Jenny. All she had left to do was to set things straight with Morgan. Morgan. She shut her eyes tight as she could, willing herself to dream of the time she'd had with him, and not of the time she'd never have.

They'd talked again on the telephone this past Friday evening. He was all right. For now he was all right. Becca tried to stay focused on his safety and not the fact that she needed to see him, to touch him, and feel his strong arms around her just once more . . . one more time before—

The silken pillow scratched against her skin. She flopped over on her back, eyes wide open now, staring blankly at the plastered ceiling overhead. Able to make out little in the darkened room, she shut her eyes against the hard reality of her life.

She'd skipped two weeks of going to the cathedral to track her mother's killer and felt every bit the coward as she tried to buy time until she could see Morgan again. One more time. Of course she *could* choose another path and run away to another town, another city, away from the dangers awaiting her in Denver. Easy enough to do, she thought, finding work along the line somewhere else. Not so easy to run away from her responsibility to her murdered mother. And not so easy to leave Morgan and the promise of what she might have had with him.

But then, she couldn't expect him to keep her as his mistress forever, much less ever marry her. He'd marry someone respectable, someone from a good family, someone to give him children and a good home. Someone else.

Becca rolled over onto her stomach, trying to make the pain hitting hard there go away. Her chest hurt, too. It hurt; it all hurt. Her life hurt.

Oh Morgan, I love you. I love you so much.

It was all her fault and she knew it. She'd let herself have feelings for a customer. *Feelings only get a whore killed.* One way or another, the saying she'd heard as far back as she could remember was true, painfully true. Likely her mother was murdered because of feelings for a customer, letting the monster in, letting him too close. Because of her own feelings for Morgan, Becca was already dying another kind of death. Fanny had always said it: *Lots of ways for a whore to die.*

Easing over onto her back again, Becca forced herself to think only on Morgan's words now, going over every word of their last telephone conversation. Only he could soothe her to sleep tonight, if any sleep would come.

"Miss Eagleton," the hotel manager reminded her a second time. "At the Windsor we do not give out information regarding the names and room numbers of our guests. It's policy, miss." Of course, it wasn't official policy, but he thought it best, given this unpleasant circumstance.

Lavinia couldn't believe this! How ridiculous! "I have the woman's name," she barked at the manager. "It's Rebecca Rose," she repeated for a third time.

"Excuse me, miss." The unmoved manager motioned for the gentleman standing behind Lavinia to come forward. He knew very well who Rebecca Rose was: Morgan Larkspur's mistress ensconced here at the Windsor in room number eight on the second floor.

"Oh, no, you don't." Lavinia shooed the man in back of her away, as if he were a bothersome fly.

The elderly, well-suited gentleman backed away, obviously giving the irate young woman in front of him a wide berth.

"Miss Eagleton," the manager scolded. "Our business is over. If you please, there are others now that need my attention."

"I do *not* please, sir. Not until you tell me the room number of Rebecca Rose. Do you know who I am?" She put her question to the manager, indignant at his despicable treatment of her.

The seasoned manager heaved a sigh. "Yes, you are Lavinia Eagleton. I'm familiar with your family name."

"Well then," she said, brightening. "There you have it. Why, next week I'm having my wedding reception here. You know, of course, I'm marrying Morgan Larkspur of *the* Larkspurs. It's *the* event of the season. Now you can tell me the room number of Rebecca Rose."

"No, Miss Eagleton. I cannot." He looked her straight in the eye.

Flushed from head to foot with embarrassment, angry as a hornet, Lavinia hoped no one overheard the manager's impudence. He was treating her abominably. If the invitations hadn't gone out weeks ago, she'd cancel her reception at the Windsor right now! "Sir," she said, trying a new tack, her tone dripping with disrespect. "Perhaps you will reconsider when I tell you I'm here representing the Ladies Aid Society. I'm here on important business," she told him, sure now he'd see things her way, her being involved with such a noted charity in Denver.

"Miss, I don't care if you're here representing Governor Pitkin himself. Our business is done. Now please step away from the desk," he ordered, unhappy with the scene she was creating at the Windsor, and unhappy that some of the rich folks in

Denver didn't have as much refinement as others.

The Windsor had standards. The Windsor kept things private. Morgan Larkspur wasn't the first prestigious gentleman to keep secrets at the Windsor, and he wouldn't be the last. The discerning manager thought of beautiful, dignified Rebecca Rose, the mistress in question upstairs. She was, most definitely, in a class above Miss Eagleton. Morgan Larkspur was one lucky man to have such a fine young woman as Rebecca Rose for mistress, but he was one unlucky man for taking such a shrew as Lavinia Eagleton for a wife.

"Next," he directed to the gentleman still in line, with only a cold stare left for Miss Eagleton.

Furious, Lavinia turned on her heel so fast she bumped into the elderly man behind her, nearly knocking him down. Barely noticing what she'd done, and barely aware of the stares from curious onlookers, she huffed across the reception area and plopped down—most unladylike—in the seating area by the bell desk. Of all the nerve! Such impudence on the part of the hotel manager! Her parents would hear about it. Morgan would hear about it. She'd never been treated so rudely in the whole of her life!

For that matter, Pastor Noah at the poorhouse had been rude to her, too. He should have told her more about Rebecca Rose. He'd been almost as impudent to her as the despicable hotel manager. Humph! She had to find the woman who'd made such a large contribution to the poorhouse, usurping her power and her position in the Ladies Aid Society. The longer Lavinia sat in the bustling reception area, the madder she got. She didn't like losing, to anyone or anything. She needed an idea, and fast.

"Help you, miss?" a young man addressed.

Lavinia guessed him to be a bellman, given his uniform and their proximity to the bell desk. Suddenly an idea struck her. "Yes." She stood and faced the young man with her warmest, most cajoling smile. There was more than one way to solve her problem.

"Do you have bags for me to carry, miss?" he asked.

"No, no bags. I'm not a guest here, but I'm so forlorn that I can't find my friend. She's a guest here and I just forgot her room number. Silly of me, isn't it?" She feigned upset, all the while keeping her eyes on the young man, needing to persuade him to help her.

"Well, just go over to—"

"The front desk?" she interrupted him. "Well I would, but I'm that embarrassed." She batted her baby blues at him, purposely setting him off guard with flattery.

The boy flushed.

Good, she thought. *Good.* "I suppose you see guests come and go all day long. I suppose you know just about everyone who stays here at the Windsor," she continued with her flattery.

"Why . . . uh . . . yes, I guess so." He grinned sheepishly.

"Rebecca Rose," she shot at him. "Do you know her room number?"

"Uh . . . I don't know that name," his face turned crimson, embarrassed that he didn't.

Caught off guard herself now, Lavinia reasoned that the woman in question must be staying at the Windsor under a different name. This puzzle was getting worse . . . and more intriguing.

"What does she look like?" the bellman asked, obviously wanting to be helpful in some way.

"Well . . ." Lavinia stalled for time. "Actually . . . you're more likely to know her as the woman who leaves here and goes directly to the poorhouse on Blake Street most every day. She's involved in charity work, just like me," Lavinia gushed ingenuously. She needed to keep the boy from asking her again what Rebecca Rose looked like.

The bellman's brow furrowed, as he apparently tried to think of the woman. There was only one young woman that came and went by herself most days: Mrs. Morgan Larkspur. Excited that he might have an answer for the beautiful blonde in distress in front of him, ever eager to help where he could at the Windsor, he gulped out his information. "Is your friend Mrs. Morgan Larkspur? She comes and goes most days by herself. I don't know where exactly, but she's very nice. Is *she* Rebecca Rose?"

"Yes," Lavinia said, her voice turned to stone. "Yes, she's the one. Her room number—what is it?"

"It's number eight on the second floor," the bellman said before he thought better of it. The unnatural look on the face of the beautiful blonde in distress in front of him scared him a little. He backed away, sorry he'd stopped to help her. When would he learn to keep his mouth shut and stay out of hotel business, other than delivering bags to rooms?

"Sally, how come yer goin'? I don't understand."

"I can't explain, Justine. I can't." The buxom, plump prostitute bent down to pick up the last of her things and shoved them into her small, dilapidated trunk. She needed to be on the afternoon train to Wichita. She needed to be somewhere safe, out of Denver and out of danger.

"Why, Sally? You only just got here a month ago from up Cheyenne way. I thought you was gonna stay here in Denver, liking it so much more than other places you've been." Justine kept on with her attempt to get Sally to stay. She didn't have many friends at the end of the line where they both lived. She'd liked Sally from the start and didn't want her to go. Things wasn't so lonely with Sally around.

Sally stopped what she was doing and turned to her new friend. "Listen, Justine. I have to go. I can't tell you why, but I can tell you I'm too scared to stay. There." She turned back to her trunk, worrying that she'd already said too much.

"Whattcha scared about?" The skinny, small-breasted prostitute was suddenly scared herself. "You gotta tell me, Sally. You gotta!"

Ah hell, Sally thought. She *had* said too much. She'd better not miss her train out of town. If he found out—the monster with the missing fingers and gold lion-head ring—he'd kill her. She knew he would. He'd told her not to say nothing, and here she'd said something to simpleminded Justine, putting Justine in danger now. God, she didn't want the girl to die 'cause of her! If she thought Justine would understand and not go off half-cocked in fear and talk to other whores, she'd tell her the whole truth. She'd tell Justine every detail about the evil monster she'd mistakenly let come in last night, who made her beg for her life more than once during his paid-for time with her. No matter how rich any john was, he wasn't worth dying over.

Sally had never been so scared turning a trick in all her years in prostitution. Nearly twenty-five, she'd been at it over ten years, mostly in mining towns but in some cities, too. Cities just like Denver. But in all that time she'd never lain with a john who'd scared her so bad with his knife at her throat, her breasts, and lower, the whole time he had his painful member inside her. He was sick. He should be in some insane asylum, not walking Denver streets playing upon unsuspecting whores like her. Goddammit! He'd threatened to cut out her womb if she didn't lie still and beg . . . beg for more sex and beg for her life. Never so humiliated with any trick before, she'd hit rock bottom with this one. One good thing came from her night with him: she was still alive. But she wouldn't be for long if she didn't leave Denver. He'd said he'd be back tonight. She couldn't imagine lying with him, enduring that kind of fear again. No, she couldn't imagine it.

"I'm not stupid, Sally," Justine broke into her dark thoughts.

"I didn't say you was." Sally finished getting her few things together.

"Well yer sure treatin' me like I am. Yer not tellin' me what or who is chasin' you out of town." Justine folded her thin arms in front of her, leveling her stare at Sally.

"All right." Sally didn't have much time. The noon train would be here soon. She had to get to Union Station, and quick. First . . . first she had to take a chance on the hope that Justine would keep silent about what she was gonna tell her. If Justine didn't, she'd end up dead. As for the others on the line . . . well, Sally didn't know them. They were on their own as far as she was concerned. "Listen, Justine, I'm going to warn you about a man, but you gotta keep your mouth shut about him to others or you could get killed. This man is a mean, evil man and he'll kill you for sure if he finds out you said something. All right? You understand?" she asked Justine, pitying the poor girl. Funny, usually Sally didn't have feelings for nobody, not no john, not no other whores. But Justine was different; she'd been nice and friendly to Sally when most of the other whores had not.

"Yes, Sally. All right." Justine tried to hold her ground, scared to death herself about what her friend was gonna say.

"Listen real careful-like 'cause this is real important. We all have rooms in these here apartments and there's no way to see who it is knocking on our door. That's the first thing, Justine. Keep your door locked. Don't leave it unlocked like you usually do. You got that?" Sally stared hard at Justine, to make sure she understood.

"Yeah, I got it," the frightened girl repeated.

"Good. Now, for the next couple of days, be sick or something. Don't take no johns. Here." Sally pulled out a five-dollar bill. "It ain't much, but it will keep you going for a couple of days."

Her eyes wide in fear, Justine took the money. "Thanks, Sally. I know it's hard—"

"Shush. Don't thank me for nothing. Do you have any money?"

"Some. I got two dollars in my trunk, I think." Justine spoke low and quiet, as if she didn't want anyone to overhear.

"Well, good then." Sally brightened a little, for Justine's benefit. "So remember what I said and don't open your door for no john for a couple of days. Then, when you do, just crack it open a little, enough to see who it is. If it's a tall, older man, dressed all gentleman-like, say you're sorry but you've got the syphilis and you don't want him getting burned 'cause of you. You know we don't get many rich-looking men here at our end, so that's your first clue to steer clear. If you happen to see his hand . . . if you happen to see his hand with two missing fingers and a gold lion-head ring, tell him straight out that you have open sores that are bleeding and all. That should get rid of him. It should, honey." Sally tried to reassure her scared little friend when she knew there really weren't any guarantees that the monster wouldn't go ahead and kill Justine for the hell of it.

Justine's knees wanted to give way. Frightened to death now, she grabbed hold of Sally's ample arms for support. "Sally, Sally, let me come with you! Please! Please!"

Sally couldn't say no to the poor wretch. "Hurry then, and get packed. You've got five minutes and that's all if you expect to make the noon train with me."

Tears welled in Justine's tired, vacant eyes. "Thank you," she whispered. "I'll be right back." She hurried out of Sally's apartment to her own. Packing everything she owned in the world wouldn't take the whole five minutes.

Chapter Sixteen

The hot summer day suddenly turned dark and chill. Becca pulled up the embroidered shade to let in more light. The gray afternoon matched her mood. The thunder outside signaled the coming storm, with lightning striking off in the distance. Becca stared at the beginning rain that was already turning the smooth street below into rows of muddy ruts. It suddenly struck her that once begun, this rain would not quit, but would pour down on her, not content until she'd been sucked into the mud below, buried deep and forgotten, like so much dust. Quick as she could, she pulled the shade down to the sill, and abruptly left the window.

What was the matter with her? Usually she loved thunderstorms. The rain made everything fresh and brand new again. When outdoors, she loved the feel of rain on her face, breathing deep of the clean, earthy fragrance. When indoors, the rhapsody of raindrops on the roof or against the window regularly lulled her into daydreams and easy sleep. Why, then, did she feel so uneasy now, unable to lie down for a nap, with no desire to go out in the welcome rain?

Someone knocked on her door. The loud knock grated down her spine. At once the storm outside pushed through the Windsor's gray and sandstone walls, coming inside, invading her privacy. Whoever it was, she didn't think it was someone she wanted to see. Despite the gnawing uneasiness in her stomach, she took deliberate steps across the room and opened the door.

"You!" Lavinia spat out, shocked to discover the identity of Rebecca Rose, the woman pretending to be Mrs. Morgan Larkspur.

Lavinia. Becca remembered her name. Shocked to find the unfriendly, unkind blonde she'd seen at Saint John's cathedral at her door, Becca's first instinct was to shut the door against this unwanted visitor. Before she had the chance to do just that, Lavinia charged inside.

"You . . . you whore! You liar! You criminal!" Lavinia had trouble getting out her accusations, she had so many of them. "How dare you . . . what are you doing here . . . at this expensive hotel? You whore! You imposter!" She continued with her rant, pouring words down on Becca much like the deluge outside.

Becca had no idea what Lavinia meant, nor did she care. She'd not shut the door yet, leaving it open for the unpleasant, apparently light-in-the-head woman to leave.

"What do you have to say for yourself?" Lavinia hadn't finished with her tirade. "I can't believe you have the nerve to stay here at such a fine hotel, in such a fine room. You can't possibly afford something like this. How many men are you sleeping with to pay for all of this, you whore? You imposter!"

"You may leave the way you came," Becca calmly announced, pulling the door open wider. She'd no idea why Lavinia had come, but no matter. Who she was and what she did was none of the so-called respectable woman's business.

Lavinia's nostrils flared. Her breaths came quick. She'd never been so angry. Her jaw clenched tight, but not enough to silence her. "*I'm* not leaving here," she spat out. "*You* are!"

Oh for pity's sake! Becca was getting a little mad now herself.

Lavinia fumed on. "I bet you earned all the money you gave to the poor house on your back! If Pastor Noah knew of your . . . your *profession,* he'd throw the money in your face! If you're not gone from here in the next hour, I'm calling the authorities to throw you out!"

All right. That was enough. "As I said, you may leave the way you came. *Now.*" Becca tried to keep her voice steady and her anger in check. The mention of Pastor Noah upset her. What did anything at the poorhouse have to do with Lavinia? Curious, she still didn't want to start up any conversation that might delay the unpleasant woman from leaving.

"How dare you tell *me* to leave? How dare you pose as Mrs. Morgan Larkspur?" Lavinia's tone turned icy.

Becca froze at the mention of Morgan's name. Surely she'd heard wrong. Surely.

"Hah! That's got you!" Lavinia gloated, seeing Becca's obvious upset.

Everything around Becca seemed to slow down. She closed the door, then brushed past Lavinia and managed to find a seat at the writing desk by the window. She caught the shade pull and raised the shade to look outside at the afternoon storm. She had to have heard this shrew wrong. She *had* to. Although it was difficult to address Lavinia with any kind of proper attention or respect, she must.

"Why did you say that? That I was posing as Mrs. Morgan Larkspur?"

"The bellman said as much," Lavinia hissed.

Ah, the bellman. That's right. Becca remembered. Morgan never bothered to correct the helpful, good-hearted young man. But then why . . . why did the bellman's mistake in thinking she was Morgan's wife . . . why did it upset this wretched woman?

Lavinia came closer, nearly breathing down Becca's neck like a predator going in for the kill. "Since *I* will become Mrs. Morgan Larkspur next week, you can understand my upset that you're using his good name to stay here at the prestigious Windsor, so you can take money from rich men, turning tricks," she rasped out, her voice intimidating, even cruel.

A clap of thunder outside made Becca shoot up from her seat. She needed to run away from the frightening noise, away from this horrible woman, away from this horrible news, away from her whole life, away from the storm that had at long last come to stay, the storm that would bury her outside in the mud, waiting to turn her into so much forgotten dust. But she'd nowhere to turn now, no place to go to get away from Lavinia— the future Mrs. Morgan Larkspur. The air in the room hung so thick now, Becca fought for every breath. *Feelings only get a whore killed.* She was dying inside; killed by the news that Morgan would marry . . . someone else.

How ridiculous for her to be upset! How ridiculous for her to think herself special. How ridiculous for her to believe Morgan loved her, really loved her. But then, of course he loved her—he no doubt loved *all* of the parlor house daughters he bedded. That he already had a fiancée shouldn't have surprised her. She couldn't blame him for not telling her. She'd never asked him, not once. Nor could she blame Lavinia. No, she'd only herself to blame—a parlor house daughter fancying herself to be something she'd never be: a respectable wife and mother, married to the man of her dreams. Morgan was going to marry the woman of his dreams. And it wasn't her.

What difference did all of this make anyway? None. Absolutely none. Her time was short. The moment she found her mother's killer, the sands would overturn for her. So what if she went to her grave without Morgan Larkspur's love and promise of marriage?

Only now did she notice Lavinia, still in the room. Never in her life had she envied anyone. And now, to envy this dark-hearted, mean-spirited, so-called "respectable society lady," who she'd never single out for a friend, broke her spirit and her confidence. Ashamed of herself, she needed to be alone. She couldn't stand being in the same room with Morgan's future wife. It hurt too much.

"Please leave," Becca said, her voice barely above a whisper.

Lavinia stepped closer, her sharp words cutting. "Not until you tell me why you picked my fiancé's name to drag through the mud, pretending to be married to him."

"I didn't pick his—" Becca stopped herself, too late.

"Then why? What?" Now it was Lavinia's turn to back away, if only a little.

Oh my God! It all made sense now. Rebecca Rose posing as Morgan's wife. She was his mistress!

Mortified, Lavinia took a few more steps away. She realized now why Morgan never touched her. He was too busy touching his mistress. Probably the whole city knew by now! Oh she could kill Morgan. She was determined to get revenge for her embarrassment . . . after they married.

Lavinia tried to calm down. It was common practice for men to have mistresses. William Byers of the *Rocky Mountain News* had one, and so did other notables like Horace Tabor. Their worlds didn't come tumbling down because of their dalliances. *Mine won't either,* Lavinia decided. Once this riffraff in front of her was gone from the Windsor, Lavinia would have Morgan all to herself again. He'd rue the day he'd ever made her jealous of some two-bit whore!

"By week's end, you'd best be gone if you know what's good for you," Lavinia growled.

"Is that a threat?" Becca still had a spark of anger in her.

"Yes," Lavinia said.

The two women had nothing left to say to each other.

Becca gave Morgan's fiancée her back.

Lavinia charged over to the door, opened it, and slammed it shut behind her.

"Great news, great news." Morgan congratulated Major General

Cook of the state militia for his success in getting Tabor's Light Cavalry to back off long enough for the miners and mine owners to agree to come to the conference table. The strike had lasted almost three weeks, and it was high-time things got settled without any more violence. This afternoon the union representatives and the mine owners would gather, Morgan included, and sit down for talks.

For his part, Morgan was more than willing to negotiate fairly. He'd do his best to convince the other mine owners to see their way clear to giving in to some of the union demands. The parties, with luck, would meet each other half way. *Damn,* Morgan hoped so.

The sooner the strike ended, the sooner he could hold his darlin' Rebecca in his arms again.

"Monty," Augusta Larkspur pressed her son for answers. "Where have you been? You were gone most of yesterday and here it's almost noon, and you're just coming downstairs. Were you out all night carousing with your friends? I needed a ride yesterday morning to my Ladies Aid Society meeting and you were not here to take me. Why, it's as if you're trying to avoid your father and me. Most unlike you, Monty." Augusta shook her head in disapproval.

Past his moment of satisfaction at the news of Spur's mistress—at how his parents would at last have a little dirt to dust off the family's fine, scandal-free name—Monty was more concerned now about the consequences waiting at home for Spur, when his parents found out about Rebecca Rose.

His mother had hit the nail on the head, all right, when she'd wondered if he'd been trying to avoid them. But Monty wasn't about to admit anything to his mother. News of Spur's mistress might make it home and was a topic of conversation Monty didn't want to have with either of his parents, especially his mother. Worse than his father's upset, his mother would be at his big brother like a ravenous bear looking for its first meal after hibernation, not leaving Spur alone until he gave up his beautiful Rebecca Rose and then gave his mother his promise that he wouldn't carry on with another mistress or frequent any more parlor houses. Monty wasn't sure if Spur would heed either of his parents and actually give up his mistress, but he didn't wish his mother's fury on anyone, least of all his brother. No, it wasn't going to be pleasant around here when Spur got home.

Dammit, what about Lavinia? Monty only just thought of her finding out. The wedding was next week, for God's sake!

Aw, hell. What about that nosy reporter, Polly Pry? Dammit, what if everything's in the *Rocky Mountain News,* out there for all to read? Spur would never hear the end of it, and maybe he wouldn't get to be in the legislature or become governor as his parents wanted. Monty settled down a little, realizing that Spur had no desire to hold any political office. They'd never discussed it, but still, Monty knew his brother, far better than his parents, he thought.

"Monty!" Augusta raised her voice. "Are you listening to me?"

Monty slouched down is his seat at the dining table. "Of course, Mother." He faked a yawn, trying to sound lighthearted. He didn't exactly feel light of heart, but he realized his mother didn't know anything about Rebecca Rose—yet. She'd be on a tear already, if she did.

"Well, then?" she demanded.

"You guessed it, Mother. I've been out with my friends carousing all night in celebration of the big wedding next week," he said, giving her his best smile.

"Humph." She touched her napkin to her mouth, and then replaced the expensive linen in her lap. "I have an afternoon appointment at Joslin's Dry Goods to meet Lavinia and her mother for the last wedding gown fitting. I need you to drive me, Monty. You'd do well to spend your time in something meaningful today, rather than celebrate with your friends. Enough time for that next week," she said dismissively, then picked up the dinner bell and rang for the maid.

"Yes, Mother," Monty agreed, as if he'd not a care in the world.

Becca found herself walking now, up Fourteenth Street and Governor's Row. She'd meant to go in another direction on Holladay Street, past Fourteenth Street toward Twenty-Third, past addresses down the line, not up it. She didn't belong in this ritzy section of Denver. Not anymore. Not since she'd found out Morgan would have a wife. Next week. No matter that she, Rebecca Rose, was from the fanciest parlor house in Denver, living now at the fanciest hotel in Denver. It didn't change the fact that she was a whore—a prostitute—and nothing more. She definitely was nothing more than that to Morgan.

She'd never been ashamed of her profession, and she wasn't now. It's just that . . . just that . . . she knew now for certain, that Morgan *was*. It wasn't his fault that he couldn't consider a prostitute for wife. He was Morgan Larkspur, an important man from an important family. She was Rebecca Rose, an unimportant woman from an unimportant family. The equation was a simple one. She just didn't measure up.

She'd tried to hate Morgan. For two days she'd tried . . . and failed.

She loved Morgan, no matter their circumstances.

He had her heart, and she'd never get it back.

The hot Thursday afternoon bore down on Becca like a blanket of stinging ants, all biting at once. She'd nowhere to go to escape her upset. Oh, how she wished Sunday would come early. The thought of just that made her turn around and start back down the hill toward the Windsor. Everything needed to be in order come Sunday: her gun loaded, her spare bullets close by, and her trunk packed and ready to go. Since she'd already given Miss Jenny her last will and testament, there was little else to do. Becca stopped short. There was one more thing she had to do. She'd rather the stinging red ants keep at her than this.

Setting her hat straight, retying the bow at her neck, Becca took unsteady steps toward the hotel. She needed to leave a note for Morgan. She'd already decided that she wouldn't call him Friday night. He'd wonder about her not calling, but really, she didn't think he'd worry about it. The strike continued, so she didn't think he'd return to Denver anytime soon. God, she hoped he'd be all right. As for what to say and how to say it in any note she'd leave for him at the Windsor, she couldn't imagine. How do you tell someone you love that you're going to stalk and kill your mother's murderer come Sunday, if you're lucky, and that you'll either be dead or in jail come sundown?

Becca knew the answer. You don't.

Writing her last will and testament had been easier than this—much, much easier. Becca picked up her step, hoping to think of something she could say to Morgan, something that wouldn't hurt him or leave him upset with her. He knew she loved him. She didn't need to say that again and didn't think she could. She knew one thing for certain in this tragedy: she knew that Morgan would have nothing to do with her after Sunday, if she were still alive.

More than once in the last few days, her mother's love had washed through her, warning her, making Becca believe that *this* Sunday was *the* Sunday of her reckoning. After Sunday, nothing much would matter. Not even Morgan.

Fanny's prophetic words resounded in her head, ringing true:

Feelings only get a whore killed.

"That's it, then." Morgan got up from his seat at the conference table, satisfied that the miners got a shorter work day out of the meeting, if little else. It was a beginning—to work eight hours a day instead of twelve—and the union, thank God, agreed. Morgan thought the workers' wages should be raised to five dollars a day, but the other mine owners wouldn't hear of it. While no decisions were made about better health and working conditions, the issues were out there being discussed. That was something, at least. Besides, the strike was over, and the threat of violence ended—for the present, in any case.

Best of all, he could head down to Denver. To Rebecca. It was Thursday afternoon now and he had more business to take care of before he could leave. The earliest he could get out of Leadville was on tomorrow's train. Excited to see Rebecca, he had some very important things to discuss with her.

His whole life had changed in the past weeks. Maybe it was the strike; maybe it was the danger the strike presented; maybe it was that he'd fallen in love, really in love, for the first time in his life; or maybe he'd just finally grown up. Whatever the reason, he'd changed. He was no longer able to consider marriage to a woman he didn't love, despite his parents' certain objection to his change of heart. He wanted to marry the woman he *did* love, and whisk her away to the ranch he'd always dreamed of owning.

Before finishing up his remaining business, Morgan headed straight for the telegraph office. First things first. He needed to telegraph his father and signal that they needed to talk. He'd wait until they were face-to-face to tell him that his marriage plans had changed. It was the least he could do. His father had stood by him his whole life. He owed his father a lot. They'd talk in detail, along with his mother and Monty, when he got back to Denver . . . *after* he'd seen Rebecca and proposed. He'd deal with Lavinia when everything else had been settled and discussed with his family and with Rebecca. Frankly, other than fulfilling her social obligations by marrying well, he couldn't imagine that Lavinia would be too upset. There were other eligible, well-bred, wealthy bachelors in Denver. She'd have little trouble finding a new one to marry.

Too excited even to stop and light a needed smoke, Morgan kept on toward the telegraph office. The streets were alive with celebrating miners, obviously happy the strike had ended. Their euphoric mood matched his, but for very different reasons.

Three o'clock. Eugene Larkspur was finishing up early at his banking office, happy to hear the strike was over in Leadville. He'd never worried over Morgan's safety. His oldest son always took good care of himself.

My son, the future Governor of Colorado, he thought. In his day, he, Eugene, could have run for office and believed he would have won. Still good-looking, with his full head of salt-and-pepper hair, still in fine form, his body lean and fit, and still on top of his game in finance and Denver society, Eugene could run still. But he'd decided long ago that Morgan would be the first Larkspur to win office, starting small then going bigger. Yes, it was all up to his oldest son.

Proud of Morgan and looking forward to seeing him return home from Leadville, Eugene felt like celebrating. It wasn't too early to start, what with Morgan's wedding to Lavinia next week. A good brandy and Cuban cigar at the Denver Club seemed called for, with all the good news. Dinner would be late tonight, as their guests were not due to arrive until eight. Augusta wouldn't be expecting him home before seven; there would be plenty of time then to change for their dinner party.

"Come in," Eugene called out to his secretary, glad she always remembered to knock. He never liked surprises, even from his loyal secretary.

The ever-efficient, middle-aged spinster, Miss Middleton, opened the glass-paned office door and quietly came inside. She nodded curtly, then handed her long-time employer the telegram from Western Union that had just come for him. "From Morgan, sir," she informed him, then abruptly turned and left.

"Thank you," he called to his secretary's back, only remembering to do so right before she closed the door. Uneasy about why Morgan would need to telegraph him, he quickly opened the folded message and read it:

> *Good news, father.*
> *Strike over.*
> *Coming home tomorrow.*
> *Have more good news.*
> *Very important that we talk.*
>
> *Morgan*

Eugene relaxed. Nothing out of the ordinary here. The strike was over and Morgan was coming home. "More good news" could mean just about anything. Whatever it was, if Morgan said it was good news, then Eugene was certain it was something good for the whole Larkspur family. Could be Morgan talked another mine owner out of his holdings and bought 'im out. His son sure was a go-getter. Eugene was proud of Morgan, more so than of Monty. He wasn't being fair to Monty, and he knew it. But Augusta had taken over raising Monty from the start. No matter. Eugene always got on better with Morgan anyway, because Morgan always stood up to him. Monty never did. Monty wasn't strong like Morgan; maybe that was why he'd let Augusta have free rein over their second son.

Eugene set the telegram down on his desk and rubbed his

eyes. More tired this afternoon than usual, he looked forward to relaxing at the club before going home. The club always did him good. Sometimes he'd even nap before going home.

Lately he had trouble sleeping. He couldn't fathom why. He wasn't really worried about Morgan's welfare in Leadville, and the burgeoning family finances were in good order. There was no danger, as far as he knew, of anyone or anything threatening the good Larkspur name. He should rest easier than he had been lately.

In a hurry now to get to the Denver Club, he pulled on his suit jacket and headed out of his office. His driver was just downstairs. He'd have that brandy and cigar in hand in fifteen minutes' time.

"There's a good man, Nelson," Eugene said, readily accepting his brandy snifter from the waiter's silver tray. He took a sip, and then set the brandy down on the stand next to him. Puffing once more on his cigar, he settled against the cushioned leather of his overstuffed wingback chair. The Denver Club was all about comfort, and Eugene felt at home there, finally able to relax after a hard day or night. He closed his eyes a moment, to better relax.

Conversation drifted across the high-ceilinged, smoke-filled room. At first Eugene paid little attention, but when he heard his son's name mentioned, he opened his eyes and strained to hear every word.

"Monty's even seen her now," one of the young men said.

"Morgan's mistress is sure a looker," another chimed in.

"Yeah, but wait until the old man finds out. He'll tan Morgan's hide for this one."

"I'd like to see that," another said, and laughed.

Eugene swallowed hard and tamped out his cigar in the ashtray by his brandy. His fingers shook. *Goddammit! Goddam-*

mit! Craning his neck, he listened to the group of men across the room, needing to hear more.

"Where did Monty see her?"

"Right in the main dining room of the Windsor. Right there in plain sight of all of us."

"Is she pretty?"

"Are you kidding? She's a beauty."

"Morgan wouldn't have it any other way, the lucky bastard. What did you say her name was?"

"Rebecca Rose, I think."

"Pretty name, too. Say, don't worry about what Morgan's old man will think. Worry about what his fiancée will think when *she* finds out!"

The whole group of young men laughed.

Eugene didn't.

"So Rebecca Rose is living at the Windsor. What, in a suite or something?"

"Yeah, I think on the second floor. Room number eight. Yeah. Room number eight."

Eugene didn't listen anymore. He got up, unbeknownst to the group across the room, and called for his carriage.

CHAPTER SEVENTEEN

Other than her morning coffee, Becca had taken in little sustenance. It was not quite four o'clock, yet she still wasn't hungry. At five, she'd go to the dining room and try to put something in her stomach. She'd be no good come Sunday if she didn't have any strength in her.

Someone knocked.

Her heart went to the floor. It could be that hateful Lavinia again. If so, she'd enjoy slamming the door in her face this time. Becca hurried to answer the knock. But she hesitated just before opening it. An eerie feeling of darkness at once settled over her, stopping her. Warning her.

A little afraid, on her guard now, she almost turned around to get her pistol . . . almost. Instead, as if something evil, something otherworldly, controlled her actions, she carefully turned the door handle and opened it. The moment she did, the moment she saw the familiar shape of the tall, foreboding man standing there, she recognized him, even though she'd never seen his face, and without needing to see his hand with the missing fingers and gold lion-head ring. She knew who it was. *Her mother's killer!* Suddenly she was four years old again, and all she could see was her mother's blood on him as he killed her mother still . . . over and over and over again.

Becca did nothing. She couldn't move, her mother's blood thick all around her. She tried to move. She tried to turn around and get her pistol from the bedstead so she could kill this monster at her door, but something held her to the spot, a prisoner already of the evil that was coming. Her heart pounded in her tight chest, each heavy thud burying her in the mud outside deeper and deeper. She felt dizzy, so dizzy she was scared she'd pass out before she could kill this demon and send him back to the flaming pits of hell where he came from.

Eugene Larkspur brushed past the frightened, admittedly lovely, young woman and entered her room, but not before shutting and locking the door behind him. He did this automatically, not even realizing what he'd done.

Becca didn't comprehend that he'd locked the door. She was barely aware he'd come inside the room. Still fighting to regain her wits, she tried to focus on her gun. Where was it, and was it loaded?

"I take it you're Rebecca Rose?" Eugene asked, more matter-of-fact than he felt. He'd make a quick business of this. No son of his would keep a mistress, no matter how lovely, at the esteemed Windsor. Eugene meant to pay her off and send her packing this very evening.

Becca didn't answer his question; she didn't even hear it.

"You are Rebecca Rose, are you not?" Eugene repeated, aware now of the young woman's fear of him. Well, good. She should be afraid, the little hussy. Still, his blood stirred a little at her fear.

Something made Becca stir into action, and she slowly pivoted and began walking over to her bedstead—and her gun.

"Rebecca Rose!" Eugene had had enough of this. This young woman was obviously touched, which was another reason to get rid of her. He wondered what Morgan saw in her. But then, of course, he knew. She was a classic beauty, a lot like . . . a lot like . . . *Ruby.*

Eugene's insides started to coil at the memory. It angered him, that this slip of a girl reminded him of Ruby.

Becca arrived at her bed. Without even looking to see where her mother's killer stood, numb inside, she pulled the drawer open and took her derringer in hand.

"Young woman, I'm talking to you!" Eugene raised his voice again, not bothering to hide his agitation. What was she doing, wandering over to the bed and not facing him?

Becca wheeled around and pointed her derringer straight at his chest. He stood only a few feet away from her now.

"What the—?" Taken aback, and all the more angry to have this two-bit whore point a gun at him, Eugene needed to talk her down. Goddammit! None of this was worth getting killed over! All of a sudden the idea of killing hit him in the chest almost as hard as the bullet he'd soon feel if he didn't handle this right. He thought again of Ruby. Goddamn if this girl didn't remind him of her. Ruby had just such a fearless look on her face when he slit her throat and killed her.

He was angry all over again that Ruby hadn't begged for her life. It was her fault, goddammit, that he was forced to kill her. All Ruby's fault. All her fault, too, that he'd had to be mean to all the whores he'd bedded after her, making them afraid. They had to beg for their life each time or else he'd be forced to kill them, too. All Ruby's fault that she didn't beg, the two-bit, no-good whore. All his other whores had to pay for what she did to him.

Eugene was losing his careful control. He could feel it draining from him, but could do nothing to stem its flow. Too late now. Too late. He'd thought of Ruby.

Angrier still, staring down the barrel of this slip of a girl's gun, he thought of Ruby's child—her brat—the brat he'd spared because he'd cared for Ruby. He'd cared so much for the mother that he didn't kill the child when he'd had the chance. Stupid, stupid, stupid! And now this girl—this child—*this brat . . .*

Well, I'll be goddamned. Now it was all starting to make sense to Eugene why Morgan's mistress pointed a gun at him, hungry to kill him, and why she looked so much like Ruby.

Well I'll be goddamned! Ruby's brat . . . after all this time . . . Ruby's brat.

Undaunted by the girl who pointed a gun at him, a changeling now from man to monster, Eugene laughed. Hard and out loud.

Becca wanted to cover her ears at the devil's thunderous cacophony, but she needed to keep her gun on him. Her hands shook. She could do this. She could. About to pull the trigger, likely signaling as much to the changeling in front of her, Becca took a deep breath, ready to mete out justice for her mother's senseless, brutal slaying.

"Oh, my dear girl." Eugene kept his taunt silky and deceptively smooth. "Now, you wouldn't go and kill *Morgan's father,* would you?"

"I'm going to kill you for murdering my mother and enjoy putting a second bullet in you for saying Morgan's name with your filthy mouth! You're no more Morgan's father than I am. You couldn't be!" She cocked her pistol.

The devil laughed at her again. "Oh, but I am, sweet Rebecca Rose. *I am* Morgan's father. You kill me and . . . well . . . he'll never look at you quite the same again, now will he?"

Dear God, it can't be true! But she was unsure now, and she hesitated to shoot. Her hesitation cost her plenty.

Easily wresting the gun from her, Eugene threw the weapon aside and grabbed hold of his prey, shoving her hard against the bedroom wall. His hands manacled her to the wall, making sure she couldn't escape. No whore ever did. Not until he was through with them. His blood sang, heady with power and knowledge of what was to come. He'd punish this whore, punish her good for what her mother did to him. He'd make the brat beg, where her mother didn't. This time he'd kill the brat!

This time he would!

Bordering on lunacy now, Eugene held on to a single thread of coherent thought, remembering his son, remembering that Morgan had taken up with Ruby's brat. This whore was Morgan's mistress, and not his. He shouldn't kill Morgan's mistress. He loved his son more than his own life. He was a good father and he had to protect his son from this whore, this whore could ruin everything for Morgan.

Getting rid of her now was the only way. Morgan would never find out. Eugene would make sure she didn't talk. A part of him rebelled at punishing Rebecca Rose—the human part that remembered how much he'd once cared for her mother. Too late now. His hard-kept control was gone, quickly and cruelly. The ugly monster had fully awakened.

Shoved up against the wall, still reeling over the impossible news that this demonic predator was Morgan's father, Becca's strength was no match for his. She couldn't move, pinned so against the wall. Her body fought inside, when it couldn't anywhere else. Her lungs pushed hard to push her attacker away. Her heart pounded, like so many nails in his coffin. Everything was already going dark around her. She couldn't think through her mounting panic; but . . . she *could* do one thing. She could hold on to her anger and not give in to her fear. Desperate to hold on to her anger, Becca fought to stay conscious with this monster at her.

Oh my God. A knife. The blade sparkled in front of her, laughing at her, ready to cut her. She'd thought she knew what to expect from this fiend, but she hadn't expected this. Her gun . . . where was it? If she could just get it in hand and kill her mother's killer. *Oh mama, I'm sorry. I'm so sorry.* Becca started to cry. She didn't want this fiend to see her tears. They weren't for him. They were for her mother, whom she'd failed. *I'm sorry, mama. Forgive me,* she wept silently.

"Yes, that's good. Cry, you whore. Cry for your life. Beg me to let you live," Eugene wheezed, poking the knife at her button-front blouse. "I need to hear you beg me."

Becca said nothing and spat in his face.

Eugene didn't wipe away the spittle. He'd have to let go of her if he did that. "You filthy whore." He poked his knife between her breasts, enough to draw blood. Seeing her blood, he felt a little better. She deserved to be punished. She didn't look afraid. "I'm giving you one more chance to beg me," he said.

Becca spat in his face a second time.

Like the viper he was, Eugene jerked her away from the wall and threw her down on the bed. He straddled her before she could get up, his knife still in hand. At first he ran the sharp edge against her throat, tempted to slash it now, but then he traced the knife down her blouse-front, cutting open each button, exposing her nakedness, making her pay for what she did to him. Making them all pay.

The pains shot up and inside her worse than any knife, worse than any strike from the most venomous snake, when he drove into her, slashing her insides with his engorged member over and over, again and again, until Becca begged for death—just as the demon wanted her to. It took all the strength left in her to keep silent; but she refused to open her mouth and give the devil the satisfaction of knowing how afraid she was. Her last conscious thought was of her mother, and how she'd soon be with her in potter's field.

Shrouded in darkness, Becca lay still. Still as the grave. Was she dead or alive? She didn't know. *Dead,* she decided. The blackness all around her told her as much. She didn't mind. In fact, she welcomed it. If she lay still, perfectly still, her mother's spirit would more easily find her.

Mama.

Desperate for the comfort of her mother's healing arms, Becca imagined crawling onto her mother's bed all those many years ago—a lifetime ago—and finding her dead, killed by the bad man with two missing fingers and the gold lion-head ring! *Oh, Mama, he killed me, too. He killed me, too.*

Just then Becca felt something hot run down her cheeks, wetting her neck. She put a hand to her face. *Tears!* It couldn't be. The dead don't cry! Quick now, she traced shaky fingers over her neck, expecting to find her skin torn and slashed. It wasn't. The darkness all around her began to fade to light. Morning light.

Along with the light of dawn filtering inside her room came the grim reality of what had taken place here the day before. Painful memories rushed at her all at once, jabbing and poking at her wherever they could find entry, reminding her that she'd been raped by Morgan's father. Oh dear God, she wished for the potter's field instead of this.

The pain she felt now, being alive, hurt worse than any pain inflicted by her rapist. She was tainted and dirtied for however many days she had left on this earth. She'd been violated beyond anything imaginable. Never could she get clean again. Overcome with sudden, hard-hitting nausea, she managed to roll out of bed and reach the bathroom area before losing the meager contents of her stomach onto the floor. She dry-heaved, unable to get a decent breath in between. The fact that she'd been raped by Morgan's father—her mother's killer—filled her with self-hate. *She* was the monster now, a loathsome human being.

Every pain that shot through her, every place on her body where she bled, every bruise, every cut . . . *I deserve.* She'd never hated herself more, and at once reached for the spigot in the tub and turned on the water. It hurt to climb into the tub. Once in, torn clothes, shoes and all, she eased against its back and waited for the tub to fill.

In a few minutes the tepid water reached her neck. She eased down farther into the welcome pool, ready to end her life. *Lots of ways for a whore to die.* This was her way. She thought of her mother, and didn't think this would be her mother's way. Nor did she think her mother would have swallowed a bottle of opium, like so many other whores did to escape the line. The water reached Becca's chin, then her mouth, then covered her nose. She kept her eyes open, going unafraid to her death.

Strong hands—someone—something—suddenly pulled at her shoulders, forcing her head above water. Becca coughed up the water she'd just swallowed and blinked hard, trying to clear her eyes enough to see who was there. No one. Nothing. The image of her mother appeared to her mind's eye.

Mama.

Becca gulped, shivering hard. It couldn't have been clearer to her than if her mother was standing in front of her now, in the flesh. Her mother had pulled her from the water. Her mother didn't want her to take her life. Her mother wanted her to prevail despite her fears, despite her suffocating melancholy, and despite the fact that she'd been raped by Morgan's father.

"All right, Mama. All right," Becca whispered aloud, ever the four-year-old obedient child. Then she stepped out of the water, her soaked clothes trying to weigh her back down. She would prevail; one way or the other she would. But, oh God, she felt so dirty, so unclean. How could she live in such a tainted world? How? Then, instead of climbing out of the tub, she ripped the rest of her clothes away, then yanked off her shoes and threw them onto the bathroom floor.

Only then did she turn off the water, which was about to overflow the tub. Grabbing the nearby bar of soap, she sank down into the cleansing water and began scrubbing herself, any and everywhere she could find. There would never be enough baths to get clean again—truly clean—but she'd do her best to scrub away memories of this nightmare every day she had breath left in her.

"Eugene, dear," Augusta began, unhappy that her husband looked so pale and sullen at the breakfast table. "Are you ill? You were so quiet at dinner last night, and barely conversed with our guests. That's so unlike you, dear." She rang the bell for the maid.

"Yes?" The crisply dressed maid came right away.

"Florence, bring Mr. Larkspur a glass of fresh orange juice."

"Yes, ma'am." The maid exited as quickly as she'd come.

"Eugene." Augusta turned her attention back on her husband. "I asked—"

"I'm fine," he said, interrupting his wife. Of course, he wasn't, but he sure as hell wouldn't tell Augusta.

"Well, well." She huffed. "You don't have to take that tone with me, dear."

This time Eugene was having more trouble than usual coming back to his normal self, to his ordered, respected life as a successful family man and wealthy Denver financier. For years now, after his time with a whore, he'd been able to put the time behind him, burying it as if it never happened until the next time. He'd been able to keep his secret life separate from his public life.

Last night and this morning, it wasn't working. In fact, for weeks now he'd found it harder to get back to his normal self. He felt his control slip a little more after each time with a whore. Sometimes he thought he was losing his mind, but he'd always come back before. Yeah, he'd thought about giving up his secret life, but that's all he'd done: think about it. Too late now, he could never give up his secret whoring. Not after Ruby.

Goddammit! He'd spared Ruby's brat again! *Stupid, stupid, stupid!*

The maid set a glass of orange juice in front of him. He reached for his coffee instead. It went down bitter, just like he felt. His insides were all mixed up, and he didn't know if they'd ever settle. Not now. Not after Rebecca Rose.

He knew why he'd spared her, and it wasn't because of her mother this time. It was because of his son. He'd hesitated to slash Ruby's daughter's throat because she was Morgan's mistress. He'd come close. He'd come oh, so close to cutting the unconscious whore's throat. But he couldn't do it because of his son. He loved his son. He couldn't kill the whore's brat because she was Morgan's.

Goddammit! The strike was over. Morgan would be coming home today. Morgan wanted to talk to him about something important. Eugene needed to get his head right before his son came home. Fighting panic for the first time in his life, Eugene realized Morgan could talk to Rebecca Rose now. He'd left her alive and she could talk. *Stupid, stupid, stupid!*

Eugene needed a plan, and quick.

"Dear?" Augusta was concerned. No matter that her husband said he was fine, and no matter that he'd all but bitten her head off a few moments ago.

Eugene stared blankly at her.

"Dear, I'm sending for the doctor this morning. I don't care what you say, you look ill," she insisted.

A plan began to form in Eugene's mind, and he felt better for it.

"Dear!" Augusta repeated, her upset obvious.

Eugene smiled at his wife and took another sip of coffee. "I am fine, Augusta. Really." He softened his tone. "As usual, my dear, you were right about last night and my behavior at dinner. I didn't feel well, but I'm improved this morning. No need for the doctor. In fact, I have an early appointment at my railroad office and need to leave in a few minutes. Would you ring for my carriage to be brought round?"

"Of course." She brightened and picked up the nearby silver-and-crystal bell.

Morgan had had trouble sleeping the night before, anxious to return to Denver and to Rebecca. Pacing beside the track by the Leadville station, he cursed the connecting spur-line from the western slope for being late. It was already half past five. He reached in his pocket to roll a cigarette and cursed that, too; he'd smoked all of his tobacco. What few cigarette papers he had left flew out of his hand. Morgan held his empty hand up to the dawning sky and studied his fingers as if counting them, making sure of them. He'd done it before, comparing his hand to his father's.

Before Morgan was born, so his father told him, his fingers had been crushed in a building accident. "Makes me strong, boy," his father used to tell him. "Like a badge of honor," he'd say, and then he'd turn the gold lion-head ring on his forefinger. "This lion has a roar, just like me, son. People take notice and step back when you pass by if you're strong. The Larkspurs are lions, Morgan. Lions. Never be anything less. Never," his father would sternly pronounce, and then ruffle the hair on Morgan's head, teasing his son into a lighter mood.

Morgan kept his hand to the mountain sky, making a fist—like a lion—and then releasing it. Just as his father had wanted, he'd tried to grow up strong and stay strong. He'd tried to do what his father wanted of him, and his mother, too. His parents had given him a lot. Quickly now, Morgan put his hand in his pocket, a reminder that he was about to displease his parents, his father in particular, with the news that he was not going to marry Lavinia Eagleton, but Rebecca Rose instead.

The whistle from the approaching locomotive broke into Morgan's dark concentration. Feeling every bit a boy again, he imagined his father ruffling his hair to tease him into a lighter mood after he found out about Morgan's changed plans. He hoped that would be the case, but if it wasn't he'd marry Rebecca anyway. She was the air he breathed now, the sun on his face, and the blood in his veins, giving him life, giving him love. She was the most important person in his life now, and he couldn't wait to see her. He knew he'd curse the slow, lumbering train the entire way down out of the mountains.

"Strike's over! Leadville strike's over!"

Becca heard the newsboy's shout from the street below. It was already early evening. Maybe he'd shouted the same news before. She didn't know. This time she didn't rush downstairs, and race outside the Windsor to buy the copy of the newspaper. That the strike was over was enough for her.

Morgan would be safe now, but he'd also return to Denver any time. Any hour. Any minute. Odd. She wasn't upset about the prospect of seeing Morgan again, excited one way or the other. Odder still, she didn't feel anything at all. How could she? She'd already been killed by the bad man with two missing fingers and the gold lion-head ring.

Lots of ways for a whore to die.

One thought kept her going now. She didn't think there was any chance she'd get pregnant from her rape, as her monthly flow was just ending right before . . . right before . . .

Refusing to think on it more, Becca continued packing her things in her trunk. Almost finished now. She hadn't packed everything. She didn't want any more to do with fancy parlor house dresses. Her intention was to head past the parlor houses, honky-tonks, saloons and hurdy-gurdies, toward the apartments and cribs at the end of the row—the end of the line on Holladay Street where she belonged. Just as well that the strike had ended. She'd finish her packing and then sit patiently and wait for Morgan to come. She should tell him goodbye. She should do that.

Of course she hadn't thought about what she'd say to him, but then, what did it matter? What did anything matter anymore, really? She had only thought as far as Morgan marrying his bride soon. And it wouldn't be her. Morgan wouldn't want anything to do with a prostitute anymore, having such a fine, respectable wife.

She'd also thought far enough to know it wasn't her fault that his father raped her. But his father had tainted her so badly that she doubted even one customer would come through her door now—at the end of the line.

Becca felt something hot roll down her cheeks. Tears again. Cursing them, she wiped them away. So what that she loved Morgan Larkspur? So what that he was the air she breathed, the sun on her face, and the blood she had left in the worn-out body that was yet giving her life? So what?

Morgan. Oh, Morgan.

Unable to hold onto her bravado, Becca collapsed into a heap on the floor and dissolved into more tears. She was soon to experience the best and the worst moment of her life. She couldn't wait to see Morgan again, yet she dreaded it all the same. She sobbed over her trunk, suddenly wanting to crawl into it and disappear.

That was it! Maybe she should leave before Morgan got here and not see him at all! *Yes.* She straightened and wiped her sleeve across her face in an attempt to pull herself together. *Yes.* She could disappear from the hotel and disappear down the line and disappear from Morgan's life! The idea of it—disappearing—helped her pull herself to a stand.

Hurrying now, she gathered the rest of her things and tossed them into her trunk. She had a few coins in her reticule, having already taken out the bills and returned them to the desk. It was Morgan's money, not hers. She had given much of his money to Pastor Noah at the poorhouse, but she didn't think Morgan would mind. But for her, no. She wouldn't take any more of his money. Her few coins would do her until . . . until she could earn more. It would be all right. She had enough. Her stomach turned at the thought of men pawing at her . . . cutting her, tainting her, killing her, over and over again for the rest of her days. Her stomach turned again. She imagined herself lying on her cot at the end of the line, pouring a whole vial of opium into her mouth, taking her last swallows. Just like Fanny.

Becca straightened her spine. No, she would not take her own life. She owed that much to her mother. She would not. Maybe she hadn't killed her mother's murderer, having failed miserably, but she would not go against her mother in this. That her mother didn't rest in peace now hurt her the most.

It was her fault that her mother's spirit didn't rest easy in the potter's field in Nevada City. Becca took some heart from the fact that when Eugene Larkspur died, her mother would rest then. Becca would ever regret that he didn't die at her hand, with her bullet killing him. Brushing off the hard reality that he wasn't dead, she glanced around the hotel suite a final time, making sure she was ready to leave the hotel—and precious memories of Morgan—behind.

Someone knocked.

Becca froze, scared to death of who it could be.

CHAPTER EIGHTEEN

The key turned in the lock.

Becca watched it, as if in slow motion. Only one other person had the key to room number eight on the second floor of the Windsor. *Morgan.*

She wished now with everything in her that his father had slit her throat last night. She'd rather be dead than have to face Morgan now. But the key was turning, and once turned, there was no going back to happier days of weeks ago, when nothing in the world mattered but their love.

The door hadn't opened yet. Panicked, Becca realized she needed to be ready—for anything. But then, there was no way for her to prepare for the unknown, no way at all. She didn't know whether to laugh or cry, so she did neither. All she managed to do was watch, wide-eyed, as the door pushed open.

Morgan stood in the doorway.

Becca had never prayed before—really prayed to God for help—but she did now. She prayed for the strength not to run into Morgan's arms, and not to tell him how much she'd missed him and how much she loved him and always would. She prayed for the right words so not to hurt him, and not to make him hate her. But she knew he would hate her after tonight. There was no other option.

Morgan stood on the threshold, as if frozen.

Much as she tried not to, Becca drank in his handsome visage, his mesmerizing slate regard, his sensual, firm mouth, and his powerful physique. It had been so long, so very long. The way he filled the doorway now, with his head almost touching the top of the door frame, as if he stood between her and all trouble, made her wish with all her heart that he did.

"My darlin' girl," he whispered, and then he started toward her.

Time stood still. Her arms hurt, the way she forced them to stay at her sides and not open to welcome Morgan. She closed her eyes and tried to shut down every part of her that ached for him. She wasn't his. Not anymore. Not since she'd been killed by his father. She belonged to the devil now. Morgan deserved better—*better than me.* Broken forever inside, she had to break now from Morgan.

"Oh, my darlin' Rebecca." Morgan reached her, putting his arms around her and pressing her hard against his chest, against his heart.

She didn't return his embrace. She didn't put her arms around him. It killed her all over again, not to. Oh, dear God. She felt a part of him. His blood flowed in her veins. His heart beat in hers. If only she could allow herself to lean into him and feel his warmth, and breathe in his male essence, and let his strong arms heal her—and fix everything broken. But even he could not fix her now.

Morgan pulled away enough to find her mouth and begin kissing her with all the love he'd been saving for her.

Becca didn't respond. She didn't open her mouth to him. *She* didn't open to him, fighting to stay shut down. She had to. She had to. She had to.

"Rebecca," he whispered against her mouth. "What's wrong, darlin'? Something's wrong."

The strain in his voice, the worry in it, and the unsure feel of his lips on hers made her all the more aware of how cruel she was being. She hated that she had to hurt him.

Morgan suddenly dropped his arms and stepped away from her.

Becca felt the sudden chill. Ice came down like a steel curtain, widening their inevitable divide.

"Rebecca." His tone changed, no longer soft. "Something's wrong. What is it?"

His pained expression almost undid her. Almost. Unable yet to find her voice, she kept silent.

Morgan didn't. "Darlin'." He spoke more softly now. "What's changed since I left? What's changed since I last talked to you on the telephone from Idaho Springs? Tell me, please," he whispered and took a step toward her.

"No, Morgan! Don't come any closer," she said at last.

He stopped short. "All right, Rebecca. Enough," he said coolly. "I'll stay put. You talk."

Here it comes! Here it comes!

She had to tell the biggest lie of her life now, in order to save his. "Since you left a lot has changed. I . . . I didn't tell you because . . . because you were away and . . . and, well, you didn't need to know until . . . until now . . . now that you're back." She struggled for every word. How she wanted to look away now. How she wanted to look anywhere but in his dark, trusting eyes. His jaw clenched hard. She could almost feel it.

Morgan kept silent, waiting. Just waiting.

"I started to see other . . . well, other customers while you were away. You see, I wanted a little more spending money . . . you know for fancy gowns and things . . . and so I did. I've seen other customers, Morgan."

There. Done.

"Other customers," Morgan slowly parroted. "You've been with other men?" He sounded incredulous.

"Yes."

"I don't believe you."

"You have to."

"All right, let's get this straight." He spoke low and clear. "I come back from Leadville. I come back to you. I love you. You love me. But now you're telling me you've been with other men, for money, since I left. Darlin', you're not making sense. This can't be about money."

Shocked that he didn't react more violently to her seeing other customers, she didn't have any words to speak back at him. What she'd said was supposed to have worked. It was supposed to have sent him away.

"Rebecca, darlin'." He came closer. "I love you. You've been worried about me. I know that. If . . . if you turned to your profession . . . if you were with other men, I . . . We need to put that behind us. I came back. I came back to you. I love you and I want to marry you," he said, his voice carrying all the emotion he felt.

Beyond shocked when she heard the word *marry*, a knife through her heart couldn't have cut worse. Morgan was proposing to her—a whore, a prostitute, a parlor house daughter. He didn't care what she was or where she came from. He didn't care. It cut her in two that the very thing she'd dreamed of, to have a home and a family with the man she loved, was just within her reach now. Close. Oh, so close. But it could never be.

Morgan's father had raped her. *His father!*

She'd been over it again and again, doing nothing but thinking about how wrong it would be to tell Morgan. It would hurt him so much to know that his own father had done such a thing to her. His father was a vicious devil. His father had killed her mother. She ached to tell Morgan that his father was a murderer, a liar, a rapist, and a monster.

But if she did tell him, it would hurt Morgan far worse than her lying to him now and telling him she didn't love him and that she wanted to see other customers. A part of her wondered if Morgan would even believe her. She couldn't take the chance.

Because she loved Morgan, she couldn't tell him everything about his father.

Because she loved Morgan, she would tell him the one thing—part truth and part lie—about his father that would forever turn Morgan against her.

"Rebecca darlin', I said I want to mar—"

"No!" She stopped him from saying it again. Anything to stop him. It hurt too much to hear him say he wanted to marry her. "One of the men I've been with is your father," she blurted out.

"Say again," Morgan said, his voice devoid of any emotion.

The room turned into a tomb. Becca could feel the carriage and streetcar wheels outside run over her body, burying her deeper in the mud. Then she felt nothing, nothing at all. "Your father is one of my customers," she repeated, making sure of her words.

Morgan backed away, recoiling from her. It was moments before he said anything. "So . . . so what you and I had . . . It was all about money. It wasn't about love was it, Rebecca?"

"No, it wasn't about love." She fought to keep her voice steady. "It was just business, Morgan. Only business."

Deadly slow, Morgan turned toward the door and opened it. "Get out," he told her, his jaw tight, his voice cold. "Get out."

Numb inside, Becca mutely bent down and closed her packed truck. It wasn't full. It would be light enough to manage herself. She grabbed the handle at one end and dragged it across the room past Morgan, then out of room number eight on the second floor of the Windsor.

Morgan slammed the door behind her.

The jarring sound hammered down her spine and echoed in her head like a death knell. *At least it's all over,* she thought as she struggled with her trunk toward the top of the hotel staircase. *At least it's over.*

She couldn't have been more wrong.

The young bellman, having spotted Becca coming down the grand staircase of the prestigious Windsor dragging her trunk, rushed up to her. "Mrs. Larkspur! Please, allow me," he insisted, and took the trunk from her.

"Thank you." She tried to smile, grateful for his help.

Once at the bottom of the staircase, the bellman hesitated. "Mrs. Larkspur, where to?" he asked, all energy and innocence.

She knew where; she just didn't want to tell him. "Young man, if you'll take my trunk outside, that will do."

"Of course, ma'am," he said, and picked up her trunk again. "I'll order a carriage for you straightaway."

"No!" She tried to call after him, but he'd already made it halfway across the reception area. She didn't want the bellman or the carriage driver or anyone else to know that she was headed up the street to the end of the line. But then, what did it matter? It didn't. There was no one to care. Morgan wouldn't. It made little difference, then, who knew where she headed. Forcing herself to catch up with the bellman and her things, she thought she had enough fare for the driver.

It was dark now. Morgan had no idea of the time. He'd sat down in the first chair he could find in the hotel suite right after Rebecca left. She'd betrayed him. She'd used him. She was nothing but a . . . a whore. From the first, she and Jenny Clayton must have lied to him about Rebecca having been untried. He'd believed it, all of it. He'd been played for a fool by both of them. All these weeks, and all he could think about was coming back to Rebecca, to the woman he loved, and who, he thought, loved him. It hurt that she'd only pretended to love him. It hurt deep down. Worse though, worse than that: *She bedded my father.* He shot up from his chair, sick at the idea of it.

God, how he hated Rebecca. He hated her now as much as he'd once loved her.

Damn her to hell! She'd cheated him out of the life he thought they'd have together. She'd cheated him out of his hope for love and marriage and children and happiness. He'd thought she was the one for him, the love of his life. She was the one, all right: the one who'd taken his life and thrown it away like so much trash. Damn her to hell!

Turning on the light switch, he looked around the rooms they'd shared. He needed to get out of there. He didn't want to remember the time they'd had together or think about the time she'd shared with other men. With his father. There was a valise in the bottom of the wardrobe. He yanked the leather case out, and then threw in the things he kept at the hotel. Still at the wardrobe, he couldn't help but notice that Rebecca had left her clothes, at least her fancy gowns. Some of her shoes, too. She must have forgotten them. He jerked them out of the wardrobe and tossed the silk and satin onto the bed.

Let the maids have them, he thought.

One last thing he checked before leaving: the desk drawer where he'd left money for Rebecca. Since she'd left her clothes, he wondered if she'd spent all of his money. He counted the bills. Fifty dollars. The rest she must have spent on the clothes piled on the bed. Maybe she forgot the money, same as her gowns. It didn't make much sense, but then, none of this made sense to him. And none of it changed the fact that Rebecca was nothing more than a lying, cheating, money-hungry *whore.*

Morgan quickly grabbed up his valise and headed, for the last time, out the door of room number eight on the second floor of the Windsor. He'd never come back to the hotel, and he'd never frequent a parlor house again, not for the rest of his days.

"Oh, Morgan," his mother gushed. "It's wonderful to have you safely back home, and just in time for your wedding next week! It will all be so grand. Lavinia's wedding gown is stunning, Morgan. She'll do you proud. And I don't think you know yet, dear. The reception will be at the Windsor, the grand Windsor. It will be the crowning event of the summer," Augusta kept babbling on.

The Windsor. Morgan would do his part as the dutiful, older Larkspur son and marry Lavinia Eagleton next week, but he'd be damned if he'd do any part of it at the Windsor. Morgan took another sip of hot coffee. It didn't go down well. He set his cup on the table hard, some of its bitter contents spilling onto the lace tablecloth. His mother was still going on about the wedding. He didn't want to hear any more. "Mother," he said over her, "where's Father? He's usually down for breakfast first. Where is he?"

Augusta picked up her coffee cup now, taking one sip, then another. She replaced the cup in its china saucer then fidgeted with her linen napkin.

"Mother?" Morgan said again.

"Yes. Well, dear . . ." The usually composed and in-control Larkspur matriarch seemed uncomfortable. She was even stalling for time.

Morgan waited. He had nothing but time now.

"I'm that sure your father had out-of-town railroad business that's kept him away from home last night," she pronounced, then picked up her cup again. "Florence!" She yelled for the maid instead of ringing the bell next to her.

"Yes, ma'am?" The maid came right away.

"This coffee's stone cold," Augusta chided. "Bring in a fresh pot immediately!"

"Yes, ma'am." The maid turned to the buffet and picked up the silver decanter, quickly disappearing back into the kitchen.

Morgan's thoughts tumbled over and over. This was unlike his father, to be away from home all night. But then, so was taking up with someone else's woman—his woman. Yeah, right. His woman.

Morgan's stomach churned at the realization that Rebecca had never been his woman, giving herself to him and him alone. She evidently gave herself to every man who had a fifty-dollar token for her. She'd given herself to his father. His own father! He hated Rebecca. And he hated his father for ever touching her. He shouldn't hate his father. His father had given him so much in life. He loved his father. But then, he'd loved Rebecca, too.

Suddenly Morgan shot up from the table.

"Spur!" Monty charged into the dining room, giving his brother a fierce hug. "Damn, I'm glad to see you, bro. I should have helped, Spur. I should have. Next time, Spur, I won't let you down." Monty swallowed hard.

Morgan's mood softened a little, seeing his good-hearted baby brother again. He'd ever be the kid in the schoolyard following Morgan around, wanting to play with the older kids, and no one letting him. "You know what, little brother? It's your turn now," Morgan said.

Monty lost his grin. His brow furrowed, and he was puzzled by what Spur'd just said. He'd been waiting to hear those words all of his life; but to hear them now . . . Something was up. He wanted to question Spur further, but thought better of it. Not in front of their mother. He'd let it go for now.

"Oh, good, Montgomery." Augusta broke into the conversation between her sons. "You're up. As soon as you finish with your breakfast, I'd like you to take me downtown. I've shopping to do." She seemed back to her old self.

"Yes, mother," Monty answered out of habit, giving his brother a nod as if they'd continue later.

Morgan gave his brother a light slap on the shoulder, then left the dining room. He didn't feel like talking anymore, to anyone.

Becca hadn't slept at all. She still sat, fully dressed, on the bare mattress of the apartment room she'd rented the night before. She'd paid for the carriage to drop her at Twenty-Third and Holladay Streets, and then dragged her trunk another block before she found an empty crib room for rent. The stale, musty odor fit her mood. She hadn't bothered to open the room's only window. It was dirty and cracked, she could see now that it was morning. She began to hear things around her that she hadn't before. People walked by out front, talking loudly, but she couldn't make out what they were saying. People were talking inside, too, muffled sounds reverberating from the other apartment rooms in the ramshackle building. She wondered about the time, but didn't bother to check her watch pin. It really didn't matter what time it was.

The next days, weeks, and months would pass. That's all. At the end of the line now, here she would live; and here she would die. She would be buried in the potter's field, having no doubt that Miss Jenny would make sure she'd rest with her mother.

Miss Jenny. Becca would need to make sure to get word to Miss Jenny about her whereabouts. After. Right now, she'd no intention of letting the dear madam know her whereabouts. But after she'd passed . . . well, somehow Becca would make sure Miss Jenny would be notified about her body. Somehow she'd make sure.

Best not to think about her death or Miss Jenny or anything else right now.

Best not to think at all.

Tired but not hungry, she didn't want anything to eat or drink. She only wanted sleep.

She lay down on the cot and shut her eyes, waiting for sleep.

Morgan didn't knock before charging into his father's library. He knew the second his father had come home. He'd paced in the front parlor until he did. With nothing left in his heart for his father now but hate, Morgan needed to get this over with.

Eugene Larkspur stood at the large bay window, his back to his son. He knew who'd just come in, and braced for it.

"Turn around and face me," Morgan said. He'd never used such a harsh tone with his father.

Eugene knew the moment his son addressed him, that his son knew. But what did he know? What had the bitch told him? What lies had she put in his head? All lies. Nothing but lies. Eugene's thoughts drifted as he slowly pivoted, doing his best to hold on to his control. He mustn't make a slip. It could cost him everything, if he did. Everything. He'd made a plan. He knew what he'd say to Morgan. Yes. Stay with the plan . . . the plan . . .

Shocked the moment his father faced him, Morgan saw a changed man. This man didn't resemble his father. This man was a stranger. This stranger's eyes were yellow and bloodshot, his complexion sickly and drawn, his hair unkempt, and his clothing disheveled. This stranger didn't stand as tall as his father. The smell of cheap perfume and cheap whiskey hung in the air between the two men.

Morgan forgot his anger, more worried about his father now than anything else.

Eugene read his son's concerned expression. Good. He'd use it.

"Father, are you ill?" Morgan spoke barely above a whisper.

Eugene answered with a wan smile, and then took a careful seat in one of the room's wingback leather chairs. "Son, please." Eugene put out his hand, directing Morgan to sit in the other wingback positioned close by.

Mutely, Morgan sat down. He still had trouble believing his eyes.

"Son, the fact is . . ." Eugene had plan upon plan now, energizing for the fight. "I am ill. I haven't said anything to your mother, and I'm holding you to it not to say anything to her either."

Morgan nodded his agreement, the smell of perfume and whiskey replaced by the cold, clinical smell of ether and carbolic acid.

"I was at the doctor most of the night and, well, he released me to come home only this morning. He thinks it might be the consumption eating away at me, but said we have to wait now. Just wait and see. This illness has run me down all sudden-like, but I already feel better, son. I had the cough while you were away in Leadville, but I'm improved. Why, I haven't coughed for days now. The doctor is pleased. Hell, I'm pleased." Eugene's lies came out easy. He *was* pleased with himself for that.

Morgan reached over and put his hand on his father's arm. "Father, I'm so sorry. Is there anything I can do?"

Hah! The moment had arrived, the moment Eugene needed. He had opportunity now and he'd best take it. "Son, I need you to listen to me about something that's not so easy to talk about. Will you do that, son?"

"Of course." Morgan thought he knew what was coming. He had to listen. His father was ill. He had to.

"I found out about your mistress, Rebecca Rose."

God, did he have to say her name?

"I went to see her at the Windsor. I went to see her to . . . I'm not proud to say it, son, but I went to see her to pay her off and ask her to leave Denver. We are the Larkspurs. You are my best and brightest son. Our future depends on you, Morgan. I knew you'd be upset with me, but I didn't want any scandal associated with your good name. You do understand, son? My good intentions?" Eugene made sure he had Morgan's eye.

"Of course," Morgan muttered, his jaw so tight he had trouble responding.

"Well, when she let me into the room, she was all smiles and sweetness, offering me a drink or a nice supper to share. I refused, naturally, but she kept insisting. Morgan . . ." He looked at his son, giddy inside that Morgan was buying it, all of it. "She . . . she began making overtures. She began seducing me. And, son . . . I'm so ashamed." Eugene buried his face in his hands, feigning upset.

It took everything Morgan had to sit there with his father and listen.

Eugene lifted his head, catching his son's eye once again. "Son, I gave in to her seductive ways. I gave in and I'm ashamed. Then after . . . afterwards, she demanded fifty dollars from me. I paid it, Morgan. I paid the money and left without demanding that she leave Denver. I failed you, son." Eugene faked a beginning cough.

Morgan put his hand back on his father's arm, worried about the consumption. He wondered though. He wondered if the fifty dollars he'd found in the desk drawer at the Windsor was his father's fifty dollars.

Eugene pulled out his handkerchief and put it over his mouth, pretending to wipe away the remnants of his pretend cough. "I was weak, son. I hope you can find a way to forgive me." He tried to inject just the right amount of penitence and dejection into his tone. Straightening in his seat, he felt better. He'd changed back to the respected, in-control, formidable Eugene Larkspur, the esteemed family man and wealthy financier.

"Father." Morgan felt like the parent now. "Nothing matters but your getting better. Put any worry about me away, and think on yourself. Mother, Monty . . . all of us will stand behind you, to help you get better."

Eugene stood. "Morgan. Remember your promise. Not a word of my illness to your mother or to Monty. You must give me your promise. I couldn't take it right now if they worried, too."

"All right." Morgan stood, facing his father. "If that's what you wish." His father did look a little better now. *I'll be damned.*

"It is," Eugene repeated quietly.

"Are you sure there's nothing I can do to help?" Morgan couldn't hide his worry.

Eugene used it. "There is, son. You can marry Lavinia come Friday at Saint John's and have the reception at the Windsor, as planned. That would make me happy, son. That would take some of my worry away."

"All right." Morgan swallowed hard. "All right."

Gotcha!

Eugene couldn't believe how well this conversation had gone. Smooth going now, all of it. Morgan wouldn't bring up his mistress again, and he would marry Lavinia Eagleton come Friday. The Larkspur name would be intact, with no more worry about it being dragged through the mud. Morgan's political future was bright, nothing but bright. The more Eugene thought about it, however, he realized there was one more thing to take care of. He had to make sure he and his son would have no more trouble with Ruby's brat.

Eugene knew what he had to do.

Chapter Nineteen

"What's the meaning of this?" Jenny insisted the moment the two uniformed police stepped into the foyer of the Palace. Such an indignity, the police coming at this hour, and on a Sunday! It wasn't yet ten in the morning. She was glad none of her girls were up, although she'd begun to wonder if one of them had taken a misstep the night before. Jenny knew only too well that it just took one.

"Miss Jenny." One of the officers took off his hat, doubtless out of respect for the noted madam.

Jenny didn't recognize either of the men. They'd never frequented the Palace, and likely had been sent by higher-ups. Humph. Higher-ups. She'd like to get her hands on them about now. Used to handling whatever trouble came through the doors of the Palace, she'd make quick work of these upstart policemen.

"Ma'am." The same officer spoke. "We're looking for one of your residents, a Rebecca Rose. We understand she lives here and we want to speak with her." He kept his tone polite, yet to the point.

Jenny's insides caved in. Becca must have . . . she must have found her mother's murderer and shot him! At least, Jenny tried to reason, Becca isn't dead, too.

What of Morgan Larkspur? Did he know anything about this? They must not be together, or the police would have already located Becca at the Windsor. Her heart broke for Becca, knowing how much she cared for Morgan.

Jenny thought of Becca's last will and testament that she'd put safely away. She thought of her innocent parlor house daughter, holed up somewhere waiting to be arrested, waiting to be buried in the potter's field in Nevada City. *Oh my sweet child. My sweet, sweet child.*

"Ma'am . . ."

"You don't have to repeat what you said, young man," she huffed. "I'm not deaf." She stalled for time, trying to think what to say, what to do. She swallowed hard. "Rebecca Rose used to live here, but she moved out some time ago. I believe she left Denver, perhaps for Kansas City. She'd talked of Kansas City and relatives there. That's likely where she's gone." Jenny spoke with authority.

"With all due respect, ma'am," the same officer said, "it would go hard on you now if you're lying."

"Is that a threat?"

"No, ma'am," he said, holding his ground with the formidable madam. "It's a fact."

"Well." She rounded on both officers now. "It's a fact that I don't lie and it's a fact that Rebecca Rose is not here, and it's a fact that if you don't vacate my house in the next minute, I'll have the police commissioner himself calling you into his office this very afternoon, asking for your badges!"

Both men exchanged a look. Then the same officer spoke. "All right, ma'am. We're leaving now, but we expect you to inform the law if Rebecca Rose gets in touch with you."

"What do you want her for anyway?" Jenny snarled.

The officer attempted a smile but didn't answer. Both men turned and exited the Palace.

Jenny shut the door hard behind them, nearly shattering the stained glass in the window frame. If only Becca would come to her before the police found her, she'd help her frightened and alone parlor house daughter. *Oh my sweet child. My sweet, sweet child.*

Morgan changed out of his frock coat and boot-strap pants, the suit he'd worn to church with Lavinia this morning. He needed to get into something that didn't feel like a damned straight-jacket. The whole time at Saint John's, as he'd listened to Father Hart's sermon, he'd wanted to get up and leave. He'd never been much of a churchgoer and didn't take to it now, especially with his wedding coming up at the very same church the end of the week.

Soured on the whole idea of marriage, he'd go through the motions for his family—only for his family. He'd even agreed to the reception at the Windsor—only for his father. His father was ill. This wasn't any time to go against his father's wishes.

Opting for loose brown trousers and a white shirt open at the collar, Morgan felt better. Everyone would still be in their Sunday best, but not him. He didn't look forward to afternoon dinner with Lavinia and her family. They'd all been invited to dine and were likely downstairs now, waiting for him to make an appearance. As far as any of them downstairs were concerned, nothing was out of the ordinary.

Morgan reached for his tobacco makings and fell into the easy chair near his bed. He rolled a cigarette and lit it, taking a deep draw. It didn't help him feel better, and, in fact, burned his lungs. Dammit, even his smokes weren't the same since . . . since . . .

He shot out of his chair, refusing to think of Rebecca. She wasn't a part of his life anymore. She was a part of his past, that's all. He quickly tossed his cigarette in the cold fireplace then stood for long moments, watching the tobacco burn down to ashes. Just like his affair with Rebecca. It was all ashes now. Nothing but ashes.

A rap on his door broke into his dark studies.

"Mr. Morgan," the familiar housekeeper's voice called through the door. "Your mother is having a fit that you're not downstairs, sir."

"Thank you, Matilda," he answered absentmindedly. "I'll be right there." Of course, he wouldn't be. He needed a few more minutes to ready himself for the afternoon ahead.

Dinner dragged on. Morgan fielded a few questions about the Leadville strike, but only a few. Their dinner guests were more interested in his upcoming wedding than in the happenings in the faraway mines. Uncomfortable even in his comfortable clothes, Morgan looked to Monty. Monty was his only safe haven. His brother sat across from him at the table, at first with little expression on his face. Morgan couldn't read him. He had no idea what Monty knew about . . . about anything.

He was anxious to talk to his little brother. His father wouldn't have said anything to Monty about his illness or about Rebecca. But then Morgan saw something in his brother's sympathetic look. Monty *did* know something. He needed to find out what.

When Lavinia rested her delicate, bejeweled hand on Morgan's arm, he wanted to shake her off. If he were not in public, he would. Dammit, he'd agreed to go through with this sham of a wedding, but he didn't know how he'd abide her touch. It was so cold, so calculating, without a drop of emotion. She'd no passion for him. He knew that, doubting if she'd have real feelings for any man. Lavinia was a lot like his mother. Lavinia was in love with power and money and position, not him. Not him as a man. Not him as a man with flesh-and-blood needs for love and companionship and passion. No, Lavinia didn't love him. She loved only what marriage to him would get her.

Morgan stared hard at her hand on his arm.

So be it.

"Cognac in the library, gentlemen," Eugene stood and announced.

Morgan couldn't get over his father's improvement from yesterday. He looked better today, even fit. No coughing, either. Morgan didn't know enough about consumption to predict how the wretched disease played out in a person. Maybe his father had more time than Morgan thought. *Good. Good on you, Father.*

Morgan stood, glad for an opportunity to lose Lavinia's cloying hand. He'd readily join the other men for cognac, anxious to corner his little brother. He was sure Monty would tell him the truth. Morgan nodded to the women at the table, then followed his father and their other male guests out of the dining room. Maybe the afternoon would pick up now. Maybe he'd feel better talking to Monty, away from Lavinia and his mother. God, anything would be better than what he'd just sat through.

But Morgan didn't feel better walking down the polished hallway toward the library. Something struck him in the chest, in the heart, as if he'd suffered an attack of some kind. He stopped a moment at the sudden, queer feeling. It wasn't exactly pain that he was experiencing, but it hurt all the same.

"Coming, bro?" Monty called from the library door.

"Yeah, be right there," Morgan said, wishing he knew what was wrong.

"Rebecca Rose?" The two police officers shoved in her door and charged inside her apartment room.

"Wh—?"

"You're under arrest," the one pronounced, while the other pulled her hands behind her back and locked them in manacles.

Becca had been up and dressed. For work. For potential customers. Yet she hadn't advertised at her window or door that

266

she was ready to have them knock. At first she had trouble telling the police officers from customers, so upset was she to have the unwanted men rush inside. With the cold steel clamped on her wrists, the reality of her assault from these police officers sank in fast.

"What do you want?" she demanded as soon as she could. She stood facing the intruders, her hands shackled behind her.

"You're under arrest for the attempted murder of Eugene Larkspur," the one who liked to talk said.

"Aw, Nate." The other finally spoke. "You don't need to go telling her anything. She's nothing but a whore. She don't need to know why she's being arrested."

"The at-attempted . . . *murder* . . . of Eugene Larkspur?" she repeated, incredulous. "I didn't . . . that's crazy. That's not true," she finally managed.

"Save it for the judge," the first officer told her. "We're just following orders." He'd dragged a lot of prostitutes to the station. This was just one more, wasn't she?

Bewildered beyond anything else she'd imagined could happen to her, Becca let the officers guide her out of her newly rented apartment crib, past onlookers, past carriages going by on the balmy Sunday evening, then put into the back of their police wagon. She stared out through the little barred window in the back of the dark wagon, suddenly afraid of what would come.

All her life she'd heard stories about what happened when the law had a whore in custody. Maybe they all weren't true, but some of them were. Some of them she believed. Her heart hammered in her chest, echoing from wall to wall in the close wagon, fueling her fear. She hated that she was afraid. She hated that the most of all.

Eugene eyed his sons talking privately in the corner of the

library. He feigned interest in his guests, all the while worried about his sons' conversation. But then, Morgan had promised he wouldn't say anything, and Monty . . . well, Monty, for all intents and purposes, didn't know anything. *Shouldn't be a problem,* Eugene rolled over in his mind. Then again, it might be.

"Listen, Spur," Monty kept on. "It just got out, that's all. I heard about your mistress from my friends during breakfast at the Windsor one morning. Next thing I knew, there Rebecca Rose sat across the dining room, looking beautiful and elegant and keeping to herself. I swear to you, Spur, I don't know who found out about her first. There's been talk at the Denver Club, too, but you know how this town talks. Hell, I'm surprised that nosy, not-so-nice reporter from the *Rocky Mountain News,* Polly Pry, hasn't spread the word all over Denver by this time. I'm just sorry, Spur, that word has gotten out this far."

"So it would be easy for anyone to find out, being at the Denver Club or the Windsor, common talk and all?" Morgan needed confirmation.

"Yeah, and then, well . . ." Monty hesitated to tell him about Lavinia's part in all of this.

Morgan bristled. "Spit it out, Monty."

"All right, Spur, but you're not going to like it."

"Little brother, there's nothing to like about any of this," Morgan gritted out, then took another swallow of his cognac.

"I don't know how, but Lavinia must have found out about Rebecca. First I heard was that Lavinia had made a ruckus at the Windsor looking for Rebecca. I know that Lavinia did see her, but as far as what happened after that, I don't know," Monty said, and downed the rest of his drink. "Mor-Morgan, where are you going?" He barely got the words out before his brother left the library.

★ ★ ★ ★ ★

"Why, Morgan, sweetheart," Lavinia dripped out the moment he entered the parlor where she and the other ladies were comfortably gathered.

"Son, this is our ladies time," Augusta chastised. "You go along back to the library." She put up her hand to teasingly shoo him away, as if he were still a child.

Morgan ignored his mother and the other ladies. He approached Lavinia. "We need to talk." He strained to keep his voice polite.

Mary Ella Eagleton sat next to her daughter. "Morgan, dear, there are no secrets here," she quipped light-heartedly. "We'll all be family come Friday. Please, let us all know what it is you need to say to my daughter," she added, a slight edge now in her speech.

"Lavinia," Morgan repeated, this time not so politely.

Mary Ella began to fan herself nervously.

Augusta would speak to her son later, in private, and remind him of his manners and his position. This week must go off without any problems. Morgan needed to be reminded of that.

Lavinia slowly rose from her seat, pretending total calm, when she felt anything but easy inside. Not until Friday was over and done with and she was Morgan's wife could she relax. No, not until then. "Of course, Morgan." She smiled innocently, then followed him out of the parlor.

"Let's go out to the gazebo," he told her, not bothering to turn around when he did so. He knew she followed, and he took the back hallway out through the door that led to the private courtyard.

More angry than worried now, Lavinia fumed inside. This was ridiculous. She shouldn't have to follow him around like some servant!

Once inside the gazebo, Lavinia took a seat. Morgan stood, facing her.

"I understand," he said through clenched teeth. "I understand that you paid my mistress at the Windsor a visit. Want to tell me about it?"

Be careful, Lavinia, she instructed herself. *Go carefully.* "Your . . . your mistress!" she stood now, too, doing her best to sound incensed. "What are you asking me? What are you telling me? That you . . . that you have a kept woman at the Windsor? Where we're to . . . we're to have our wedding reception? Oh Morgan!" She feigned upset, even tears, and collapsed back down on the gazebo bench.

Morgan's jaw clenched harder. "Are you telling me that you *didn't* pay a visit to Rebecca Rose at the Windsor?"

Be careful, Lavinia. Go carefully.

"Well . . . well . . ." Lavinia took out her handkerchief, sobbing into it, stalling for time. "I did go see a woman—Rebecca Rose as you say—but it was about my worries over the Ladies Aid Society and her interference in our charity work. I . . . I didn't know *that* woman was your . . . your mistress." Lavinia grinned inside, knowing she'd win this.

"Go on."

"Yes, well . . . I suppose you want to know the details of it all, Morgan." She sniffled. "First, I . . . I forgive you for keeping a mistress . . . you having just told me . . . and . . . I'm humiliated, of course." She chanced a look at him to make sure he knew of her distress and everything that he'd put her through. She needed to play on his guilt. "You need to know how Rebecca Rose humiliated me with the Ladies Aid Society. I searched her out because of her interference with our good work. Morgan, she was down at the poorhouse on Blake Street, acting as if she wanted to help and giving money, lots of it, to the poor souls sheltered there. Well, you can imagine my upset when I arrived to roll up my sleeves and to get out my money. She'd already come, doubtless to show me up. The very nerve! And now that I find out she's nothing more than a . . . a . . . *prostitute!*" Lavinia tried to sound as if she'd never uttered such an offensive word before.

She fanned herself rapidly with her handkerchief. "To think that those poor souls, those poor innocent children at the shelter, were being fed and clothed and cared for by a prostitute . . . by Satan's hand . . . why it's horrible, just horrible!" Lavinia couldn't read Morgan now. It worried her that she couldn't. "You can understand, can't you dear, why I rushed to find her and get her to stop—to leave town, even. I'd no idea she was your . . . your . . . Oh, Morgan!" She dissolved into fake tears yet again.

Morgan relaxed his jaw, if only a little. He had no idea if Lavinia spoke the truth about any of this. If she did, then Rebecca was a saint and not Satan's handmaid. If Lavinia didn't, then he'd no business marrying her because she was a liar, no matter how prominent and proper a wife she'd be for him. He'd just rid himself of one liar. He sure as hell didn't want to saddle himself with another.

Uneasy now, unsure of what to believe about Lavinia or Rebecca, he thought about the money he'd left in the hotel suite, in the desk drawer for Rebecca. If she didn't use it on herself to buy expensive clothes, but gave it to the poor . . . *if it's true* . . . then there might be other lies being told about Rebecca. Maybe his father wasn't telling the—

No!

His father wouldn't lie to him.

His father was dying of consumption. His father wouldn't go to his Maker with lies on his last breath. His father would never hurt him. But lying, cheating, unscrupulous women like Rebecca, would.

Lavinia wanted to stand up and cheer, but thought better of it. She'd won. She could tell from Morgan's pained expression.

"It's getting cold out here," he said, his throat tight. "Best get you inside."

"Not through the front of the station house, Nate. We need to take her around back," Becca overheard one officer saying to the other.

"What's the deal?" the other one asked.

"Just drive around to the back, Nate. We're to take her in the back way, put her in isolation, forget her charges, and forget we ever saw her."

Becca scooted back farther on the wagon seat and pulled her knees up as a child might—a four-year-old child afraid of the dark, without the protection of her mother. A four-year-old child who knew about all the frightful things that could go bump in the night.

The police started to talk again. She covered her ears, wishing them away, wishing it all away, wishing with everything left in her that the good fairies—the ones her mother had summoned to protect her when she was a child—really did exist and would find her alone, inside the dark jail . . . and would rescue her from harm. Hating herself for it, she wished for something else. A bottle of pure, potent, poisonous opium, so she could escape the line once and for all.

Eugene noticed nothing out of the ordinary with his sons for the rest of Sunday evening, and he breathed a little easier. Whatever had transpired between Morgan and Monty, they'd kept it to themselves. Whatever it was, given Monty's pleasant demeanor, Morgan hadn't revealed anything to Monty about him, and had kept his promise. *Just like the good son Morgan's always been,* Eugene thought.

Still, Eugene worried. He needed to make sure nothing would go wrong now. Of course he could rely on Morgan to keep quiet. He believed the lies he'd been told. But he couldn't rely on Ruby's brat to do the same thing. Yes, she was a whore, and no one would believe her, especially not against the word of Eugene Larkspur. But still, Eugene worried.

Twice now, he'd made the mistake of leaving Ruby's brat alive. *Stupid, stupid, stupid!* Using his connections with the law, he'd asked the city judge to keep everything quiet, and to arrest Rebecca Rose and get her off the street so she couldn't threaten anyone else. It hadn't been difficult to convince his friend, Judge Wells, that he'd met up with her by accident, fallen prey to her, and then found himself at the end of her gun when he didn't pay up enough for her time. Eugene didn't think his jurist friend would bat an eye at the fact that he'd been with a soiled dove, and he'd been right.

"A prostitute like Rebecca Rose needs to be put away," he'd informed the judge. "A prostitute like her could have killed me. There are other unsuspecting men out there, and she shouldn't be given any more opportunity to take their money or their lives."

Judge Wells had agreed to have Rebecca arrested and put in isolation, then transferred to a prison out of state. She'd be nothing but a bad memory in a few days' time. But right now Eugene still worried. He worried she might say something in the Denver jail. Even in isolation, someone might find her; someone might ask questions. Could he take the chance? Could he risk leaving her alive and letting her be transferred out of state?

No, probably not.

The first one down to breakfast Monday morning, Morgan wasn't hungry. He'd slept little. He wanted coffee and the newspaper, anything to keep his mind off Rebecca.

The maid entered the dining room, nodded her good morning, and then set fresh coffee on the server. An efficient maid, Florence knew Mr. Morgan liked to serve himself.

He returned her nod but didn't feel like talking. His insides were raw and his nerves worse. Having filled his cup and sat down at the table, he opened the *Rocky Mountain News* and sipped his coffee. He was curious to read how the paper had covered the strike ending in Leadville. He hoped they set everything down right. The story had broken last week, but coverage would still be heavy. The paper got things wrong sometimes. He wanted to make sure the Denver paper didn't play favorites, supporting the mine owners over the miners, and leaving out some of the legitimate complaints the miners had, and which had forced them to strike in the first place.

Morgan read the front page covering the silver strike, and then the second. The paper did a decent job presenting both sides. Good. Morgan had wanted more for the laborers, but at least a shorter working day was a start. And, the laborers' complaints were now a matter of public record. He set down his coffee cup and read on to page three for more of the day's news.

Then he saw it, the headline of Polly Pry's gossip column:

PROSTITUTE ARRESTED FOR THE ATTEMPTED MURDER OF EUGENE LARKSPUR!

CHAPTER TWENTY

Morgan didn't believe what he'd read. He didn't want to make any connection between the scandalous headline and his father. Between the headline and Rebecca. Papers didn't always print the truth. Certainly not Polly Pry. Much as he didn't want to, Morgan read her gossip column once, then again. It had to be lies, all of it. Had to be.

But then, he thought again.

The part about Rebecca being a prostitute wasn't a lie.

The part about his father being with her wasn't a lie.

But the part about Rebecca trying to murder his father . . . That had to be a lie.

His father would be down soon. Damn, he didn't want him to see the trash printed about him in the newspaper. God only knew how long his father had left, ill with consumption as he was. This news could send him to an early grave. Morgan heard voices. His parents were coming. Quickly, he shoved the paper under his chair, out of sight.

Anything to keep his mind off Rebecca.

Becca hadn't slept. A jailer had brought her bread and water, but she didn't want it. She just wanted out. Out of this jail, out of this life. Just out. She didn't want anything else. Just out. Tired of being so afraid, she tried not to jump at every sound. She felt buried already, buried alive, alone in her cold cell, isolated, apart from the rest of the world. Being shut away so, she tried to shut down all thoughts, all feelings. All memory of Morgan. If only she could stop thinking about him, and needing him close. If only she could see him . . . just for a moment . . . one more moment—

Stop it! Stop it! Stop it!

Feelings only get a whore killed.

That truth never rang so true.

Becca climbed off her cot and stood dead center in her cell. There was a tiny, barred window at the back wall and nothing but stone walls on either side. Slivers of daylight sneaked inside. The entire front of her cell was barred and locked shut. She saw nothing through the iron bars but another locked door ahead, this one wood, solid and heavy. Walking to the bars, she leaned into them and tried to see out on either side.

"Step away." A gruff jailer, this one new to her, made her jump.

He'd appeared in front of her as if by magic. *Dark magic,* she thought. She hadn't seen the jailer and wondered where he'd been sitting.

"Need the necessary?" he asked, still gruff.

She shook her head no and stepped back.

He unlocked her cell and shoved in a chamber pot. "Here. In case you do," he said, then relocked her cell.

"Do you . . . do you know anything about the charges against me? Do you know how long I'll be here? What will happen?" She was quick with her questions, surprised she even had them. She wasn't so scared at her jailer's presence now. She didn't think he wanted to assault her. That he didn't try to touch her gave her the confidence to speak.

The jailer looked at her, his expression ponderous. But he said nothing, only shaking his head back and forth. No. Then he mysteriously disappeared, as quickly as he'd appeared. Disappointed that he didn't answer her, she realized now that she really did want to know. She did want to know how and when it would end for her. She wanted to get it over with, that was all.

The bell to the Larkspur mansion rang loudly several times. A maid scrambled to answer.

Mary Ella Eagleton came charging inside, newspaper in hand. "Where's Mrs. Larkspur? I must see Mrs. Larkspur right now!" she insisted.

The maid showed her into the front parlor. "Wait here, please," the maid said, then hurried to find her employer.

Mary Ella fanned herself with her handkerchief. It was hard to wait, with such news to discuss.

Augusta Larkspur soon entered the parlor. "Hello, my dear. How nice to see you—"

"Augusta!" Mary Ella got up from the velvet-cushioned settee. "What do you make of this, Augusta? What do you make of it?" She bristled, shoving Polly Pry's gossip column into her friend's hands.

"What on earth? What's this about?" Augusta took the news page, and then took a seat. "Please sit down, Mary Ella. Please calm down. What has you in such a dither?"

Mary Ella gasped. "Oh, my dear, you don't know then, do you? You poor dear. You don't know."

Irritated by her friend's insulting posture, Augusta didn't appreciate Mary Ella's feigned sympathy, either. Humph. *Poor dear, my eye!* Whatever it was she didn't know, Augusta didn't care. "Dear." Augusta tried to keep her tone polite. "Why don't you take your little news home with you and come back later for afternoon tea." Getting up, Augusta dropped the paper in Mary Ella's lap.

"Augusta Larkspur!" Mary Ella stood, paper in hand. "How can you be so smug, so unfazed about all of this? I declare, it's a scandal like none other! I might be inclined to be smug about it, too, if it didn't affect *my* daughter and *my* family!"

"What do you mean *your* daughter and *your* family?" Now it was her turn to feel sorry for poor Mary Ella. Quickly, she grabbed the paper back from her friend. There must be something scandalous in Polly Pry's gossip column about the Eagletons. She needed to find out and set things right before Friday, for mercy's sake. The wedding was Friday! Whatever was wrong, Augusta would make it right. She had great influence in the city, in Denver society. She'd go see Polly Pry, herself, if need be, this very afternoon.

Augusta sat back down, heaved a sigh, and then straightened out the newspaper.

Mary Ella sat across from her, nervous, on the edge of her seat

At last finding the gossip column, Augusta began reading:

PROSTITUTE ARRESTED FOR THE ATTEMPTED MURDER OF EUGENE LARKSPUR!

Another bawdy prostitute was arrested last evening on Holladay Street, which in and of itself is nothing to write about. But that this prostitute was arrested for the attempted murder of one Eugene Larkspur is worthy of print in this column.

The young beauty, Rebecca Rose, had been living at the Windsor Hotel for some time, the room doubtless paid for by more than one wealthy gentleman. This columnist has her suspicions, but I refuse to name names at this time. Of course, one might speculate that the esteemed Eugene Larkspur quite possibly is one of the wealthy gentlemen in question. One might also speculate that with two sons, it's not outside the realm of possibility that one of his sons—say for instance, Morgan Larkspur—secured Rebecca Rose's rooms at the Windsor in the first place.

I think you'd all agree that this slight dalliance on the part

of the Larkspurs gives new meaning to the term family business.

Don't let this little column prevent you from attending Morgan Larkspur's wedding to Lavinia Eagleton this coming Friday. I plan to be there. It's guaranteed to be the event of the summer social season. There may not be a seat for me at the reception table, but you can count on me to be there. By the by, isn't it just too delicious to think that the upcoming Larkspur wedding reception will be at the Windsor? The same Windsor that housed the unfortunate Rebecca Rose. The Larkspur men should rest easily now that she's in custody. I've no doubt she'll be sent away to prison for many years. Her punishment should be a lesson to other soiled doves who get such ideas in their heads!

We are all thankful that Eugene Larkspur remains unharmed. Now that the murderous prostitute in question is behind bars, we can assume he will remain unharmed. We cannot assume, however, that his wife won't do him harm when she hears of this.

The arrest of Rebecca Rose is yet another in the long line of prostitutes arrested along Holladay Street. Never fear, gentlemen. There are hundreds upon hundreds of soiled doves still at work in Denver, in the oldest profession in the world. Never fear, ladies. I will make sure you know about each and every one of them.

I'll be back next week and tell you all about the Larkspur wedding party at the Windsor.

Until then,

Polly Pry

Augusta let the paper fall from her hands. She didn't need to read the article again to make sure of it. Rebecca Rose might as well have her gun pointed at Augusta now, for the damage done. The trigger had been pulled and the bullet let go.

There was no making this right. In time perhaps things would be right again, but not now, not yet. *Yes, time is all that's needed. Just a little time,* Augusta mused silently. "Mary Ella," she said softly, and then stood. "Mary Ella, I'd like to get a bit of rest, if you don't mind. I'm that tired. Don't think ill of me, dear, for leaving you now." She smiled as if nothing were amiss, then started up the stairs to her room.

Morgan had no choice. He didn't want to see Rebecca again, but he had to go to the city jail and see if there was something to be done about her being sentenced to prison. The idea that she'd be sent away to rot in some godforsaken jail upset him as much as knowing that she'd tried to kill his father. Why did she do it? It didn't make any sense to him. His father never said anything about her trying to kill him, not a word. He said he'd paid her fifty dollars and then he left. His father wouldn't lie, but . . . his father might try and protect him from her. His father might try to shield him from knowing that his mistress was so low-down and dirty.

Morgan rubbed his temples. His head hurt worse than ever from thinking on all of this. On top of everything else, his father was ill with consumption. Then there was the considerable problem of their family name being dragged through the mud in the *Rocky Mountain News.* Morgan didn't care about scandal for himself or for Monty. They'd be fine. It was his parents he worried about. They wouldn't be fine. His father's condition would worsen and his mother would never recover from the disgrace. The die was cast. His family would never be the same.

Morgan thought about the feelings he'd once had for Rebecca. They sure as hell would never be the same again, either. He'd let himself have feelings for a whore. He'd let himself fall in love with her, fancying being married to her, settled down, with children underfoot. She'd played him for a fool. Even so, he should try to keep her out of prison. His worst enemy didn't deserve that.

With the morning paper safely hidden, his parents wouldn't learn of their family misfortune . . . yet. He wanted to be home with them when they did. If he went downtown to the jail now, he'd be back soon. This wouldn't take long; he'd make sure of it.

"You!" Becca cringed when she saw Eugene Larkspur suddenly appear at her cell door, showing up as mysteriously as her guard had. She'd expected anybody but him. Morgan's father. Her mother's killer. Her rapist!

Now she was afraid again. Now it would all end. Somehow she'd known he'd come to kill her. Somehow she'd known she'd die at this monster's hand. How she longed for opium. Just one little killing bottle.

A guard came to the bars, this one new. This one looked mean. This one didn't care what fate might bring her way. He unlocked the cell door and opened it. "You stay back, missy," he ordered Becca. "One wrong move and you'll pay for it. I'll see to it," he promised.

Eugene stepped inside her cell, and then turned to the officer. "I want some privacy with this whore. Make sure of it," he said, pulling out a handful of bills.

The officer took the money. "You betcha, Mr. Larkspur," he said, a crooked smile on his face.

When the officer didn't move, Eugene rounded on him. "That means you, too," he spat out. "I don't want anyone coming in and disturbing us."

The unsavory jailer tossed Eugene a knowing smile, then disappeared from view.

Becca heard another door shut. She was alone now . . . alone with the devil. It made her sick to look at him. Her stomach rebelled and she started to retch, crumbling into a heap on the stone floor, cold as the grave. Nothing came up.

"Get up, bitch," Eugene snarled, pulling her to an abrupt stand. He shoved her against the farthest cell wall.

Pinned so, with edges of stone jutting into her back, Becca felt the devil's hot breath on her skin, the oppressive, fetid odor of pure evil holding her to the wall as much as his hand. It was hard for her to get a breath now. One killing hand—the hand with two missing fingers and the gold lion-head ring—was at her throat, while the other . . . The other held her gun, her very own derringer! He must have taken it when . . . after he . . . She wanted to laugh at the irony of it all, but she couldn't. He meant to make a mockery of her death by using her own gun.

Eugene put the gun to Becca's temple.

She didn't try to fight him off. She kept her eyes shut and waited. Just waited.

Eugene wasn't ready to kill her, though. Not yet.

"Mr. Larkspur, you can't see the prisoner," the unsavory officer announced the moment Morgan came inside the isolation unit of the jail. The officer didn't want to have to part with the money just given him, and he needed to keep Eugene Larkspur's son at bay. It would be too much to assume the son would give him a bribe, too. Hell, he was damned mad at the front desk. How'd they let Morgan Larkspur through, anyway? Must be a greenhorn out there, dammit!

Morgan was suspicious. This officer put him on his guard. "I'm here to see Rebecca Rose. *Now*," he insisted.

"Where's your order from the judge to see her?" the officer asked, contriving.

"I don't have one," Morgan growled.

"Well then, you'd best turn and leave. Can't get in without a legit order," the officer said, and then he turned away as if to dismiss Morgan.

"You go get me permission," Morgan said. "You go get a *legit order,* and I'll wait right here."

"Hold on, now." The officer started to worry—about his job and the visitor already inside Rebecca Rose's cell. "All right. I'll be back in a minute," he mumbled, trying to stall for time. He needed to figure something out, and fast, but all he could think of was to put Morgan Larkspur off until his father was through with Rebecca Rose. He could let Eugene Larkspur out the other door and no one would be the wiser. "You stay put," he told Morgan, then slipped out in the direction of the front desk, thinking he'd left both doors to the isolation cell good and locked.

Morgan had no intention of waiting to see Rebecca. Something was wrong around here, and he needed to find out what. He tried the door by the officer's desk. It was unlocked. Morgan cracked it open. He heard a voice, a man's . . . *his father's!*

Morgan pushed the door open wider and stepped inside the cell area, out of sight of Rebecca and his father, but within earshot. Everything around him slowed to a halt—everything but the two people inside the isolation cell, the two people he loved most in the world. His father was talking. Morgan listened hard.

"Beg. I want to hear you beg," Eugene hissed, the monster in him fully awakened.

Becca didn't respond. With his mangled hand pressed against her throat, she couldn't speak anyway.

"Your mother never begged," Eugene snarled. "It could have saved her if she had. I had feelings for your mother. I had *feelings* for her . . ." His voice trailed off.

Frozen to the spot and to the moment, Morgan dared not breathe. This wasn't his father talking. This was a lunatic, a monster.

"A whole year I came to see your mother, a whole year!" Eugene's anger flared. "She threatened to tell my wife about us. Imagine that. A two-bit whore, trying to make a Larkspur jump through hoops! I told her. I told Ruby she shouldn't threaten me. I warned her."

Becca *could* imagine it—all of it. She was afraid for her mother all over again.

Eugene pushed the gun harder against Becca's temple. "Ruby wanted me to marry her and be a father to you. When I refused, when I told her I was already married and had children, she asked me to take you home then, and raise you with my sons. Me, with a respectable family, taking in a whore's brat! Imagine that!"

Becca saw it all painfully in her mind's eye.

Morgan saw it, too, although he couldn't believe what he was hearing.

"I had to kill her. I had to slit Ruby's throat. She made me. She didn't beg for her life. She made me." Eugene sounded more like an upset child now than a lunatic murderer. "I should have killed you then. I knew you were there somewhere, lurking, watching. I knew. I knew you'd grow up and come after me one day. I should have slit your throat the night I killed Ruby."

Morgan knew now, without any doubt, that his father was insane. His father had killed Rebecca's mother! Dear God!

"You can imagine, my dear," Eugene said, his tone darkening, "my surprise when I found out you were Morgan's mistress. You, Ruby's brat! You! Thinking yourself good enough to be with my son! You, a two-bit whore! I fixed things good so Morgan wouldn't want you."

"You . . . raped . . . me," Becca managed to rasp.

"Yes, well, my son will never know that," Eugene taunted. "I'll make sure of that this time."

Morgan tried to move, but he couldn't. The jail floor had

turned to quicksand, holding him, not letting him free.

"This time I'm going to finish you. I'll be done with Ruby once and for all, once I finish you, once I get you to beg for your life. Just beg. Just give me that before I pull this trigger. Just give me that," Eugene whined.

Morgan found his legs and raced to the cell door, in view now of Rebecca and his father. Dear God. His father had a gun to Rebecca's head. *Dear God!* It took everything he had in him to hold his voice steady and to try to get through to the human part left inside the monster before him. "*Father*, put down the gun."

Becca heard Morgan now, only Morgan.

Eugene turned slightly, enough to be eye to eye with his son.

In the time it takes for a heart to stop beating, he put the gun barrel against his temple and fired. He was dead instantly. His body collapsed to the floor. A trickle of blood oozed from his head and onto his misshapen hand, the gold lion-head ring becoming smothered in red.

Becca stepped over the lifeless body and ran into Morgan's arms . . . loving him . . . loving him.

"Darlin'," he whispered against her hair. "Oh, my darlin' girl."

Their bodies pressed close, they stood in each other's arms, holding onto each other for dear life.

"Have you had the doctor over to see mother again?" Morgan quizzed his brother, worried their mother might not recover from the shock she'd suffered.

"Of course," Monty reassured him.

The brothers stood in the vestibule of the courthouse, waiting for Rebecca and Jenny Clayton to join them. It was Friday, Morgan's appointed wedding day. There would be no service at Saint John's and no fancy reception at the Windsor, but there would be a wedding all the same, between the right two people—the two people right for each other.

It would take time for the scandal surrounding the Larkspur family to die down. But die down it would, as others erupted to take its place. The Larkspur family name might be tarnished, but not their fortune. It was Monty's turn now. Morgan had every confidence that his little brother would handle the family business interests just fine. Monty was smart. Monty was ready. Monty had never been given the chance. Now he had it.

Both brothers worried about their mother, but only Monty grieved over their father. Morgan refused to think of his father. He'd thrown away a lifetime of memories the moment he saw the gun at Rebecca's head.

Morgan, with Rebecca, had gone to the Larkspur mansion right after Eugene's suicide. Morgan had refused to leave her alone, and Becca had hoped to be of some help. They'd quickly agreed not to tell Monty or Augusta all the sordid details surrounding Eugene's death. There was no point in telling them that Eugene had gone mad and was a murderer and a rapist. It was bad enough that he was dead. It would be too much for Augusta to know the whole truth.

As far as the newspapers were concerned:

Eugene Larkspur shot himself dead at the city jail, unable to deal with the public scandal brought on by his private involvement in the sporting life. It is believed, too, that the deceased suffered from long-standing melancholia, a secret he kept well-hidden. A respected family man, an astute businessman, Eugene Larkspur is survived by his wife, Augusta Larkspur, and his sons, Morgan Larkspur and Montgomery Larkspur.

When Morgan had gone upstairs after his father's suicide to see his mother, Augusta greeted him and gave his hand a pat. She'd spotted Becca standing behind him, and asked the lovely young woman to come around so she could see her.

"My, you're so pretty. So pretty. Lavinia, isn't it? Yes, so pretty . . ." her thoughts had soon trailed off. Morgan and Monty realized then that she wasn't in her right mind. She wasn't ready to hear that her husband was dead.

"Spur, don't worry." While they stood waiting in the vestibule, Monty tried to reassure his big brother again that their mother would come around in time, and that he'd take care of her, as always. "Today's a day for celebration. You're getting married today. You'll have a whole lifetime of tomorrows with your beautiful Rebecca Rose."

"We won't be far away, little brother. The ranch I'm buying on the front-range is within a day's ride. Maybe in time mother will want to come and stay with us. Maybe in time she'll accept Rebecca and our children," Morgan said.

"Of course she will, Spur. Of course." Monty was playing the big brother now.

At just that moment, Becca and Jenny Clayton came through the front doors of the courthouse.

"Darlin'." Morgan took hold of Rebecca's hand right away. "Are you ready?"

She squeezed his fingers. "I've been ready my whole life. For you," she answered, her throat tight. His handsome smile took her breath away. He already had her heart. She loved him so. It was a powerful feeling, a heady feeling, to love someone so much you could near burst from it. She'd loved before. She'd loved her mother, and Fanny, and Miss Jenny. But her love for Morgan answered a different need, a—womanly need to love and be loved by a man, a womanly need to be a wife and a mother.

She thought again of her mother, her beloved Ruby Rose. *You can rest in peace now, Mama. Now you can.* Her mother would ever smile down on her from heaven above, knowing her parlor house daughter would have a respectable life with the man of her dreams.

I love him, Mama. I love him.

Still hand-in-hand with his Rebecca, Morgan nodded to Monty and Jenny, and then he guided the wedding party inside the courtroom, ready to get married.

Humbled by the moment, overcome with emotion, Becca felt first one tear and then another escape down her face. She let them fall and didn't blink against them, no longer needing to hide her feelings, no longer believing that *feelings get a whore killed.* She was living proof of it.

ABOUT THE AUTHOR

Joanne Sundell lives in Grand County, Colorado, with her husband and their entourage of felines and huskies. Their three children are grown and off on their own adventures.